P9-DHN-856

She was being followed

He was taking his time, hugging the row of buildings, a dark silhouette in the streetlight's anemic glow.

As she started to sprint across the bridge, Jordan heard a sickening sound, a dull, muffled thump, like a dart imbedding itself in a bale of straw. Acting on instinct, she sprawled on the bridge as another bullet whined just inches from her.

Pressing herself against the slimy, wet cobbles, Jordan listened to the measured steps approaching along the canal. He was going to find her soon. Jordan's eyes darted to the narrow gap beneath the bridge railing. The space was so tight, it would be difficult to squeeze through, but it was her only escape route.

One. Two. Jordan mentally counted. *Three!* With a sudden burst of energy, she scooted beneath the rail and into the murky water. Blind panic gripped her as the icy, oily water engulfed her....

ABOUT THE AUTHOR

A native of Little Rock, Arkansas, Laurel
Pace attended New York University and the
School of Visual Arts in New York City. She
worked in advertising as a producer of radio
and television commercials before turning to
professional writing. Many of her story ideas,
including the one for *Broken Lullaby,* come
from the three years she spent living in
Europe. She now makes her home in Atlanta,
Georgia, with her musician husband and
their five very loving cats.

Books by Laurel Pace

HARLEQUIN INTRIGUE
112–DECEPTION BY DESIGN
174–GHOSTWALK

HARLEQUIN AMERICAN ROMANCE
192–ON WINGS OF LOVE
220–WHEN HEARTS DREAM
312–ISLAND MAGIC
370–MAY WINE, SEPTEMBER MOON

Don't miss any of our special offers. Write to us at the
following address for information on our newest releases.

Harlequin Reader Service
P.O. Box 1397, Buffalo, NY 14240
Canadian address: P.O. Box 603,
Fort Erie, Ont. L2A 5X3

Broken Lullaby

Laurel Pace

Harlequin Books

TORONTO • NEW YORK • LONDON
AMSTERDAM • PARIS • SYDNEY • HAMBURG
STOCKHOLM • ATHENS • TOKYO • MILAN
MADRID • WARSAW • BUDAPEST • AUCKLAND

If you purchased this book without a cover you should be aware that this book is stolen property. It was reported as "unsold and destroyed" to the publisher, and neither the author nor the publisher has received any payment for this "stripped book."

ACKNOWLEDGMENTS

Special thanks are due four wonderful people for their help in getting *Broken Lullaby* beyond the notes-on-napkin stage:

To Violet Vestal,
whose love of genealogy inspired Jordan's career;

To Margot and Gerhardt Ludwar,
who graciously filled the gaps in my knowledge of Vienna and the Opera Ball; and

To Ronald F. Tunkel,
Special Agent, U.S. Treasury Department, Bureau of Alcohol, Tobacco & Firearms, whose introduction to weapons and forensic technology proved indispensable

Harlequin Intrigue edition published August 1992

ISBN 0-373-22191-6

BROKEN LULLABY

Copyright © 1992 by Barbara M. Wojhoski. All rights reserved. Except for use in any review, the reproduction or utilization of this work in whole or in part in any form by any electronic, mechanical or other means, now known or hereafter invented, including xerography, photocopying and recording, or in any information storage or retrieval system, is forbidden without the permission of the publisher, Harlequin Enterprises Limited, 225 Duncan Mill Road, Don Mills, Ontario, Canada M3B 3K9.

All the characters in this book have no existence outside the imagination of the author and have no relation whatsoever to anyone bearing the same name or names. They are not even distantly inspired by any individual known or unknown to the author, and all incidents are pure invention.

® are Trademarks registered in the United States Patent and Trademark Office and in other countries.

Printed in U.S.A.

CAST OF CHARACTERS

Jordan MacKenzie—She searched for her client's past and found danger.

Nick Rostov—He was determined to find the Radetsky Music Box at all costs.

Kitty Ridgewood—Was a dark secret hidden in her forgotten past?

Daria Rostov—A gifted dancer, she had inherited her great-grandmother's talent.

Natalie Gallinin Rostov—A betrayer's treachery had cost her everything.

Maria Rachmanova—She lived among the ghosts of the past.

Guddrun Mayes-Cooper—She was as ruthless as she was beautiful.

Count Boris Radetsky—How far would he go to protect his inheritance?

Bertie Waxx—A tabloid reporter, he hounded the rich and famous.

Dirk Arvidsen—Murder was his business.

Chapter One

"Yes?" The voice sounded remarkably clear, despite the several thousand miles separating Milan from Beverly Hills.

"Good afternoon, Ms. Ridgewood. It's Jordan MacKenzie."

"Good *morning,* Ms. MacKenzie!" Kitty Ridgewood chuckled as she reminded Jordan of the multiple time zones lying between them.

Jordan grimaced, mentally calculating the time in Los Angeles. "I'm sorry for calling so early," she began.

Kitty brushed aside her apology. "I start my day before most people have breakfast. But tell me what you've learned," she demanded with unapologetic directness of someone accustomed to quick answers.

"Nothing since the last time I spoke with you." At the sound of muffled footsteps from the hotel hallway, Jordan instinctively dropped her voice. She realized it bordered on paranoia to suspect anyone of eavesdropping outside her door. All the same, she waited until the damped footsteps had evaporated into silence before resuming her conversation. "I only arrived in Milan an hour ago, but I wanted to let you know that I'll be meeting with Dr. D'Antonelli this afternoon."

"The art historian?"

"Yes. I'll also be speaking with an art expert in Vienna tomorrow, someone who responded to my inquiry only last week," Jordan felt obligated to add. Given the disappointing response her blizzard of letters to various art experts had yielded, she wanted to offer Kitty some evidence of progress, however meager. As a professional genealogist, Jordan's business was to wrest family trees out of the slimmest leads. If it were easy, she always reminded herself, people would simply do it for themselves. Still, she shied away from building false hopes in Kitty.

To Jordan's relief, Kitty seemed satisfied with the news. "Excellent. You'll keep me informed if you discover anything of interest?"

"Of course," Jordan assured her.

Kitty Ridgewood cleared her throat. "Ms. MacKenzie, I know I needn't remind you..." She hesitated before going on in a lower voice. For a powerful woman who must be a millionaire several times over, she seemed oddly ill at ease. "You will be *very* discreet, I'm sure, but I must remind you once again of how important confidentiality is to me. No one can know that you're investigating my past. Absolutely no one. As I've told you before, several senior executives in my company are currently under investigation for federal tax fraud. The publicity has been horrendous! Right now, my name is always in the news, and there's nothing that can be done about that. But if you were to find any members of my family, I wouldn't want them to be dragged into this mess, be embarrassed on my account."

"Certainly," Jordan agreed. Every time they talked, Kitty never failed to remind her of the scandal overshadowing her cosmetics firm, Regime, and of the secrecy she wished to maintain. No wonder she was beginning to regard hotel staffers with beady-eyed suspicion, Jordan reflected.

"You'll be meeting these art people alone?" Kitty prompted.

"Yes," Jordan replied. "Occasionally, however, on complicated assignments such as this one, I have to hire specialists. For example, someone to translate information. Whenever possible, though, I handle everything myself, with my secretary helping out with the preliminary research." Jordan paused, giving Kitty Ridgewood a chance to give her approval. She could understand Ridgewood's aversion to publicity, but as a professional she could not make promises she would be unable to keep. "You have my word that I'll reveal your identity to no one."

"I appreciate your discretion, Ms. MacKenzie," Kitty conceded in a brittle tone. "In the meantime, I'll look forward to hearing what enlightening information this Dr. D'Antonelli can provide."

Jordan was a little intimidated by Kitty's confidence in her investigation. *She thinks it's all sewn up, that I'll call her in a week with a huge list of relatives going back four centuries. How can I tell her she's probably nursing false expectations, that the leads she's given me are hopelessly flimsy, that public records in central Europe are a nightmare after two world wars, that orphans, under the best circumstances, have rotten luck with family trees....*

As if she could read Jordan's mind, Kitty hastened to conclude the conversation. "Good luck, Ms. MacKenzie," she said by way of parting. "You're going to need it."

As she replaced the phone on the bedside table, Jordan remembered the first time she had met her current client. In keeping with her boss's obsession with secrecy, Ridgewood's secretary had spent weeks sounding Jordan out before finally sending her a first-class plane ticket to Los Angeles. Even then, Jordan had known only that she was flying west to meet a top executive with Regime. Coming on

the heels of her successful reconstruction of Senator Geri-
cault's family tree, she had suspected something big was
brewing. Jordan had been startled when she was at last
alone with *the* Kitty Ridgewood in her private office. In
contrast to the media's portrayal of Ridgewood as an iron-
willed autocrat, all she had seen was a fearful, uncertain
woman confronting her painful past. Jordan still winced at
the memory of Kitty's embarrassment when she had admitted that she was an orphan and did not even know her true
date of birth.

During the two-hour interview, Kitty had revealed that
her earliest memories were of an orphanage in Austria,
where she guessed she had been left when she was very
small. In keeping with the prevalent child-rearing philoso-
phy of the day, however, none of the orphanage nuns would
ever tell her anything about how she had come to be there,
so little Käthe Davidov, as she had been called then, grew up
ignorant of her origins.

Käthe remained at the orphanage until she was fifteen,
when she was hired out as farm girl. Fortunately her knack
for tending children garnered her a better position a few
years later as a nursemaid with a well-to-do family in the
village. When the clouds of war began to gather in the mid-
1930s, Käthe's employers emigrated to England. Kitty had
confessed that in the new country, where no one knew she
had been a penniless farm maid, she quickly constructed a
new identity for herself. Käthe Davidov became Kitty Davis,
a polished young woman whose flawless English and so-
phisticated manners admitted her to new and exciting social circles. Her escape from the past seemed complete when
she met and fell in love with American air force Colonel Bud
Ridgewood. After the war they married and moved to California, where he became a pioneer in the aerospace indus-
try and she founded her cosmetics firm.

Jordan would never forget the desperate look in Ridgewood's clear blue eyes as she had recounted the loss of her husband. "I was so happy all these years, Ms. MacKenzie," she had whispered, almost as if she were praying. "Only when I lost Bud last year did I begin to feel this *need* again." Kitty had pressed her fist against her stomach, as if to still the gnawing emptiness. "We never had any children, and now that he's gone...I have no one. If I have any family left, anywhere, I want to find them." Kitty's husky voice had sounded as if she were making a vow. "Can you do that for me, Ms. MacKenzie?"

"I'll try my very best, Ms. Ridgewood." Jordan had been so moved by Kitty's story that, for once, she wished she could promise miracles.

Now, two months later, Jordan reflected that she was going to need nothing short of a miracle. If only Kitty had been able to give her more concrete details, something to go on besides the two enigmatic relics of her sundered childhood.

Shifting on the edge of the hotel bed, Jordan unlatched her briefcase and removed a manila envelope. She opened the envelope's flap and carefully lifted out a fine gold chain with a tiny heart-shaped locket. Cradling the delicate jewelry in her palm, Jordan frowned. No engraving, no picture inside, no clues. Kitty had insisted the locket was one of the two "treasures" that she had jealously guarded at the orphanage. But where had she gotten it in the first place?

The item Jordan next slid from the envelope was even more puzzling. She placed the sepia-toned photograph on her knee and studied the faded image. Jordan regarded the solemn-faced little girl in the picture, dressed in the starched muslin of the Belle Epoque. The child was standing next to a spindly table in one of those curiously awkward poses favored by turn-of-the-century photographers. Could the child have been Kitty? Jordan wondered. Ridgewood had insisted that she was already living in the orphanage by the time she reached the girl's probable age, but who could be sure, given Kitty's amnesia-fogged recollection of her childhood?

Jordan studied the child's pose. Her tiny hand had been positioned, just so, on the edge of a polished wooden box occupying the center of the table. The box itself would have been unextraordinary, save for one remarkable feature: the large artificial egg mounted on its lid. Jordan squinted over the egg, studying its filigree-encrusted surface.

No, she hadn't misled herself in her eagerness to grasp at any available clue. The egg was either one of the famous art objects fashioned for the last Russian czars by the jeweler Carl Fabergé or a good enough fake to fool the average person. Even the privacy-obsessed Kitty had initiated a few furtive attempts in the past to contact museums, based on her conviction that the egg was a Fabergé.

As she slipped the photograph and the locket back into the envelope, Jordan sighed. Genuine or fake, the whimsical egg was not simply the best concrete clue they possessed. At this point it was the *only* one.

VITTORIO D'ANTONELLI'S apartment felt more like a museum than a private home. Jordan instinctively lightened her step on the polished marble floor as she followed the servant across the circular foyer. She glanced at the solemn-faced busts ensconced in the foyer's wall niches, resisting their blank-eyed stares.

The servant stepped aside to make way for a short, white-haired man hurrying toward them. "Signorina Mac-Kenzie!" He bowed slightly. "I am Vittorio D'Antonelli. Welcome to my home!"

"Thank you, Dottore D'Antonelli. It was very kind of you to have me here today." Jordan studied the lined face, recognized the eagerness waxing behind the cordial smile. Could this ivory-towered art scholar somehow suspect that she was representing Kitty Ridgewood? After all, Kitty had said she had contacted museums in the past, hoping to find the egg. What if...? Jordan quickly squelched the utterly ridiculous notion.

If D'Antonelli had noticed the flash of suspicion in her eyes, he graciously pretended otherwise. "Art is my life, Signorina MacKenzie. I am always happy to assist those with similar interests." He touched her elbow lightly, guiding her into a large room opening off the foyer.

Four Palladian windows bathed the salon in a soft golden light, enlivening the rich tones of the oil paintings displayed on the walls. A brocade settee and two chairs were drawn up beside the tiled fireplace where a few logs crackled pleasantly, filling the air with the clean scent of simmering hardwood. The inviting atmosphere was wasted on Jordan, however, for she pulled up short the moment she spotted another man standing in front of the windows.

D'Antonelli could not have mistaken her consternation, but he went on smoothly. "Signorina MacKenzie, I have taken the liberty of inviting another art expert to join us this afternoon."

Not waiting for their host to make introductions, the strange man strode past the settee and offered his hand. "Nick Rostov, Ms. MacKenzie. It's a pleasure to meet you. Vittorio tells me you may have a photograph of a very remarkable artifact." His voice was low pitched, with the trace of an accent that was impossible to place.

"I think so, but then I'm no expert." When Jordan glanced down at her leather briefcase, she noticed Nick

Rostov's gaze following hers. He smiled quickly, but not fast enough to mask the interest in those dark sapphire blue eyes.

The servant had reappeared, bearing a tray of crystal glasses and a decanter. *"Un aperitivo, signorina?"*

"Si, grazie, signore," Jordan replied, grateful that her measly knowledge of tourist Italian had stood her in good stead so far. While the drinks were being dispensed and handed around, she took the opportunity to gather her wits and observe her host and his surprise guest.

Vittorio D'Antonelli was much the way she had imagined him during their brief phone conversation: dignified, almost courtly, a well-bred gentleman of the old school. He even looked the part of the renowned art historian, with his impeccably trimmed white beard and wire-rimmed spectacles. Yes, those thick, owlish lenses were definitely not glasses, but spectacles, Jordan thought, smiling behind her aperitif glass.

Now Nick Rostov was another matter altogether. He certainly didn't fit her image of an art expert, but perhaps she excepted him to be old and slightly fusty only because Hollywood always depicted scholars that way. Certainly, no central casting mogul would ever dream of putting Rostov in such a role. Why waste someone with the attributes of a sexy secret agent or a handsome cavalier in Napoleon's army? Not only did he have the looks—a tall, muscular frame that would stand out in anything from tux to jeans, curly dark hair, and midnight blue eyes with just enough edge to keep those chiseled features from being too picture perfect—he even had that enigmatic accent.

"Nicholas is a specialist in Russian artifacts," D'Antonelli was explaining. "I must confess we are both exceedingly interested in seeing this photograph you described."

Jordan nodded, forcing her thoughts back to the issue that had brought her to Milan in the first place. Seating herself on the edge of the settee, she placed the empty aperitif glass on the marble table and then hoisted the briefcase onto her lap. As she snapped open the lid, she was keenly aware of the two pairs of eyes trained on her, following her every move.

"These are enhanced enlargements of the photograph. I think you can see the detail more clearly than in the original." She handed D'Antonelli and Rostov each a copy.

Rostov's intense blue eyes took in the picture in a sweep. "This is only a portion of the original photograph?"

"An enlargement of the entire picture would have been as big as a poster. And, anyway, the egg is the only thing of real interest." *To you, at least,* Jordan added silently to herself. She tried to look nonplussed, as if his question made no sense. After all, what could an art expert care about the anonymous little girl posed beside the Easter egg?

She pretended to rearrange some papers in the open briefcase, trying to quell her paranoia. And she *was* paranoid where Kitty Ridgewood's identity was concerned. Otherwise she would never have taken such pains to crop the picture to show only the egg. Jordan had made sure that even the tips of the little girl's fingers, resting only inches from the egg's base, were safely excised from the enlargement. It was a long shot, she knew, but she did not want to risk someone's recognizing Kitty's resemblance to the child.

"So what do you think?" Jordan prompted. She folded her hands on her lap, right at the point where her short skirt skimmed her knees. She caught Rostov's eye as it wandered to her leg, causing him to look quickly away.

The older man had taken his copy to the desk. Nick Rostov joined him, leaning over his shoulder while D'Antonelli inspected the egg's image through a magnifying glass. The convex glass hovered over the filigree base, then glided slowly over the egg's dark, mottled surface. "Unquestionable," Jordan heard the white-haired gentleman murmur under his breath. When the lens reached the figure of the tiny horseman crowning the egg, it trembled in D'Antonelli's hand.

Nick Rostov peered at the intricately crafted figure, but Jordan noticed him stiffen when she walked up behind him. "Any clue as to what it might be?" she asked quietly.

Rostov exchanged a guarded glance with D'Antonelli. Then the elderly man cleared his throat. "In my humble opinion, the egg depicted in your photograph is a genuine Fabergé," he began.

Jordan nodded, but she looked puzzled. "But which one? I must have gone through dozens of books on the subject and found no egg that matched this one's description."

D'Antonelli smiled indulgently. "You would not have found this particular egg in any existing catalog."

"Why not, Dottore D'Antonelli?" Jordan persisted.

"Because no one is certain exactly how many eggs Carl Fabergé fashioned for the last two Russian czars, Signorina MacKenzie. Some art historians maintain it was fifty-seven, others fifty-eight. And then there are those—" he gave Rostov another of those significant glances that were beginning to irritate Jordan "—who believe the correct number is fifty-nine. The question becomes more muddled when one takes into account the pieces that were not specifically commissioned as Easter presents for the czarina. You see, Fabergé produced a quantity of miniature eggs, as well as several full-scale pieces to mark special occasions."

"You believe this egg falls into the latter category?" Jordan fixed D'Antonelli with the sort of uncompromising gaze Kitty Ridgewood would have adopted under the circumstances.

"Yes, I do," D'Antonelli conceded slowly. "I think this egg is part of the Radetsky music box."

"The Radetsky music box?" Jordan pronounced the name carefully.

D'Antonelli nodded solemnly. "In 1913, Czar Nicholas II commissioned a specially constructed music box for Count Radetsky in gratitude for Radetsky's foiling an assassination attempt against the czar and his family. The black marbled egg was fashioned not only as a decoration, but also as part of the music box's mechanism. One twisted the little horseman perched atop the egg in order to make the box play its tune. I did not believe a photograph of the egg existed. Until today."

"We could be more specific if we could see the original photograph," Nick interposed. "Of course, the best possible determination could be made from examining the piece itself."

"I don't have it," Jordan told him. For a second, Rostov only continued to stare at her, as if he were waiting for her to change her mind and admit she was carrying the thing in her briefcase. "I don't," she repeated, a little defensively, and immediately felt annoyed with herself. A man with his looks was undoubtedly used to hearing what he wanted from women; the thought that he wouldn't from her gave her a perverse pleasure. *Sorry to disappoint you, Mr. Rostov.*

"But you do have the original photograph," Rostov reminded her.

"Not with me," Jordan told him truthfully. "And even if I did, I wouldn't be free to show it to you." Drawing a deep breath, she glanced at D'Antonelli and then back at Nick Rostov. "I'll be honest with you, gentlemen. I am researching a family tree for a client who wishes to remain anonymous. My client has forbidden me to let anyone see the photograph in its entirety." Kitty had not actually said as much, but Jordan felt sure she would agree with the spirit of the statement. "I've solicited your help in identifying the

Fabergé egg in the hope that it could lead me to some of my client's relatives.''

"Then a member of your client's family has the music box?" Rostov posed the question aggressively.

"I didn't say that," Jordan told him coolly. Her eyes locked with his, warning him to back off. She watched Rostov's face relax into a conciliatory smile, but she wasn't about to be taken in that easily. Thank God she hadn't let the matinee idol good looks blind her to the ambitious art collector they disguised. It was obvious to her now that Nick Rostov was present at that meeting for one reason: he saw her as a link to the precious music box. "The egg—or rather, the music box—is only a remote clue to my client's history, and probably not a very reliable one," she added to emphasize her point.

Rostov nodded, but he raised his brows as if he didn't believe a word she had said. The skeptical expression in his cobalt blue eyes was infuriating, and Jordan felt hard-pressed to control her anger. Of course, maybe it was to her advantage that he believed she knew more about the music box than she actually did. "I suppose this item would be very valuable to a museum or a private collector," she remarked. She paused, waiting for a ripple in the dark blue curtain of Rostov's eyes.

"Extremely valuable, Ms. MacKenzie." Rostov's voice was as even as his unbroken stare. "But I'm sure you know that already."

In spite of herself, Jordan frowned at Rostov's insinuating tone. "No, I didn't, Mr. Rostov, at least not until today."

Nick Rostov gave her a cynical smile. "So you haven't sought an appraisal previously?"

Jordan shook her head. "Actually, only one other person has responded to my inquiries besides you, *dottore*."

She nodded politely to the silver-haired scholar who, next to the probing Rostov, was beginning to seem more like a genial ally with every passing moment.

Rostov pounced on her remark. "Who, may I ask?"

No, you may not. The snappish retort danced through Jordan's mind before she replied evenly, "A Dr. Gudrun Mayes-Cooper. She's meeting me in Vienna tomorrow morning. Do you know her?"

Rostov's shrug failed to mask the annoyance reflected in his steely blue eyes. "I've heard of her," he conceded shortly.

D'Antonelli's instincts for preserving a genteel atmosphere apparently prompted him to intercede. "Many collectors have long coveted the Radetsky music box. But of course, only one may possess it."

Something in the older man's voice, a hint of things unspoken, caused Jordan to turn. "Dottore D'Antonelli, do you have any idea who last owned the music box?"

D'Antonelli looked down at his hands. He studied their floury, wrinkled contours for a moment as if he were noticing them for the first time. When he looked back up at her, he smiled faintly. "Why, Count Radetsky."

"Then I should definitely get in touch with the count's family. I suppose they live in western Europe now," Jordan guessed. The quick yet knowing look that passed between Rostov and D'Antonelli made her feel like a child excluded from a playground clique.

"The Radetsky family presently resides in Austria," D'Antonelli informed her with the slightest trace of indulgence. "But I do not think it would do you much good to contact them, *signorina.*" He cast another meaningful glance at Rostov, whose face had become an impenetrable mask.

"Why not?" Jordan insisted.

D'Antonelli heaved a worldly sigh. "The present-day Count Radetsky has never laid eyes on his ancestor's precious treasure. You see, Signorina MacKenzie, the music box vanished during the Russian Revolution. No one has seen it since."

"So, my friend, was meeting the charming Signorina MacKenzie not a worthy reason to travel to Milan?"

Nick ignored Vittorio's remark for the moment and continued to gaze out the window at the Titian-haired woman walking across the courtyard below. He waited until Jordan MacKenzie had disappeared through the gate before turning to his companion. "That all depends on what she really knows."

"Ah, Nicholas! What a contrary young man you are sometimes! You are brilliant in your field. Few people—and certainly none your age—can recognize an art forgery as quickly as you. The great galleries of the world clamor for your services. If you chose, you could be a curator at one of the best museums, respected, a little richer perhaps, famous."

"Fame I can do without," Nick cut in. Then he gave Vittorio's shoulder a comradely jostle. Just because his hackles rose at the very thought of a public identity was no reason to snap at his old friend. After all, without Vittorio's encouragement and guidance, he would probably still be drifting around in limbo, a washed-up competitive skier with a bad knee and an empty future. Nick had seen what could become of people like himself, living off the currency of a daredevil image and a family name that had meant something a century ago. He still shuddered to think how he could have squandered his life—how he almost had.

Nick folded his arms as he walked to the enormous open fireplace. Although he could tell Vittorio was eager for a postmortem on their meeting, Nick was still trying to sort through his conflicting impressions of Jordan MacKenzie, and he avoided his old friend's prompting gaze.

"A splendid job you did with that last assignment," Vittorio remarked in a transparent attempt to penetrate Nick's silence. "To think that the British Museum was on the very brink, teetering on the precipice, if you will, of buying a *fake!* And at such an outrageous price!" His pale eyes beamed with admiration. "But I must say you could have made things a bit easier on yourself if you hadn't deemed it necessary to break into the forgers' workshop."

Nick studied his hands outstretched before the comforting fire. "That seemed the best way to find out what they were up to."

"But dropping through the skylight? Really, Nicholas!"

"I believe in the direct approach."

"Still, with so much money involved, it is a good thing they were not armed."

"A couple of them were, but they never knew what hit them." Nick shrugged indifferently.

"My God!" Vittorio gasped in spite of himself. "Someday, Nicholas, you are going to find yourself in what the Americans call a real jam. Can you not find a more *peaceful* way to go about your work?"

"I'm always open to suggestion." Nick turned to face the older man. "For instance, I'd be interested to hear your ideas for getting to Miss MacKenzie, short of mugging her and getting a look at what's really inside that briefcase."

Vittorio looked dubious, as if he were not quite sure how much of Nick's statement he should take seriously. "Please, Nicholas, I hope you have nothing so violent in mind."

Nick relished the doubt lingering in Vittorio's eyes. "Don't worry. I wouldn't dream of harming a single red hair on her head." Seeing Vittorio's face relax, he hastened to add, "I might get caught."

"Nicholas!" Vittorio exclaimed. "But of course you are only making a joke," he reassured himself.

"This is no joking matter," Nick reminded him. "What do you know about this Jordan MacKenzie, anyway?"

Vittorio's white brows drew into a wispy line of concentration. "Only what she has told me, that she is a professional genealogist researching the family tree of an unnamed client." Vittorio grimaced slightly. "A curious profession, I would think, wandering about in graveyards, looking for dead relations."

"You think she's telling the truth?" Nick pressed his friend.

"I do not believe that Signorina MacKenzie has ulterior motives," Vittorio began carefully. "She certainly does not *seem* like someone equipped to bargain a black-market art deal. She appeared very intelligent, but from an expert's standpoint her questions were rather naive, don't you think?"

Nick conceded a reserved nod of agreement. During the brief meeting, he had recognized the same qualities in the American genealogist, but had resisted taking them at face value. He had reminded himself not to be taken in by a guileless front—especially with a woman as attractive as Jordan MacKenzie.

"Indeed, I perceived a certain candor in her that is rare in our business," Vittorio went on. "I am inclined to believe that Signorina MacKenzie means what she says. She has somehow acquired this photograph and simply wants to identify the piece."

"Let's not forget who her next contact is—Gudrun Mayes-Cooper." The name left a faintly repellent aftertaste on Nick's tongue. "You know as well as I that Gudrun doesn't do any favors. If she's flying in from London to meet Ms. MacKenzie, there's got to be something in it for her."

Vittorio's shoulders rose in another eloquent shrug. "Perhaps I am wrong. Perhaps this Signorina MacKenzie knows far more than we suspect."

Nick shifted in front of the fireplace, folding his hands behind his back. This was not their first lead on the Radetsky music box; there had been others in the past, all of them false. Already he had been forced to fight the emotions that the grainy photocopied picture had stirred within him, had struggled to maintain a coolly skeptical view of this latest possibility.

Vittorio waited a few moments before he lost patience with Nick's silence. "So? Are you interested in pursuing the case?"

"You know me too well to ask that question, Vittorio. I'll do whatever I can to recover it." Nick was startled by the hoarseness that had crept into his voice. "The Radetsky music box has already cost two people their lives. It's time the truth was made known."

Chapter Two

The Russian Revolution! The phrase was still darting around in Jordan's mind like a video game gone haywire after she left D'Antonelli's apartment and turned down Via Manzoni. She had been so encouraged when the art historian had responded to her inquiry, had come to Milan with high hopes of getting a conclusive lead on the Fabergé egg, only to learn that it had been swallowed up by a cataclysmic revolution!

Of all the wild cards a genealogist could draw, a revolution had to be one of the worst. Records destroyed, families divided, whole communities scattered to the four winds—Jordan almost winced at the chaotic image. In her work, she had run up against revolutions before; sometimes she had been able to piece together shattered fragments of family history. More often, however, she had been left with frustrating blank spots, truncated, leafless branches in her client's family tree. The thought that Kitty Ridgewood's case might fall into the latter category added an extra chill to the damp wind hounding her down the street.

Given the remote chance that the Radetsky music box would ever surface again, little wonder Nick Rostov had pounced on the news that she had a photograph of the piece. She could imagine herself doing the same thing in her line of work, dashing after every scrap of information, pressing anyone who might have the flimsiest clue to her client's past, even bristling a little when a possible informant scurried behind the barrier of confidentiality. She was inclined to think more kindly of Rostov now that she found herself cut adrift in a similar boat.

She had probably bent over backward to resist his probing precisely because she found him attractive. A professional to the core, Jordan loathed the disproved-but-still-tenacious myth that emotions influence a woman's business decisions; strict separation of business and private life had always been her rule. Now if she had encountered Nick Rostov under different circumstances . . .

Jordan shifted the heavy briefcase and fought the temptation to bemoan yet another bit of bad luck. Her eyes drifted in passing to a department-store window, populated with beautiful-people mannequins dressed in exquisite evening clothes. Two of the figures had been arranged in a tango or another impossibly romantic dance that no one bothered to learn anymore.

For a minute Jordan paused to smile at the window-dressing fantasy. Her mother had loved those dances—the merengue, the rumba, the cha-cha—and had practiced with records in their living room until she could glide through the complicated steps. She remembered her father's teasing. "Who do you think you are? Ginger Rogers?" Only later had she realized the disappointment her mother must have felt that he never danced with her, not even just for fun in the living room.

"See anything you like?"

Jordan started at the question—and at the unmistakable accent of the man who posed it. Blinking, she focused on the reflection overshadowing hers in the plate-glass window.

"Mr. Rostov! You startled me!" Impossible as it was, Jordan had the crazy feeling that he could tell she had been thinking about him, simply by looking at her.

"I'm sorry." The expression in the dark blue eyes seemed more amused than contrite, but the smile that complemented it was too genuine to doubt. "You left Vittorio's apartment in such a tear, I was afraid I'd never catch up with you."

In truth, Nick had cursed himself for lingering so long in Vittorio's salon. Fortunately, Jordan MacKenzie had not been too preoccupied with her mission to resist the distractions of Via Manzoni's elegant shops.

"Well, you caught me." The briefcase dangled from both hands in front of her, her chin was thrust up at him, and Nick could imagine Jordan adding, "Now what do you intend to do about it?"

Nick heaved a quick sigh. "So I did." He glanced across the busy street, seeking inspiration from the great city rising about them. He found it in the inviting arcade of the Galleria Vittorio Emanuele. "Look, I know you're probably tired of talking about Fabergés." He hesitated, giving her a chance to nod—which she graciously declined to do. Encouraged by that slight show of restraint, Nick went on. "But if you're not in a tremendous hurry, I'd like to invite you for coffee."

Nick noticed that Jordan MacKenzie had the sort of wide, full mouth that could curve with maddening ambiguity. Was she pursing her lips slightly in disdain? Were the corners twitching impatiently, a full-fledged frown held back only by civility? Or was she tempted to smile? Nick decided to push his luck and go with the latter.

"You'll have a hard time convincing me you're in a rush. Remember, I caught you window-shopping," Nick reminded her with a grin.

The lush coral lips expanded into an unequivocal smile, but her voice was as even and businesslike as it had been earlier at Vittorio's. "It isn't time that concerns me right now, Mr. Rostov. It's what you have in mind over that coffee. Ten to one, the Radetsky music box is going to crop up somewhere in the conversation."

"You're right." Nick hesitated, trying to gauge the appraisal of him going on behind the luminescent cat's eyes. "I'll be honest with you," he began. He sensed that subterfuge would be wasted on Jordan. Either she would respond to a straightforward request or she wouldn't, period. "I only want to talk with you for a few minutes."

Jordan could not imagine what additional information she would be able—or willing—to furnish Nick Rostov, but the thought of retreating into the arcade and enjoying a cup of thick Italian cappuccino with him prompted her to agree. "All right."

The Galleria was thronged with well-dressed Milanese, shopping, browsing through the racks outside bookstores, chatting over their afternoon coffee and pastry. Jordan let Nick escort her past several attractive cafés before they reached the one he had in mind. She slid into a chair, grateful to be rid of the cumbersome briefcase, and waited while a blur of rapid Italian passed between Nick and the waiter.

"Will you have espresso or American-style coffee?" Nick asked as he draped his garment bag over a chair and then slid into the seat across from her.

"Well, actually I was hoping for a cup of cappuccino." Jordan's voice trailed off. She must sound exactly like a kid in a soda shop, holding out for the triple fudge malt!

"Good, that's what I want, too. Can I tempt you to have some *gelato* with me? The chocolate here is fabulous."

Nick's stomach had been grumbling for something more palatable than the airline fare he had consumed earlier that

day, and he could scarcely believe his good fortune when
Jordan nodded eagerly. For most of his adult life he had
associated with women who were perpetually dieting. He
had grown accustomed to eating alone while they picked
away at a few lettuce leaves and sipped Perrier, but he had
never really liked it. Even when he had been in athletic
training, under coach's orders to eat heartily, he had always felt like a lone pig who had somehow ended up in an
aviary by mistake. Thank God Jordan MacKenzie was con-
tent with the curvaceous figure nature had bestowed on her!

Jordan's green eyes sparkled with unabashed delight
when their order arrived. Nick watched, fascinated by the
unfamiliar spectacle, as she plunged into the ice cream, un-
abashedly savoring every bite.

"You're not hungry?" she commented, glancing at his
melting portion.

"Oh, but I am!" Nick caught himself and quickly tasted
his own *gelato*.

Jordan licked the spoon and then placed it on the saucer
beneath the empty ice cream dish. "That was delicious. It's
a bad habit, but I often eat when I'm frustrated. And Dottore D'Antonelli's news about the Radetsky music box was
pretty frustrating."

Nick paused, holding the cup of cappuccino midway between the table and his mouth. For a brief interlude the refreshments and Jordan MacKenzie's enjoyment of them had
pushed the Radetsky treasure to the back of his mind.
"What were you hoping to hear?"

Jordan's laugh was flat and humorless. "*Not* that my research was going to run up against the Russian Revolution!" Shaking her head ruefully, she cut her spoon through
the cappuccino's frothy cap. "You can't imagine how difficult it is to trace even the simplest personal milestones—
birth certificates, marriage records, property exchanges—

after a revolution has swept a country. Or maybe you can?'' She cut her eyes up at him and regarded him thoughtfully.

Nick grimaced. "Works of art fare as poorly as official records during a revolution—if not worse. If your client is of Russian heritage, you're going to be dealing with the same obstacles I've confronted in trying to locate the Radetsky music box.''

"How long have you been looking for it?" Jordan asked.

Nick took his time swallowing the last spoonful of *gelato. As far back as I can remember? Since I was a child at my grandmother's knee?* What could he honestly say? "A long time" seemed a reasonable compromise, and that was the one he chose.

Jordan apparently found his answer acceptable, for she nodded her understanding. "I wish I could help you, Mr. Rostov. I honestly do. But I don't even know where that photograph came from originally." She straightened in preparation for a battery of unwelcome questions she could not answer.

"Your client must have some inkling."

Jordan's waving Titian hair rustled against the collar of her Burberry as she shook her head. "I've told you, Mr. Rostov. I'm not free to divulge my client's identity." She sounded a bit impatient, as if she were tired of repeating herself.

"Somehow this discussion wouldn't seem so adversarial if you'd quit calling me Mr. Rostov. Nick will do just fine."

False chumminess was one of the oldest manipulative tricks in the book, but then hadn't she been relying on "Mr. Rostov" to hold him at arm's length? She, too, could be accused of some subtle game playing, Jordan reflected. She sensed that Nick preferred first names between them for the exact reason he had offered: it felt more natural. "Okay,

Nick. But by whatever name I call you, I still can't reveal my client's name."

"What if I didn't ask you to?" Nick toyed with the ice cream spoon, giving her a sideways glance.

Jordan leaned forward slightly and frowned. "But I don't see how you hope to learn anything about that photograph if—"

Nick lifted a hand to ward off her protest. "Vittorio can't be the only person you plan to contact while you're conducting your research. You've already mentioned that you have an appointment with Gudrun Mayes-Cooper, correct?"

"Yes, that's right," Jordan began.

"And I'm confident you don't intend to tell Dr. Mayes-Cooper or any of your other contacts who your client is. Yet you must be hoping to extract a lot of information from these people about your client's past. Right?"

"Well, yes," Jordan conceded reluctantly. She had the peculiar feeling of being led somewhere she wasn't quite sure she wanted to go, and she was casting about for some ballast to slow the process.

"Very well. Why not pretend I'm just another of the people you'll be interviewing? Don't tell me your client's name. Simply share some of the other information you surely have. You can't be wandering around Europe without some leads to go on. Let me in on them. It's a long shot, I know, but the clues that might shed light on your client's background could also help me find the Radetsky music box."

Jordan crossed her arms across her chest and frowned. "I don't know, Nick."

If he leaned any farther across the tiny table, he would be in her lap. "I swear I won't press you about your client, and

I'm a man of my word. Let's work together, Jordan. We can help each other."

He had an utterly charming way of pronouncing her name, his tongue cutting neatly between the two syllables. With a sensitive case like Kitty Ridgewood's on her hands, the last thing Jordan needed was that low voice insinuating its way into her subconscious with words like *together.* She focused on a leather-goods shop across the arcade, anything to avoid the handsome, persuasive face directly in front of her.

"If you would tell me something about your client, I might be able to tie it in with other attempts I've made to locate the Radetsky."

Jordan shifted in her chair to face him. "So you know more than you let on in Dottore D'Antonelli's apartment today?" she said, snatching the chance to turn the tables.

Nick relaxed back in his chair, suddenly looking all too comfortable for Jordan's taste. "That depends on what you mean by 'let on.'"

"Oh, no, you don't, Mr. . . . Nick." Jordan tapped the marble tabletop with one finger. "If we agree to cooperate, one of the first ground rules will be no coy games."

"So you accept my offer?"

"I said 'if,' " Jordan reminded him.

Nick lapped an elbow over the back of his chair and gave her a tolerant smile. "Careful that you don't violate your own ground rule with this *if* business. But I see your point, and I'm willing to abide by it," he added before Jordan could formulate a suitable retort. "What more do you ask?"

"I need some time to think it over," Jordan told him. Despite her misgivings, she couldn't bring herself to give him a flat "no" out of hand. Then, too, his suggestion had its merits. She needed to consider the offer from all angles—without the distraction of Nick's startling blue eyes trained on her.

"Thank you for the coffee, but it's getting late. I really need to go." Jordan glanced up at the sky darkening above the arcade's glass dome. As she reached for the briefcase stowed beneath the table, Nick leaned forward and lightly placed his hand over hers.

"When will I know what you've decided!"

Jordan withdrew her hand, but her eyes lingered on the long, tapering fingers resting on the table. "I'll make up my mind before I leave Milan."

"And when is that?" Nick rose, mirroring Jordan's movements.

"Tomorrow." Jordan sidestepped, seeking an avenue of escape.

Nick obligingly moved aside and then fell in step with her. "I suppose we ought to make some arrangement to get in touch, then?"

"I'll leave word with Dottore D'Antonelli, if that's all right with you." Now that she was on her feet, once more in motion, she was thinking more clearly. The brain definitely needed plenty of oxygen to work efficiently. Another minute slouched in that bentwood chair, and who knows what she would have agreed to. Jordan picked up her pace as a safeguard against further lapses.

When she reached the street she abruptly halted, driven back into the arcade by a pelting rain. Silently cursing her short, straight skirt, Jordan tried to support the briefcase on one knee while she fumbled in it for her umbrella.

Nick took the briefcase and held it open for her. "Don't you think that's rather chancy, leaving word with a third party?"

Jordan flicked the umbrella open and reclaimed her briefcase. "Dottore D'Antonelli seems like a very responsible person." She lunged into the stream of pedestrians bent against the now-driving rain.

Nick flipped up his collar, walking sideways beside her. "It isn't that I don't think we can depend on Vittorio, but I'd prefer you contacted me directly."

Jordan narrowed her eyes against the droplets spattering her face. "Okay, give me your card."

Garment bag slung over his shoulder, Nick slapped his pocket with his free hand and then shrugged. "That wouldn't do you any good, since I'm not going to be at my telephone number in Vienna."

"Then give me the name of your hotel." Jordan shook the water from her hair, feeling as exasperated with Nick as with the rain. When she glanced over at him, however, she had a sudden change of heart. Sodden dark curls were plastered to his brow and collar. The fabric of his camel-hair coat was beginning to resemble the fur of a freshly bathed dog. "Oh, for heaven's sake! Get under this thing!" Jordan lifted the umbrella over his head.

"Thanks." Nick gave her a wet smile as he looped an arm around her shoulders and hunched down beneath the skimpy umbrella.

"There's my hotel." Jordan seized his arm, dragging him along with her as she made a break for the welcome sight of the Hotel Sabbiodore's striped canopy.

Inside the hotel lobby they shivered and shook themselves like two drenched retrievers. Mopping her leather briefcase with a soggy tissue, Jordan edged toward the concierge's desk. "If you give me the name of your hotel, I promise to call you."

Without speaking, Nick walked to the desk and fished one of the hotel's cards from the display case next to the bell. When he presented it to Jordan, she could only stare for a moment.

Nick gathered up his wet coat and the garment bag. "I just flew in from Vienna this morning, too early to check into a hotel. So, if they have an available room, I suppose..."

"You'll be staying here," Jordan supplied. While he filled out the registry, she tried to glare at him—not an easy feat for someone who must have borne at least a passing resemblance to a drowned rat.

Nick dotted an *i* with a flourish and then returned the pen to the smiling concierge. "I guess this takes care of our communication problem. You can phone me right here in your own hotel." He gave her a deceptively innocent grin. "Who knows? Perhaps you can simply knock on the wall."

"I doubt that." Jordan shoved a tangled strand of wet hair off her brow and turned toward the elevator. Juggling the wet coat and briefcase, she stabbed the button impatiently. From over her shoulder she saw Nick wave the bellboy away. When the elevator door creaked open, he caught it and then sidled into the tiny car beside her.

Jordan stared up at the flickering numbers as the elevator began its creeping ascent. She *would* have ended up with a room on the very top floor. Nick had apparently given up badgering her and was trying to wear her down with silence now. She kept stealing glances at him, waiting for him to get off, but he kept his eyes glued to the lighted numbers until they reached her floor. *Oh, God! He is going to be able to knock on the wall!* she thought as the car finally lurched to a halt. Then again, he could just be following her.

Not waiting to find out, Jordan charged out of the elevator and then wheeled. "Okay, look, Nick. I said I would consider your offer, and I will."

"If you're leaving tomorrow, we need to work something out quickly." Nick blocked the elevator door with one broad shoulder.

Jordan took a step back and bumped into a portly man trundling two suitcases. *"Scusi, signore!"* she mumbled, trying to recover her take-charge expression as she looked back at Nick. "Remember the time I requested to think this thing over alone?"

The fat man dropped one of the heavy suitcases, shoving it in front of Jordan. He grunted as he scooted the other piece closer to the elevator door.

"I remember." Still holding the elevator door, Nick gave the overweight man a dubious look.

"I meant what I said." Jordan stepped aside to accommodate the man struggling with his luggage.

Nick jockeyed from side to side, trying to circumvent the man's ponderous bulk. "But maybe if we could just—" In desperation, he broke off. Grabbing one of the suitcases, he hoisted it into the elevator.

"Grazie, signore!" The corpulent man's face flooded with relief as he seized the remaining bag and began to tug it backward into the elevator.

"No maybes, Nick." Jordan nudged the suitcase with her knee, giving it the shove it needed to clear the elevator's threshold.

"Molte grazie, signora!" The chunky man sagged against the wall, spent from his efforts.

"Jordan..." Nick began.

Smiling sweetly, Jordan waved with her fingers as she watched the doors close in front of Nick Rostov's exasperated face.

EVEN WITHOUT NICK'S assertive blue eyes to prod her, Jordan had a difficult time weighing the pros and cons of his offer. With a secretive and demanding client like Kitty Ridgewood, she needed to justify every risk carefully, regardless of how tempting the bait might appear. However, as she showered and dried her hair in the modest little hotel room, Jordan began to question her elaborate efforts to evade Nick's probing.

She had encountered a handsome man with an intriguing accent in the heart of Europe, but that was no reason to react as if she were a character in a spy movie. From a practical viewpoint, much could be said for working with Nick. Motives aside, he unquestionably knew enough about the Radetsky music box to save her weeks, perhaps months of laborious research. As an art world insider, he might even harbor a few tips that she would never be able to unearth on her own. And what did it matter to her if their collaboration led to his locating the Radetsky music box? After all, Kitty Ridgewood had hired her to find lost relatives, not art treasures. If she chose to tap Nick's resources, she need only stay on her toes to prevent any accidental slips that might give Kitty away. It was the "only" that continued to bother Jordan as she rummaged through her suitcase and dressed for dinner.

In spite of her attempt to play devil's advocate for Nick's case, she narrowly cracked the door and gave the corridor a furtive inspection before leaving her hotel room. Had the tiny pension offered room service, she would never have risked running into Nick on her way to a restaurant. Fortunately the lobby was empty, save for the night clerk snoozing behind the front page of a newspaper. Safely out of the hotel, Jordan chose an inconspicuous trattoria without even glancing at the menu displayed in the window. Over risotto and roast chicken, she continued to ponder her dilemma.

The very factors that recommended working with Nick underscored the pitfalls of involving him in her search. If the music box did prove to be a vital link with Kitty's past, tracing it might inevitably reveal her identity. Jordan had experienced too many surprise twists in her career as a genealogist to predict where any case would lead, especially in the early stages of an investigation. By the time she had returned to her hotel room, she had accumulated enough compelling reasons to prejudice the most stubborn jury against Nick Rostov's case.

He wouldn't be happy with her decision. Based on her limited experience with Nick, he didn't seem the kind to give up easily. She could imagine him pressuring her, bombarding her mind with rational arguments while his charm insidiously disarmed her defenses. Worse still, she had innocently revealed that Vienna was her next destination, something she would never have done had she realized that city was his home. She could not afford to have him complicating matters as she began her investigation in Vienna.

It was not cowardly, only practical, to get out of Milan without another face-to-face encounter with Nick Rostov. With this thought in mind, she phoned the airline and changed her reservation to a red-eye commuter flight that would have her miles above the Alps before Nick had even ordered his morning coffee. Satisfied with the concierge's promise that a cab would be waiting for her in plenty of time to reach the airport, Jordan tried not to feel like a sneak—with moderate success—as she prepared for bed.

THE DESK CLERK WAS nowhere to be seen when Jordan slipped into the dim lobby the following morning. She tapped the bell gingerly and was relieved when he appeared in a door cut in the wall of cubbyholes and keys. *"Buon giorno, signorina!"*

"Buon giorno, signore." Jordan squinted through the window at the still-dark street outside. While she waited for the clerk to fill out the American Express slip, Jordan penned a note to Nick.

"After carefully considering your offer, I've decided that my client's best interests prevent me from accepting."

Jordan hesitated. That sounded awfully perfunctory, as if she were turning him down for a used-car loan. She frowned, trying to think of a way to soften the comfortless sixteen-word sentence. None had occurred to her by the time the clerk pushed the charge slip across the counter. There was no point in dilly-dallying around, Jordan scolded herself as she dispatched both signatures and headed for the cab the concierge had ordered. If she felt like a thief slipping away in the night, so be it. She would slough any irrational guilt regarding Nick Rostov much faster than she would live down a serious gaffe with Kitty Ridgewood.

The cab driver tossed his cigarette into the gutter before taking Jordan's garment bag and stowing it in the Fiat's trunk. He opened the rear door of the vehicle and waited for her to climb in.

Jordan was already half inside the dark cab before she saw the man slouched in the corner.

"Good morning, Jordan." Stifling a languid yawn, Nick straightened his lanky form and smiled at her.

Chapter Three

Jordan pulled back so abruptly she bumped her head on the roof of the cab. "What are you doing here?" she demanded.

Nick's drowsy smile widened. "The same thing you're doing, I suppose. Taking a taxi to the airport."

Jordan took a deep breath, trying not to let her irritation cloud her ability to think clearly. Her eyes scanned the street in the vain hope that another cab would emerge from the gray fog.

Nick shook back his cuff to check his watch. "If you're going to make that early flight, you'd better get in. We're cutting it pretty close as it is."

Jordan glanced at the cabbie, who looked as if he were beginning to have serious doubts about this early-morning fare. The man probably spoke as little English as she spoke Italian, too little to offer any assistance in a matter that was becoming more ridiculous by the moment. Swallowing hard, she edged onto the back seat. "*I* ordered this cab," she informed Nick under her breath as the palpably relieved driver pulled away from the curb.

Nick raised an eyebrow, looking, to her great annoyance, not at all discomfited by the situation. "I know. The desk clerk told me."

Jordan rolled her eyes in disbelief. "I can't believe you actually *spied* on me!" she finally managed to get out.

"Spy is rather an extreme word, don't you think? I mean, it does smack of wiretaps and binoculars and those clever little devices Q fashions for James Bond." Nick's smile never faltered.

"While you're listing surveillance techniques, you might include pumping a hotel employee for information. A primitive but apparently effective means of keeping tabs on someone," Jordan put in with an acerbic smile.

Nick grinned, easing his shoulders comfortably into the plump upholstery. "Someone, you might add, who had every intention of skulking off without leaving a trace."

"I was not skulking off!" Jordan insisted, suddenly sitting up straight. "And I did leave you a note. I kept my part of the bargain."

"I appreciate that." Nick nodded graciously. "May I ask what the note said?"

Jordan stared out the window for a few moments before answering. "No."

"No, I may not ask?"

Jordan gave him a withering glance. "Yes, you may ask, and my answer is no."

Nick shook his head and chuckled. "Thank God we have the whole flight together to discuss things further."

"It won't do you any good, Nick. I've made up my mind."

"I can't count the times people have told me that—usually right before they make the very concession I've been angling for."

Jordan regarded Nick in exasperation. Given his appalling bravado, she wondered how he managed not to look smug, but somehow he did. Perhaps it was the mischievous twinkle in those dazzling blue eyes.

Nick's smiling eyes locked with hers, teasing her. "See? You're already reconsidering, aren't you?"

Jordan kept her gaze steady. "Actually, I was trying to think of a suitable punishment for that talkative desk clerk that wouldn't land me in an Italian prison for the rest of my life."

Nick burst out laughing. "Okay, the score is even. If we can seriously discuss working together, I promise to keep everything aboveboard." He clapped a hand over his breast briefly. "You have my word. No more spies. But can we talk? Please?"

Jordan caught the word *aeroporto* on a passing road sign, a sure indication that they were approaching their destination. Thank God she need hold him at bay only a little longer. Whatever maneuver he pulled, she was not going to let him wrangle a seat next to her on the plane. She would see to that even if she had to ride with the cargo.

She folded her arms across her chest and shook her head. "We've already talked, Nick, and I've explained my situation to you. My client—"

"Insists on absolute confidentiality," Nick put in impatiently. "And I've told you I'll respect those wishes. I can help you, Jordan."

Jordan glanced out the window at the broad field of moored aircraft. "Perhaps you could. But I've weighed the issue from all angles, and I've decided it's best that I work alone."

"Contacting dozens of people all over the Continent certainly doesn't constitute working alone," Nick scoffed, but his voice took on an edge of urgency as the taxi jolted to a halt outside the airport rotunda.

"I don't intend to tell anyone more than I've told you." Jordan suppressed a smile at Nick's uncharacteristic chagrin. While he was fumbling for his wallet, she counted out the fare plus a generous tip and then climbed out of the cab. By the time Nick caught up with her, she had shouldered her garment bag and was on her way into the terminal.

"I could save you a lot of trouble if you'd let me. For instance, what do you know about Gudrun Mayes-Cooper?"

Jordan resisted his challenging tone. "That she's a well-known art expert who's negotiated some important acquisitions in recent years."

Nick's laugh was short and hollow. "Anyone who reads back issues of *Newsweek* in the dentist's office would know that. But do you have any idea how she obtained some of those treasures?"

"Well, I suppose..." Ripping her plane ticket from the pocket of her shoulder bag, Jordan frowned at the line leading to the counter.

Nick's humorless chuckle was peculiarly annoying. "No supposing, Jordan. How did she pull off the Gorky Madonna deal, for instance?"

"I don't know." Making the admission irritated Jordan as much as his needling. "I've never even heard of the Gorky Madonna, but I fail to see what that has to do with my investigation." Gathering up her bags, she hurried for the customs gates without waiting for Nick. With his usual speed he caught up with her while the customs official was inspecting her passport.

"The Gorky Madonna is an extremely valuable Byzantine triptych, a picture of the Madonna in three connected pieces. After the turmoil of 1917, it remained hidden in a monastery for years. Word of its survival finally reached the West, but by then it was in the hands of black marketeers."

As he followed her to the boarding area, Nick adopted the monotone of a slightly bored lecturer. "Gudrun put out the word that she had an inside track on the Gorky Madonna. Not surprisingly, a wealthy collector pounced on the bait."

"Did she get it for him?" Jordan broke in. Shifting her garment bag, she impatiently followed the passengers shuffling toward the boarding ramp.

"Oh, yes." Nick lapsed into a silence obviously intended to whet her curiosity.

Jordan shot him a sarcastic smile calculated to deflate his attempt at melodrama. "Good."

"Would you like to know how she pulled off this feat?" he asked after a few moments.

"I'm sure you're going to tell me, anyway." Jordan nodded graciously to the flight attendant. Sidestepping a man digging pillows out of an overhead bin, she edged her way down the aisle.

Oblivious to the passengers pressing behind him, Nick paused beside the row of seats where Jordan had safely ensconced herself between a motherly-looking woman and a man in a three-piece suit. "As it turned out, Gudrun was dealing with fairly unscrupulous types—not an unusual situation on the black market. One of the 'mules' her contacts used to transport part of the triptych to the West was a ballet dancer who planned to defect. It seems that, over the years, this dancer had been bringing more to the West than stunning performances and smuggled artworks. At any rate, the spy dancer went into hiding while he was waiting to be granted asylum. Of course, Gudrun wasn't interested in espionage or any of that. She simply wanted the icon. She employed some rather heavy-handed fellows to track down the dancer, thugs who weren't particularly sensitive to a defecting spy's need for secrecy. Gudrun got her missing piece, though."

"And the dancer?" The grim look on Nick's face made her almost afraid to ask.

"The police found his body floating in the Danube." At last yielding to the bottleneck building behind him, Nick moved to the rear of the cabin, but not before adding, "I imagine a lot of people were relieved when they ruled it a suicide."

Nick's chilling curtain line had effectively robbed Jordan of any peace she had hoped to enjoy during the flight. While the elderly woman napped contentedly beside the window and the businessman pored over a report, Jordan was left to ponder Nick's revelation and its implications about Gudrun Mayes-Cooper. Of course, he could have exaggerated, deliberately twisting the story to cast Mayes-Cooper in an unflattering light. But what if he *wasn't* stretching the truth? Jordan was still considering that troubling possibility when the plane landed in Vienna.

As she had expected, Nick was right behind her before she was out of the boarding area. "Still looking forward to your tête-à-tête with Dr. Mayes-Cooper?"

Pulling up short, Jordan wheeled to face him. "Okay, Nick, I've had enough games."

"I'm glad to hear that. I wasn't looking forward to relying on bell captains' gossip to keep up with you. Talking with you directly is much more productive—not to mention enjoyable." He flashed her one of those devastatingly appealing smiles.

Jordan fostered an expression that was all business. "I want to know exactly what sort of help you can offer me. What should I expect from Gudrun Mayes-Cooper when I meet her this morning?"

"Does this mean we're working together?" Nick hedged cannily.

Jordan refused to budge. "It could."

Nick cleared his throat. "Simply put, Gudrun will do anything to get what she wants. She'll connive, lie, cheat, double-cross, consort with the most ruthless people you'd ever care *not* to meet—whatever it takes to win. Don't fall for any tips she might offer about the Radetsky music box. Believe me, if she had any valid leads on it, she would have followed them long ago. And don't tell her anything that's even remotely confidential, although you don't seem to have a weakness in that area," he was quick to add.

Jordan grimaced. "Well, at least I'm forewarned. Thanks."

"My pleasure. Now what do I get in return?"

Jordan was startled by the directness of his question. For all his appeal, she needed to remember that Nick Rostov could drive a bargain as hard as any she had in mind. "It all depends on what you want."

An insinuating glint flickered across the deep blue mirrors of his eyes for a fleeting moment, causing Jordan to wish she had chosen slightly different words. "Meet me in Demel's for coffee this afternoon and let me know how your meeting with Gudrun went."

"Okay," Jordan agreed.

They had been walking through the terminal and had now reached the taxi stand. Nick opened the rear door of the nearest cab and held it for Jordan. "If I was driving into the city, I'd offer you a lift, but I'm afraid I'm headed for the suburbs. My sister has been keeping my dog, and I need to take him off her hands before he devours all of her furniture." The mercurial smile altered once more, giving him a winningly boyish look.

Given the enormous amounts of energy she had spent eluding him, Jordan was surprised by her disappointment at the abrupt parting. "What time should we meet this afternoon?" she asked, rolling down the cab's window.

"At four, like all good Viennese." Nick stepped back as the cabbie ignited the engine. "Enjoy your kaffeeklatsch with Gudrun."

"She sounds delightful," Jordan remarked dryly through the open window.

Nick's enigmatic laugh carried over the airport din. "Oh, but she is. Utterly charming. That's what makes her so dangerous."

WITH THE PRECISE MUSCULAR control he had practiced so often as an athlete, Nick carefully nudged the door of the Porsche shut. He winced as the lock engaged, emitting a brief click. The sound should have been imperceptible to any creature more than a few feet from the parked car, but where sharp ears were concerned, Pedro defied normal physical laws. The raucous bellow from the two-story house warned Nick that today was no exception. Whatever his ragamuffin dog might lack in pedigree, he more than compensated in the auditory department.

As Nick hurried to the front door, a series of jubilant yelps was punctuated by the sound of claws scrambling for traction on slippery parquet. The door swung open, releasing a forty-five pound trajectory of wiry white fur.

"Take it easy, Pedro." Nick scooped the squirming dog into his arms. Wrinkling his nose at the large pink tongue swiping his face, he grinned at the slim woman standing in the doorway. "Were you a good boy while I was in Milan or did you wreck Tante Daria's house?"

Daria smiled indulgently. "For the record, he ate two African violets, but they were near death, so I won't take off any points for that. Other than sleeping on a dance costume I'd left on the bed, he was almost the model child this time."

"You must be getting old, Pete." Nick scratched the dog's ears as he carried him back into the house.

"He probably would behave better if you didn't confuse him with so many different names," Daria remarked, giving her brother and the wiggling dog a wry glance.

"Pedro. Pete. Pietor. It's all the same, and he knows it. Don't you, fellow?" Nick ruffled the stiff hair sprouting over the dog's eyes as he placed him on the floor.

Daria shook her head. "You're hopeless, but it's good to see you, anyway."

"It's good to see you, too." Nick gave his sister a warm hug.

Holding her brother at arm's length, Daria scanned his face. "Was the trip worthwhile?"

Nick nodded. "It appears that Vittorio's hunch was on target."

Daria glanced cautiously down the hall and then pressed a finger to her lips. "I want to hear all about it," she said in a low voice. "But I think I should warn you that Grandmama and Maria Rachmanova have come for coffee this morning. They've talked of nothing else since you left for Milan, and they will be clamoring to know what you've learned."

"I should never have mentioned Vittorio's call to Grandmama." Nick castigated himself. "At her age, she doesn't need to have her hopes raised only to see them dashed once more. And poor Rachmanova, she's even older than Grandmama!"

"I don't think we need treat Grandmama like a child, Nick," Daria began. She broke off as a door at the end of the hall opened. She smiled affectionately at the two white-haired women who appeared.

"Welcome home, Nick!" Nick's grandmother rushed to greet him. She embraced him as if he had been away for two years, not a scant two days.

"You're looking wonderful as always, Grandmama," Nick told her sincerely. He smiled into the face that seventy-plus years had left remarkably unlined.

His grandmother accepted the compliment with easy grace, a gift she had honed during her many years as a prima ballerina. "You are a flatterer, but I love you for it! You are going to join us for coffee, aren't you?" Not waiting for his answer, she slipped her arm through his, leading him back to the doorway where the other woman stood.

"Good day, Nicolai Rostovitch." Although Maria Rachmanova, like his grandmother, had lived most of her life in Vienna, she still clung to the Russian forms of address she carried from her youth. Indeed, the elderly woman often spoke as if time had frozen for her in 1916.

Nick nodded cordially and returned the greeting. Just as Grandmama had mothered him and Daria while their parents flitted from New York to Paris to Monte Carlo—wherever the next sports-car rally or charity ball demanded—so also had Maria Rachmanova played a similar role in their orphaned grandmother's life, albeit under very different circumstances. In 1920 Grandmama had been the only member of her family to survive the flight from Russia. Like Grandmama's mother, Maria Rachmanova had been a member of the famed Kuzov dance troupe. Although scarcely more than a girl herself, she had taken the hapless child under her wing. He would always be grateful to the eccentric and somewhat forbidding lady for the kindness she had shown Grandmama.

"So, Nick, tell us what you have learned in Milan," Grandmama demanded as soon as they were gathered around the dining table.

Regardless of his reservations about raising false hopes, Nick realized that any effort to evade his strong-willed grandmother's questioning would be futile. Over coffee and

Kuchen, he gave the women an abbreviated account of the meeting in D'Antonelli's apartment and the photograph that Jordan MacKenzie had mysteriously acquired.

"To think you've seen an actual picture of the music box! You *do* think it is authentic?" Grandmama added, a questioning note tempering the excitement in her voice.

"Both Vittorio and I do. The problem isn't the picture, but all this idiotic secrecy surrounding it. I believe I've reached an agreement with Jordan MacKenzie. I'll have to see where that leads." Nick shot a glance at Daria, appealing for her help in keeping expectations in check.

"We've been disappointed so many times before," Daria commented, picking up the cue. "I suppose we must simply hope for the best."

As Nick had feared, Daria's cautious appraisal was wasted on their grandmother. "When will you speak with Miss MacKenzie again?"

"This afternoon. She has a meeting with a rather shady art dealer this morning, and I'm anxious to hear what comes of that."

The papery-fine skin of Maria Rachmanova's brow drew into a frown. "Are you certain this Miss MacKenzie can be trusted?"

Nick hesitated. His immediate impulse was to say, "Yes, of course." Following almost instantaneously on the heels of that urge was the troublesome reminder that he had only the most superficial—and intuitive—basis for that assessment. "I think she's a decent person who has no idea what the Radetsky music box really represents." When Rachmanova's grave stare remained unaltered, he went on. "I do agree that extra precautions are in order. A friend from my college days is in a position to provide the necessary information, and I plan to call him this evening."

The aging ballet dancer appeared only partially placated by his assurances. "You should not bestow your trust too easily, Nicolai Rostovitch," Rachmanova warned him.

"And I don't, as a matter of personal policy." Nick strove to keep his tone even. Ordinarily, he felt no great need to defend his position. That he found Jordan extraordinarily attractive, however, made him especially sensitive to criticism in this case.

Grandmama came to his defense, but her face, too, had grown solemn. "I know you will be careful, Nick. But you must remember. You well know from your profession the great lengths to which people will go to acquire a valuable art treasure." Her eyes traveled to her slim hands folded nervously on the edge of the table. When she looked up at Nick, a thin bead of moisture rimmed her eyes. "Think of how much more someone would be willing to risk to keep two murders secret."

SURELY NICK ROSTOV WAS being facetious when he applied the word *charming* to Gudrun Mayes-Cooper. For now, Jordan preferred to give him the benefit of the doubt. Given the way her meeting had been going that morning, she couldn't bring herself to face another disappointment and admit that Nick was the kind of man who would see anything attractive about the arrogant, manipulative woman sitting across the hotel tearoom table from her.

Not that the art expert wasn't pretty, Jordan allowed. In fact, she was stunning. Unfortunately, her model-perfect looks began to fade—at least in Jordan's eyes—after about five minutes of conversation, just long enough for her high-handed, calculating manner to assert itself.

Nick had insisted that Gudrun was a snake, but with that peculiar dichotomy of the male mind, he could still think she was a knockout. Not that his opinion of the woman's looks mattered a damn, Jordan snapped at herself. Frowning, she checked her watch, recrossed her legs and waited for Mayes-Cooper to complete her inspection of the photocopy.

The halo of spun-sugar blond hair was bent over the picture of the Fabergé egg. Mayes-Cooper was taking an awfully long time to examine the photocopy, far longer than Dr. D'Antonelli or Nick had. Probably for effect, Jordan thought uncharitably.

"Very interesting, *very* interesting," the art expert murmured to herself in a low, breathy voice.

One exquisitely manicured hand guided a magnifying glass over the photocopy while the other toyed with a wisp of platinum hair. When she finally looked up she ignored Jordan for a few moments, making an elaborate production of putting away her magnifying glass and rearranging things in her briefcase. The cynical violet-blue eyes settled on Jordan only when she reached to retrieve the photocopy.

Jordan flashed a sweetly poisonous smile as she returned the copy to her own briefcase. "Do you recognize the piece?" she asked. She had decided in advance to play dumb and let Mayes-Cooper be the first to identify the Radetsky music box.

Gudrun regarded her warily, sizing her up. "Hasty, ill-considered evaluations serve no purpose, Ms. MacKenzie. Given time and the opportunity to examine the original photograph—"

Jordan interrupted the condescending voice. "As I've already told you, that's impossible. I do have some extra copies of the picture. If you like, you may have one." She pulled a copy from a pocket of her briefcase and slid it across the table.

Gudrun looked at the photocopy as if it were an insultingly small tip. She made no effort to conceal her distaste when she at last picked it up. "The resolution is perfectly wretched," she complained, her glossy lips pursing into a pout.

"The original isn't much better," Jordan assured her. She sighed, surveying the porcelain coffee service arranged on the table, and then scooted her chair back slightly. "Well, forgive me for taking up so much of your time. Thank you for meeting with me today."

As Jordan stood, Gudrun lurched forward in her seat. "Wait!" She caught herself and eased back slightly. "I mean, you shouldn't be discouraged simply because I haven't been able to give you an immediate identification. I will be more than happy to research this object thoroughly. It *is* an intriguing piece." She forced a makeshift smile.

Jordan pretended to consider the matter for a moment. "I imagine that could become very time-consuming. I would have to consult with my client first before committing to such expensive research. But I do appreciate your offer."

As Jordan picked up her briefcase, Gudrun Mayes-Cooper jumped up from the table. "The cost would be negligible. Truly."

Jordan shook her head, now thoroughly relishing the quagmire into which she had lured her opponent. "That's very kind of you, Dr. Mayes-Cooper, but I couldn't possibly ask an expert of your stature to expend valuable time on what might be a fruitless search."

"The service of art cannot be evaluated in mere money, Ms. MacKenzie. Discovering a great work to share with the world is the real reward I seek."

Jordan stared at her in amazement. Lying wasn't a skill she admired, but Mayes-Cooper was certainly an unabashed master of the art. "I'll speak with my client and then get back in touch with you. How long do you plan to be in Vienna?"

"As long as necessary," Gudrun said smoothly. For a split second, a glimmer of malice cracked through the earnest facade. "But don't worry, Ms. MacKenzie. If you don't find me, I'll certainly find you."

"I CAN'T BELIEVE she managed to say that with a straight face! 'All I care about is art. Please let's not spoil things by discussing dreadful, nasty money.'" Nick imitated Gudrun's gushy-hushed voice. His hearty laugh carried over the clinking china and subdued conversation filling Demel's elegant pastry shop. "That's our girl, all right! Vintage Gudrun." He shook his head.

Jordan's amusement was more restrained. "She impressed me as a real operator, and I spent less than an hour with her."

"From the sound of things, you held your own rather well." A flash of admiration sparked Nick's brilliant blue eyes.

Jordan wrinkled her nose and carefully stirred her coffee. "I feel pretty stupid now, letting her meet me in my own hotel. I'd like to change hotels to shake her, but I've already used that hotel as my local address in correspondence. I sent a letter by messenger to Count Radetsky this morning, and I'd hate to risk having his response go astray."

"Save yourself the trouble of packing again, and stay put. You can take Gudrun at her word when she said she would find you. She's a veritable bloodhound." Nick speared the bite of apple strudel remaining on his plate and popped it into his mouth. "Chances are she's already made friends with most of your hotel's staff, and we've already seen where that leads."

Jordan lifted the coffee cup, frowning through the fragrant cloud of vapor. "I'm not sure I like the sound of that.

Maybe I'll move, just to give her a little extra work. I'm going to Spitzdorf tomorrow, anyway."

"Oh, really? What's in Spitzdorf?" Nick's tone was deliberately nonchalant.

Jordan took a long sip of coffee before answering. Much as she shared her mother's romantic affinities for candlelight dinners and schmarmy old movies, she was her father's girl, too. And veteran FBI agent Jack MacKenzie never committed himself without thinking twice.

"A convent." Jordan lowered the cup, settling it silently on the saucer. "It used to be an orphanage. I have reason to believe that my client spent her early childhood there."

Nick whistled softly under his breath. "Your client is an orphan? This must be a really tough case."

"I don't have much to go on," Jordan admitted.

"Perhaps the good nuns will be able to enlighten you. In any event, the Tyrol is a beautiful part of the country. At least we can enjoy the scenery."

"We?" Jordan's brows rose questioningly.

Nick nodded. "I'll drive you."

"Thanks for the offer, but I've already bought a train ticket." Nick had no reason to look so crestfallen, Jordan told herself, nor did she need to explain her rationale—but she did, anyway. "I'm planning to use the travel time to catch up on paperwork. I have other cases in the works, you know, and I swore to my secretary that I'd courier a bundle of material to her by the end of next week."

"I understand," Nick agreed affably. "If I can't interest you in a chauffeur, you'll still need an interpreter. Remember, I promised to help you."

Jordan laughed and shook her head. "You just don't give up, do you?"

"Never."

"You'll have to keep trying, then. I speak German."

"Ja, aber wahrscheinlich verstehen Sie nichts in Spitz-dorf." Nick adopted the singsong rhythm of the Tyrolean dialect.

"I caught the word 'Spitzdorf,'" Jordan insisted defensively.

Nick chuckled. "Good for you. Which proves what I just said. You probably won't understand anything in Spitz-dorf. Come on, Jordan. I'm sincerely offering you some valuable help. I'll do all the talking you need to get you inside that convent and in touch with the right people. Then if there's something you'd rather I didn't see or hear, I'll let you go it alone." He threw up both hands. "And I won't ask any questions that you don't want to answer. What better deal can I offer you?"

Jordan gave him a skeptical grin. "As my father used to say, there ain't no free lunch. If it's a deal, you must be expecting something in return."

"To be sure." Nick's face eased into a smile of supreme confidence. "You, my dear Miss MacKenzie, are going to help me find the Radetsky music box."

THE HOTEL ROOM WAS SMALL and dingy, but Arvidsen had seen worse. He had slept in countless rooms like this one, cramped holes with lopsided pictures covering the stains on the cheap wallpaper. The shabby respectability was familiar to him by now, even homelike. And this place was clean. That was one commodity on which Arvidsen insisted—cleanliness—even when his work took him to some third-world hellhole.

He could have done far better for himself in Vienna. A room at the Imperial or the Sacher Hotel would have scarcely made a dent in the money his latest client was paying. He wanted to keep a low profile, however, and that interest was better served in a fallen-down pit like this hotel.

He would be leaving shortly, anyway, as soon as he received orders from his client.

Arvidsen let the bulky gray-and-beige desk phone buzz a half-dozen times before picking up. He waited, listening to the anxious breathing on the other end of the line for a few seconds, enjoying the nervous fear that lay behind it.

"Herr Brenner?"

Arvidsen smiled at the code name he had given the client. "This is Brenner."

He could hear his client swallow, force moisture through a throat constricted with apprehension. They were always like this, the ones with money and reputations, afraid of going too far to turn back. He laughed to himself. Didn't the fools realize that once they had contacted him, there could be no going back?

Arvidsen listened to the tight voice giving him instructions. When his client started to repeat the information, Arvidsen cut in abruptly. "I understand."

A tense silence intervened. Arvidsen was about to hang up the phone when the anxious voice caught him.

"I want no unnecessary violence. If you must . . . do anything, it must be clean, without any traces that could lead back . . . back to me. Is that clear, Herr Brenner?" An empty pause followed. "Herr Brenner?"

Arvidsen only chuckled into the phone. He held the receiver for a long moment before letting it drop back onto the cradle. Then he walked to the wardrobe and pulled out a flat, rectangular case hidden behind the hem of his black leather coat. He placed the leather case on the dresser and opened it, adjusting the table lamp's faded shade to illuminate the sleek steel components secured inside the case.

There were newer, more powerful handguns than the Ruger Mark II Government Target Automatic, but the gun was still Arvidsen's weapon of choice. It was perfect for his style, a .22 caliber that functioned with pinpoint accuracy. Arvidsen liked to work at close range, liked to see the look in his target's eyes just before he pulled the trigger. His fingers slid the length of the barrel, caressing the tempered steel. His eyes rested on the dismantled gun and silencer for a few moments. Then he closed the case and snapped off the light.

Chapter Four

As Nick had predicted, the glorious Tyrolean landscape, with its glacier-crowned limestone peaks and valleys rippling with evergreens, relieved the tedium of the half-day's journey to Spitzdorf. What he had not foreseen was that he would be the principal beneficiary of the postcard-perfect scenery passing outside the train's windows. Apparently Jordan had been serious about catching up on her work during the trip.

As far as Jordan was concerned, they might as well have been traveling in a windowless baggage car. Except for a couple of brief pauses for coffee and lunch, she had buried herself behind a stack of legal folders bulging with photocopies and smudgy faxes. At first he had interrupted her to point out a particularly spectacular sight. Jordan would smile, make a politely appreciative comment, and then promptly retreat to her work. After a while Nick gave up distracting her and turned to the Frederick Forsyth paperback he had fortunately brought along.

Normally he could have lost himself in the novel's suspenseful plot. Today, however, his mind kept wandering to the enigmatic photograph of the Radetsky music box and the equally intriguing woman who had brought it into his life. Despite his best efforts, he was still fighting a pang of guilt at delving into Jordan's background behind her back. Looking at the lovely face half-concealed behind a fat, spiral-bound document, Nick realized that under any circumstances he would have wanted to learn more about her, albeit in a more straightforward fashion.

The early-afternoon sun streaming through the train's window had awakened the fire hidden in her dark gold hair. That hair reminded him of a Titian painting he especially liked. Nick had always marveled at the great master's rendering of those burnished shoulder-length waves. Something in their wondrous texture tempted the viewer to touch the canvas, as if he could run his fingers through the exquisite silkiness of that glorious hair. Nick caught himself as the conductor strode by their cabin and announced the approach of Spitzdorf.

Jordan looked up from some copies she was studying. She quickly flipped through the remaining pages, then snapped open her briefcase and shoveled the entire mess of papers into it.

"So this is Spitzdorf?" She leaned forward, craning for a peek at the vista just opening through the mountain pass. "It's beautiful!"

Nick surveyed the snow-banked, half-timbered buildings nestled at the feet of the jutting mountains and shrugged. "You missed a dozen equally charming sights on the way," he grumbled good-naturedly.

Jordan grinned. "This *is* a business trip, remember?" she reminded him. "I think it's time you got to work, Mr. Interpreter."

"At your service." After the train had halted, Nick collected both their bags and then slid open the compartment door. He led the way across the platform and upstairs to the station. Nick deposited their bags in a locker before heading for the taxi stand.

Pausing beside one of the two Mercedes taxis, Nick turned to Jordan. "What was the name of that monastery again?"

"Convent," Jordan corrected him. "It's called the Kloster des Heiligen Florians."

Nick dutifully instructed the cab driver before ushering Jordan inside the cab. As the big sedan plowed through the snowy streets, he gave her a bemused smile. "You know, you're going to have to tell me *something* about this mystery client of yours or I'm going to be pretty useless asking questions for you at the convent."

Jordan reluctantly shifted her gaze from the row of attractive shops lining the narrow street. "I had planned to brief you," she insisted.

"Better start." Nick nodded toward the taxi driver, who had slowed the Mercedes to a crawl. "It looks as if we're about to reach our destination."

"I'm looking for records from the early 1920s regarding a child named Käthe Davidov."

"Do you know when the girl was admitted to the orphanage? Where she came from? Who brought her?"

Jordan shook her head. "Those are a few of the questions I'm hoping to answer this afternoon."

The cabbie had braked in front of a three-story fortresslike building, bordered on either side by a gray stone wall. The sidewalks of the cul-de-sac were so narrow, Nick opened the taxi door carefully to avoid scraping it against the facade of the forbidding-looking structure. Looking up at the cold, stark walls, he winced for the orphaned and abandoned children who had spent their young lives there.

While the taxi driver wrote a receipt for Jordan, Nick tugged the ancient bell chain dangling from the door frame and waited for someone to respond. A small face, framed by a nun's starched white wimple, soon appeared in the steeple-shaped peephole cut in the door. After introducing himself and Jordan, Nick briefly explained the purpose of their visit. To his surprise, the young nun broke into a wide smile.

"Please, one moment," she said in heavily accented English.

Considerable rattling and grating issued from the hallway as the door's medieval lock yielded to admit them to the convent foyer. The nun clasped her hands in front of her and beamed at Jordan.

"You are from America? Then you must know of Notre Dame!" When Jordan nodded, the little nun went on eagerly. "My brother, Thomas, studied at this university for one year as an exchange student. Go, Fighting Irish!" She giggled shyly and made a small rah-rah gesture with her fist. "When we visit, I tell him we must speak English so that I may improve. My English is not so good as his."

"Oh, but you speak excellent English," Jordan was quick to assure her, with a pointed glance at Nick.

Sister Berthe, as the nun had introduced herself, was obviously delighted to have the opportunity to practice her language skills. "I will be very happy to help you. It has been many years since our sisters cared for orphans." Her lively dark eyes scanned the vaulted ceiling, and she frowned. "Like little flowers, young ones need light and air to grow well. They have now a better place. But come. I will take you to our Mother Superior."

Jordan turned to Nick, but he was already prepared for the next obvious step. "I don't suppose you'll be needing me any further for now."

"No, but thanks for getting me this far." Jordan sounded genuinely grateful.

"My pleasure. What time should we plan to meet?"

Jordan conferred with Sister Berthe before answering. "Let's say around seven, at the train station. That should give me plenty of time to do my research, and I think we can still make the last direct train back to Vienna. You could check the exact departure time, if you don't mind."

"I'll be glad to. Good luck, then," Nick told Jordan. After thanking Sister Berthe for her help, he retreated to the snowy street.

The taxi had long since departed, but that was just as well, Nick decided. With more than five hours to kill, he was in no rush to get anywhere in the tiny village. As he trudged through the street winding to the village square, he felt strangely frustrated. If he looked at matters realistically, the chances of Jordan discovering anything of earth-shattering importance that afternoon were slim. And if she did uncover a valuable lead, Nick was confident he could justify his participation in the next phase of her investigation, just as he had inveigled the chance to accompany her to Spitzdorf. No, something besides his quest for links to the Radetsky music box was bothering him.

He enjoyed working with Jordan, and he felt excluded. Nick grappled with that realization as he wandered past the eighteenth-century fountain that marked the center of Spitzdorf. From the start of his unorthodox career as an art appraiser and acquisition agent, he had preferred to work alone. He had always contended that partners only complicated things, arguing for caution when bold action was needed and blundering ahead when restraint was in order. Yet none of his reliable stock of arguments seemed to apply to Jordan. In the brief time he had known her, she had impressed him as being bright, energetic, strong-minded enough to hold her own, and blessed with a sense of humor that kept obstacles from becoming insurmountable nightmares. Her stunning looks did nothing to detract from his opinion. A visceral stirring stung Nick at the thought of that lush, inviting cascade of reddish blond hair, and he took quick measures to rein in his emotions.

He still didn't know that much about her, Nick reminded himself. After all, if appearances were an accurate reflection of character, Gudrun Mayes-Cooper would have been an angel. That sobering thought prompted him to retrace his path to the town's post office. When he had spoken with Peter Clements last evening, his old college friend had promised to dig up some background information on Jordan MacKenzie in less than twenty-four hours. If Jordan was really a stalking horse for an underhanded art collector, now was as good a time as any to find out. Despite his resolve, Nick felt an unfamiliar queasiness in the pit of his stomach as he waited for the call to go through to the American consulate in Vienna.

As Nick had hoped, Peter picked up on his direct line. "Clements here."

"Hey, Peter! It's Nick. Did I catch you at a bad time?" To Nick's surprise, he almost wished Peter would say yes.

"No worse than any other. I guess you're calling to see what I've got on Ms. MacKenzie? Hang on a sec."

Nick listened to the muffled sound of papers being shuffled. When they had been college roommates, Peter's side of the room had suffered from chronic disorder, and Nick guessed that his present office fared no better.

"Okay, here it is." Peter sounded out of breath, as if his search had been an arduous one. "I gave my buddy in Washington the info you had on her. Her business appears to be on the up-and-up, licensed, Silver Spring, Maryland C of C member, all the conventional stuff. As far as her personal life is concerned, he didn't come up with much. She has a few parking tickets, all paid, but nothing criminal."

Nick felt a stupid smile of relief spreading across his face. "So you don't have anything that would indicate this genealogy business is a smoke screen."

"If it is, she's spent almost nine years establishing it. That seems kind of farfetched to me."

"Me, too," Nick hastened to agree.

"Oh, Chris did find one choice tidbit."

Nick's heart did a two-step between beats. "What?"

"Her dad retired from the FBI two years ago. Remember the Poconos Stalker, that serial killer who preyed on hikers and campers? Well, Jack MacKenzie is responsible for nailing him." Peter chuckled. "If his daughter is anything like her old man, she's a sharp one. I wouldn't try to put any funny business over on her if I were you, Nick."

"If her story is as straight as you've led me to believe, I won't have to," Nick assured Peter. "Thanks for the help."

"Anytime. Get in touch when you're back in town. Joy and I would both love to have you over for dinner some weekend."

After promising to take advantage of Peter's invitation, Nick thanked him again and hung up. An emotion akin to elation seized him as he left the post office and set out for the train station. His instincts had been right about Jordan. He could trust her. The thought glowed in his mind like a newfound treasure.

A light snow had begun to fall, and Nick flipped up his collar while he studied the train schedules posted outside the station. He was checking his watch, trying to decide how he should while away the remainder of the afternoon, when an unmistakable face caught his eye through the smeared window of the station café.

Nick instinctively retreated behind the sheltering cover of the train schedule board, safely out of Gudrun Mayes-Cooper's range of vision. She hadn't seen him, he was sure.

She was too preoccupied with signaling the café's waitress to her table. Nick watched while the art expert scowled and gestured over her order. He was well out of earshot, but the pantomime made clear that Gudrun was very displeased with the tea and biscuits she had been served.

This isn't your customary five-star restaurant, Gudrun. What the devil *was* she doing in a rail station café, anyway? And in Spitzdorf, of all places? She had to be trailing Jordan. There was simply no other rational explanation for Mayes-Cooper's appearance in an obscure village with scarcely fifteen hundred inhabitants and no museums or galleries. She was lying in wait for Jordan, no doubt, ready to pounce on her and pump her for information when she returned to the train station.

What better task could he have found than making Gudrun Mayes-Cooper uncomfortable, Nick thought with a gently malicious smile as he headed for the café. He paused just inside the door to adjust his coat collar and brush the snowflakes from his hair, giving Gudrun a good chance to spot him, which she immediately did.

"Good afternoon, Gudrun." Nick relished the anger that darkened her violet-blue eyes to the shade of overripe plums.

"Hello, Nicky." Mayes-Cooper's voice was as frosty as the opaque moisture clinging to the streaked windows.

Nick surveyed the room and was delighted to find a free table directly opposite Gudrun's. He took time making himself at home, removing his coat and pulling the paperback out of his pocket. Gudrun was doing her best to ignore him, but the pink flush coloring her neck gave her away. Every time he caught her eyes drifting to his table, he smiled and nodded cordially. At last she shoved the half-empty teacup away from her and stood up. Tossing a few ten-schilling notes onto the table, she stalked toward the door.

"On your way back to London, Gudrun? You must have decided to take the scenic route." Nick gave her a pseudo-innocent look guaranteed to raise her hackles even further.

"You win this one, Nicky," Gudrun conceded. She paused in the doorway, her lips curling into a bitter smile. "But I'm warning you. The game isn't over yet."

"SO MANY ORPHANS! It is always so after a war." Sister Berthe shook her head sadly as she brushed dust from the yellowed papers wedged into the box she had just opened. "So, we shall continue with 1921?"

"Yes, please."

Jordan let Sister Berthe divide a handful of the documents. She adjusted the green glass shade of the desk lamp, funneling light onto the faded pages. They had spent over two hours examining the records from 1920, much longer than she had anticipated, but given the quirks of orphans' backgrounds they dared not skip a single document. The handwritten entries were difficult to decipher, some almost illegible. Equally tedious were the printed portions set in the old German script that neither Jordan nor Sister Berthe read with any speed. Even the paper required careful handling, for it was brittle with age and crumbled easily. At this rate, Jordan figured, she would need to spend the night in Spitzdorf and continue her work tomorrow. Still, there were no shortcuts to the painstaking task.

"I am sorry that the files were not kept in order, *B* following *A* and so forth." Sister Berthe murmured the apology, holding a page up to the light.

"I'm just grateful that they were kept at all," Jordan consoled her.

They had been working for some time in silence when Sister Berthe suddenly grabbed Jordan's wrist. "I believe I have found little Käthe!" she exclaimed.

Jordan anxiously rushed around the table to peer over her companion's shoulder. She could barely contain her excitement as Sister Berthe's finger traced the entry.

"Davidov, Käthe. Date of birth—unknown. Age—unknown." Jordan translated as she read aloud. "The spaces for her place of birth and parent names aren't even filled in. And what does this mean?" She pointed to a smudged sentence.

Sister Berthe studied the blurred letters for a moment. "It says that she was transferred to the orphanage on March 3, 1921 from..." She hesitated, wrinkling her upturned nose over an ink blot. "From the Marienlazarett in Vienna."

"The Marienlazarett?"

Sister Berthe's veil rustled when she nodded. "That would be a hospital. I am sorry we have so little information about this poor child, but perhaps the hospital's records will be more complete."

"You have been extraordinarily helpful," Jordan assured the friendly nun.

After helping Sister Berthe return the records to their storage box, Jordan took time to thank her and the Mother Superior again before setting off for the train station. It was not quite six o'clock, but perhaps Nick would have wandered back to the station already. She was exhilarated from her find and anxious to share the good news with him.

Jordan halted on the curb. As she waited for a van laden with ski equipment to pass, she wrestled with the conflicting impulses thinking about Nick Rostov always elicited. They had agreed to be partners, and no matter how she qualified that arrangement, he was entitled to a certain amount of candor. Hadn't she already revealed to him Kitty's original name? In any case, he would no doubt be familiar with the Marienlazarett and could help her penetrate the hospital's bureaucracy. In light of his cooperation so far, perhaps their goals did not necessarily lead to conflict.

A surprisingly warm feeling filled Jordan as she caught sight of Nick, slouched over his paperback and coffee in the station café. The emotion was akin to what people feel at a reunion with an old friend, someone who remembers lots of shared birthdays and laughs at silly private jokes that no one else thinks are funny. She had no reason to feel that way about someone she had just met, didn't know at all really, Jordan told herself. Nonetheless, she was glad to have reconciled her misgivings about working with him.

Nick looked up as she was scampering across the snow-crusted street. Breaking into a big smile, he snapped his book shut and hurried to meet her.

"You must have had a productive search."

Jordan regarded him quizzically. "How do you know?"

"When I saw you running across the street, your smile was bright enough to light up these mountains." Nick's hand swept the icy air, gesturing toward the shadow-cloaked peaks.

"It did go rather well," Jordan admitted, at the same time trying to control her exuberant expression.

"I hope you can tell me about it over dinner." Nick slid his arm easily around her shoulders, guiding her into the station.

Jordan nodded decisively, her head grazing the soft wool of his coat. "Not only will I fill you in, but I may have another assignment for you."

"That's what I'm coming along for." Was it her imagination, or had Nick given her shoulders a little squeeze?

Jordan glanced up at him, smiling slyly. "No, Nick, you're coming along to find the Radetsky music box," she reminded him.

Nick's uproarious laugh echoed through the cavernous train station. Still chuckling, he shook his head. "Apparently I'm not the only one, either."

Jordan pulled them to a stop. "What do you mean?"

Nick's arm gently urged her forward. "While you were digging away through the convent's records, I happened to bump into our old friend Gudrun Mayes-Cooper."

"Here?" Jordan balked in her steps once more.

"Uh-huh. Specifically, she was sitting in the station café, berating a waitress, when I spotted her. It was a warm encounter, as you can imagine, but I'm sure she would have much rather run into you." Nick released his hold on Jordan to fish the locker key from his pocket.

Jordan groaned. "How did she know I was in Spitzdorf?" When Nick glanced up from the locker latch, she waved him back. "Please, I don't want to hear about bribing bellboys and the like. Oh, God, don't tell me this woman is going to become my shadow. How am I going to get rid of her?"

Nick slung both their garment bags over his shoulder before linking arms with Jordan and heading for the platform. "Short of wearing a string of garlic around your neck, I don't know. But don't worry about her right now. You've made some progress, and that's cause to celebrate."

Jordan paused on the railcar's lowest step. "I'm game just as long as it's a moderate celebration. Let's not tempt the gods."

"I don't think wine over dinner is excessive."

"Nor do I," Jordan agreed happily.

She waited while Nick asked the conductor to reserve two sleeping compartments for them. Ordinarily, she had no one but her dedicated secretary, Molly Bledsoe, to share the trials and small victories of her work. Teaming up with Nick apparently offered some fringe benefits that went beyond linguistic skill. Jordan felt her remaining reservations begin to melt as Nick escorted her to the dining car.

To his credit, he waited for her to bring up the discovery she had made at the convent that afternoon.

"Have you heard of the Marienlazarett in Vienna?" Jordan asked while they were inspecting the menu.

His eyes lingering on the brief wine list, Nick shook his head. "No, but there must be dozens of hospitals in Vienna."

Jordan slowly closed the menu. "According to the convent records, Käthe Davidov was transferred to the orphanage from this hospital. That's the sum total of my big discovery. Other than that scrap of information, the records offered nothing, no names of parents, not even a birthday."

Nick shrugged as he hailed the waiter. "At least it's a start." After he had ordered wine, he touched Jordan's hand lightly. "Don't worry, Jordan. We'll find the hospital, and chances are its records will be much more complete than those at the orphanage. Now let's forget about all these complicated matters and enjoy our dinner."

Jordan was more than pleased to follow his suggestion for the remainder of the evening. During a delightful dinner of schnitzel and tiny dumplings, their conversation zigzagged from topics as diverse as New Age music to the Washington Redskins. Never once did either of them so much as allude to the Radetsky music box or Käthe Davidov's shrouded past.

Not that she was having any trouble keeping her mind off business, Jordan reflected. Nick possessed talents custom-tailored to distract a woman from her worries, the almost-too-good-to-be-true combination of devastating good looks and manners to go with them. Whether refreshing her glass of wine or ordering dessert, Nick orchestrated the evening with the unobtrusive hand of a man who performed such niceties as a matter of course. Best of all, he seemed to be enjoying the time as much as she. They were still lingering over brandy long after the waiter had extinguished the other dining tables' lamps.

"Do you travel much in your work?" Nick's low voice sounded pleasantly intimate in the dimly lighted car.

Jordan gazed at their dual reflections in the dark window. "Yes, but most often in the United States. Occasionally I get a case that takes me abroad, when I'm lucky enough to have a client who can afford such expensive research." She broke off abruptly, before she could chat her way into the mine field of wealthy clients—like Kitty Ridgewood. "But usually I find myself in places like Graniteville, Vermont or Blowing Rock, North Carolina. I suppose an art expert never finds much need to visit those places." It was a corny, freshman-mixer sort of comment, but Jordan felt comfortable enough with Nick to dispense with phony sophistication.

"You'd be surprised. I've made acquisitions in some out-of-the-way places. The only difference is that my little villages tend to be in places like Yugoslavia or Greece."

"Must be nice." Jordan held up the brandy snifter, capturing the table lamp's subdued light in the amber liquid. "I love delving into dusty old county court records, but sometimes I wish I could do it in slightly more exotic locations. I guess I'm doomed to keep Greece and Yugoslavia on my vacation list."

"My work may sound exciting, but I'm certain that if we were to trade places for a time, you would be just as glad as I to get home at the completion of an assignment."

Jordan smiled over the rim of the snifter. "You're probably right. Where do you call home, anyway? Try as I may, I still haven't managed to place your accent, but I'm certain you can't have lived your entire life in Vienna."

Nick chuckled. "I've lived so many places, I fear my speech is permanently screwed up."

Jordan smiled and glanced up at the chiseled face illuminated by the misty light. "There you go again. Just listening to you talk, I would swear you grew up in France or Switzerland. But then you throw in a phrase like 'screwed up' and ruin my whole theory. At least give me a hint."

"I lived in southern France until I was eight years old. Then my parents separated. Mother is an American, so my sister and I lived part of the year in New York with her. Or rather in boarding school," Nick quickly amended. "The rest of the time we spent with my paternal grandmother in Austria. And if that isn't complicated enough for you, I did my undergraduate work at the University of Colorado. I suppose Vienna is where I really feel most at home. My grandmother and sister live there. And I have an apartment in the city. And my dog." He broke off. When Jordan caught his eye he grinned, a little awkwardly as if he had just made an embarrassing revelation. "I guess that sounds rather weird."

He looked so vulnerable, if only for that split second, that Jordan did not have to fake the warm smile she gave him. "Anyone who makes a living digging up the marriage records of someone's great-great-uncle Caleb and great-great-aunt Hortense would never presume to accuse someone else of being weird. One thing I will say for you. Some twenty-first century genealogist is going to have a field day tracking you down for your descendants."

"You sound as if you would relish such a task. Somehow I get the idea that the more challenging the case is, the better you like it.'' He picked up the conversation so quickly, Jordan sensed he was looking for a good opening to let her talk about herself and get him off the hook.

''That's my dad's genes at work. He's an FBI agent.'' Catching the amused smile playing on Nick's handsome face, she hastened to explain. ''Believe me, he isn't a thing like those tough-talking G-men you've seen in old Hollywood movies.''

Nick made an obvious effort to sober himself. ''Oh, I'm sure. I was thinking of something else, really. But tell me more about your parents. Whom do you take after?''

Jordan thought for a moment. ''Well,'' she began slowly, ''I guess I inherited Dad's practical skills and Mother's fascination with romantic things. Put 'em together, and what do you get? A genealogist.''

''Your parents must have known what they were doing when they got together,'' Nick commented.

He was looking at her so intently that she was grateful for the waiter's arrival to pick up the check and give them their sleeping berth reservations. ''We should probably call it a night pretty soon,'' she remarked, glancing around the empty car. ''The train is due into Vienna at five in the morning.''

Nick checked his watch and sighed. ''Please don't spoil a wonderful evening by bringing up such barbarisms.'' He reluctantly gathered up their garment bags and followed her out of the car. They jostled single file down the narrow corridor. At the junctures between cars, Nick would slide open the door and they would both scurry across the windswept platform to the next car. When they reached the first sleeping car, they paused to chafe their cold hands.

''Brr! This is certainly a far cry from February in Florida.''

''Is Florida a favorite vacation spot of yours?''

"Since Dad retired, my parents spend part of the winter there, and I usually manage to visit them for a couple of weekends." Jordan chuckled. "Dad loves deep-sea fishing, and he enjoys having someone to listen to his fish stories."

"I gather your mother isn't crazy about fish?"

"Not catching them! But she finds plenty to keep herself occupied while Dad's out conquering nature. She paints big, dramatic seascapes. Writes poems about the pounding surf. Takes moonlit walks along the beach."

"That's something they could do together," Nick suggested.

Jordan's laugh took on a bittersweet edge. "Only if Mother wants to hear about the dangers of stepping on jellyfish and yucky bits of flotsam. I'm afraid my father was born without a romantic bone in his body. I suppose that's why opposites attract. If two dreamers got together, they'd probably have a hard time muddling through life."

"I wouldn't be so hard on dreamers, Jordan. I've stepped on a few jellyfish myself, but I'm none the worse for it. Far better than never to have seen the moonlight rolling over the waves."

Something in that low, insinuating tone sent a warm rush through her, and Jordan was grateful for the meager light that helped conceal the heightened color in her cheeks. She took a deep breath. "Well, I guess we need to decide who gets which sleeper. Do you have any superstitious preference for numbers?"

"None." Nick made no effort to move.

"Okay. Then I'll take 110."

Jordan backed toward the compartment. When the train rocked unexpectedly, she lurched to one side. Nick caught her, but as she regained her footing his hand remained firmly clasped to her arm.

Facing him in the close corridor, Jordan could sense the outline of his tall frame, the way it fit around her shadow, lean where she was curved, hard muscled where she was softly rounded. Her own body tingled with awareness of him. This wasn't supposed to be happening, she told herself. She wasn't supposed to be feeling this way about a man whom she had met only two days earlier, a man who might want something from her she wasn't free to give.

When his hand slid down her arm, she started. His blue eyes had darkened to the color of a fathomless ocean. She thought she saw a tremor pass beneath the tanned skin, scarcely perceptible but enough to alter the entire cast of his face. Jordan measured her breathing, unable to move as his fingers gently skimmed her hair, following the waves' wayward path from her temple to her shoulder. For an infinitely long moment she wanted to close her eyes, lift her chin to his touch, offer her parted lips to his. For a good part of that moment Jordan wished she had never heard of Kitty Ridgewood and her faded old photograph.

But she had. Jordan blinked, hard enough to bring herself back to reality. She felt his fingers drift through a long strand of her hair, loosing their hold as she stepped back toward the door.

Nick dropped his hand at his side and gave her a long, maddeningly unreadable look. Then he slid open the compartment door and hung her garment bag on the hook. "Good night, Jordan."

"Good night, Nick."

Jordan retreated into the compartment and pulled the door shut. This was what she got for having wine *and* brandy, she told herself as she flicked on the light and began to rummage through her bag. She was lucky she hadn't made a real fool of herself back there in the corridor. In spite of her self-recriminations, however, Jordan was still smiling when she emerged from the compartment a few minutes later, armed with toothbrush, soap and towel, and made her way to the rest room. *You won't find much to grin about at five in the morning,* she reminded the weary-eyed reflection in the mirror. With this sobering thought in mind, she made short order of her bedtime toiletries.

Although the rhythmic clack of the train's wheels effectively muffled her steps, Jordan instinctively tiptoed past the occupied sleepers. Near the end of the corridor she hesitated and frowned. She was almost certain she had left the light on in her berth, yet every compartment she had passed had been dark. Jordan retraced her steps, straining to read the numbers in the low light. She found 110, but no light showed through the opaque glass panels. She must have turned it out, after all. Thank heavens she could at least remember the number! *That's it for you, old girl. No more brandy!*

Jordan yanked at the door and was surprised when it resisted. She gave the handle another, more forceful tug. It yielded slightly, enough to allow her to shove aside the garment bag wedged against it. The damn thing must have fallen off the hook and somehow jammed the... Jordan froze as something in the dark compartment moved.

"What—" Jordan felt the words crammed back into her throat, held in check by the bundle of bedding shoved into her face. She was grappling with the unwieldy mattress when the train took a sudden curve, throwing her off balance. Jordan landed heavily on her back. As she struggled to regain her footing, she heard the compartment door slam shut. Jordan lunged for the door and threw it open.

"Help! Stop! Thief!" As she tore down the corridor, Jordan shouted and pounded her fist against the closed doors, anything to signal the escape of her assailant.

Drowsy faces began to emerge from the sleepers, but Jordan didn't slow her pursuit. Whoever had been lurking inside her compartment had fled, as evidenced by the half-open door at the end of the corridor.

"Stop!" Jordan cried as she rushed into the next sleeping car.

A door to her left slid back and a groggy-looking Nick Rostov, dressed only in his slacks, appeared in the opening. "Jordan? What's wrong?"

"I caught someone prowling in my sleeper!" Jordan pointed frantically toward the end of the corridor.

Nick was instantly alert. "Wait here for the conductor."

As Nick raced toward the door, Jordan ignored his order and followed. The awkwardness of trying to hurry along the coaches' narrow corridors was eclipsed only by the clumsiness of moving through the cold passages connecting one car to the next. A stitch began to nag at her side, aggravated by her nervous, gulping breaths. She clutched her midriff when Nick abruptly halted at the end of a car. He held the door for a moment while they both stared at the parallel lengths of glistening track cutting through the snow behind the train's last car. Whoever had invaded Jordan's compartment had managed to elude them.

Chapter Five

"You say that nothing was taken? No jewelry or valuables?"

Jordan was almost too tired to shake her head. "My briefcase had been opened, but nothing is missing, as far as I can tell."

"You cannot describe the intruder?" Herr Komm, the police inspector who had boarded the train in Radstadt, had asked Jordan these questions at least twice already. As he filled out his official report, however, he seemed determined to repeat them in his precise, textbook English.

"No. I've told you I couldn't see anything. Whoever it was shoved the bedding into my face."

"Yet you pursued someone the length of the train." Herr Komm tapped the report with the tip of his pen. "You cannot offer at least an estimate of his person's height?"

"I didn't really see the person I was chasing. When I managed to get out of the sleeper, the door at the rear end of the corridor was partially open, so I assumed the prowler had fled in that direction."

The police inspector said nothing, but when his eyes met Jordan's she could tell that the same depressing thought had occurred to him: whoever had invaded her sleeper might well have run in the opposite direction and simply closed the railcar door behind him.

Jordan closed her eyes, shutting out for a moment Herr Komm's gaze and the train compartment's harsh overhead light. She felt Nick's hand close around hers, and she gave him a grateful smile.

"You were not able to identify the person from among the other passengers?" Herr Komm mumbled to himself as he checked off the next question.

"How could Miss MacKenzie identify someone she didn't see in the first place?" Nick cut in. Up until now he had left most of the talking to Jordan. The edge in his voice, however, suggested that fatigue and frustration were beginning to take their toll on him, too.

The police inspector looked up from his report to fix Nick with a cold stare. "I am sure you understand that I must complete my report."

Nick drew a heavy sigh. "Certainly." He watched in silence while Komm filled in the time and date and then offered the report for Jordan's signature.

"I apologize for the unpleasantness you have suffered, Miss MacKenzie. I must advise you, however, that the chances of a suspect being apprehended are very poor." Herr Komm eased his glasses forward to massage the bridge of his nose. "The intruder could very likely have leaped from the train while it was in motion. He could simply have climbed out at the station before I was summoned. Or he could still be aboard. In any case, if you did not see him, we have no way of identifying him."

"How can you be sure this person is a man?" Nick interposed.

Herr Komm's wiry brows rose at the heretical suggestion. "I cannot, of course. It is possible that the intruder was female," he conceded a little huffily. "May your journey be a safe one, Miss MacKenzie.'' He gave Jordan and Nick a stiff nod before leaving the compartment.

Jordan reached to pull the door securely shut behind the departing police inspector. ''You think Gudrun Mayes-Cooper was the person I caught pilfering through my things?''

Nick frowned as he stretched his long legs out in front of him. ''Right now, can you think of a better candidate? A common thief would have gone for your purse or the garment bag, not your briefcase. And look at the evidence. We know Gudrun was in Spitzdorf. We can be sure she wanted a look at the contents of your briefcase. Now how would she go about it?'' Not waiting for Jordan to fill the blank, he went on. ''We took our baggage with us to the dining car, so that ruled out any snooping while we ate. She had to opt for the next-best thing. She waited until you left the sleeper, assuming that you would spend a good while fussing over your hair and face, like she probably does. She sneaked into your couchette and had just opened the briefcase when you surprised her. Regardless of what Herr Komm thinks, you don't need to be a power lifter to pick up that thin mattress and push it into someone's face.''

Jordan nodded thoughtfully. ''Makes sense, but how did she manage to get away? Somehow I can't see her taking a flying leap into a snowbank.''

''She could have ducked into one of the empty compartments while you were scrambling with the mattress.''

''I didn't scramble very long,'' Jordan insisted. ''And we tried to look into the compartments while we were running the length of the train.''

Nick shrugged. ''A lot of them were dark. She could have crouched. And, you know, since we never saw anyone, we aren't even certain we were searching the right portion of the train. I don't know, Jordan. I just have a funny feeling that

Gudrun kept her cool and nonchalantly climbed off when the train stopped in Radstadt.''

"If only I could have gotten to the light switch."

Nick pulled his legs back and turned to face Jordan. He slid an arm around her shoulders and gave them a comforting squeeze. "You stopped her before she got away with any of your materials. You should feel good about that."

Jordan refused to be mollified. "I was lucky this time. But what next?"

"Next, we try to get some rest." Without relinquishing his grasp on her shoulders, Nick leaned to switch off the compartment light. "Close your eyes."

Jordan felt his hand glide lightly over her brow, and she dutifully complied. Exhaustion had blunted her senses, allowing a comfortable familiarity to supplant, for the moment, the intense sensations his closeness would normally have awakened. Cushioned by a foggy half sleep, she was dimly aware of the train's swaying, punctuated by brief intervals of motionlessness accompanied by garbled announcements and the shuffling feet of boarding and departing passengers.

"JORDAN." NICK'S SOFT voice gently penetrated her mental haze. "We've arrived in Vienna."

Yawning, Jordan forced herself to sit upright. "I must have fallen asleep."

Nick smiled. "Uh-huh. And now we're going to get you back to your hotel so you can sleep some more." Gathering up their garment bags, he guided Jordan off the train. His hand remained securely anchored at her waist until they reached the taxi stand.

Accustomed as she was to managing for herself, Jordan ordinarily would have resisted being shepherded about like a child. Right now, however, she was simply too tired to assert her capability. Besides, it felt good to have someone else take care of practical matters for a change—especially someone as attractive as Nick. Had she really become such a self-sufficient robot that she had forgotten how to accept support? If she needed practice in that area, Jordan decided, she could think of no better place to acquire it than at the hands of Nick Rostov.

When they reached her hotel Nick bade the driver wait while he escorted Jordan into the lobby. Smiling, he dangled her briefcase in front of her, just out of her reach. "Remember, you're to take the morning off and sleep. No work."

"I have so much to do, Nick," Jordan protested. "I need to find that hospital and—"

"The hospital will still be there this afternoon or tomorrow, for that matter. Besides, you'll be more efficient if you're fresh."

"Maybe you're right." The elevator's arrival gave Jordan the chance to reclaim her briefcase, along with her garment bag. "Thank you. For everything."

"I'll ring you up later," Nick promised just before the elevator door glided shut between them.

Nick was so thoughtful, Jordan mused as she unlocked the door of her hotel room. If she wasn't careful, she could get addicted to that sort of pampering. Contrary to her earlier misgivings, he was turning out to be an unqualified asset. And with the likes of Gudrun Mayes-Cooper lurking in dark corners, she needed every ally she could get.

The thought of the cutthroat art dealer raised a host of unpleasant memories—and unanswered questions. While Jordan changed into her robe and slippers, her mind kept returning to the troubling incident in the sleeper. The scenario that Nick had painted made sense. Who besides Gudrun Mayes-Cooper had a motive for rifling the briefcase? All of the pieces fit together perfectly.

Too perfectly. The words reverberated in her mind as if Jack MacKenzie himself had intoned them. Her dad always claimed that the obvious clues were never the right ones. If you saw something easily, it was probably because someone wanted you to.

The room was suddenly very still. Jordan sat on the side of the bed and swallowed slowly. *Who besides Gudrun Mayes-Cooper has a motive for rifling the briefcase?* Her mind rebelled at the answer it could not ignore. Nick had offered such a precise reconstruction of events. *As if he had thought it through beforehand.* She hadn't actually seen Gudrun in Spitzdorf, only had his word for it. Nick could just as easily have followed the plan of action that he had outlined for Gudrun. After stalling her with the bedding, he would have had more than enough time to run back to his own couchette and pretend to join her pursuit a few minutes later. Even his solicitous behavior afterward could have been no more than a smoke screen.

It was this last possibility that stuck in her mind like a vicious thorn. *But Nick seems so sincere!* she heard her hungry emotions wail inwardly. Her logic would not be placated, however. Chris Palmer had seemed sincere, too, she reminded herself with brutal accuracy, had showered her with compliments, even talked about dangerous things like love. And she had believed him until she learned, quite by accident, that he was still married to a woman who had no intention of giving him a divorce.

Of course, Nick might not be at all like Chris, but she could ill afford to take unnecessary chances. For the time being, she would conduct her research without his help until... *Until when?* The thought that the trust and under-

standing they had briefly enjoyed might never be restored
was too bitter to contemplate.

One thing was certain, however. She would go nuts if she
did nothing but sit around the hotel room and think about
Nick for the rest of the morning. Fortunately, she had plenty
of work to keep her mind occupied. After phoning the hotel tearoom to order coffee, Jordan reached for the city
telephone directory.

Her heart sank when she could find no listing for the
Marienlazarett. Still, she should have expected as much in
a city that had undergone the sweeping changes that Vienna
had weathered since the 1920s. Jordan turned to the historical and cultural information on Vienna that she had stored
in her briefcase. After inspecting one of the tourist guide-
books, she decided to phone the Historical Museum of the
City of Vienna. The staff members of large museums were
often veritable fountains of information, and they were
usually multilingual. Frau Probst of the Historical Museum proved to be exemplary on both counts.

"Ah, yes, the Marienlazarett." Frau Probst sounded delighted to be of service. "It was an infirmary established
during the reign of Empress Maria Theresa. In this century, the patients treated there were primarily indigents and
those requiring quarantine."

"When was it closed?"

"In 1945. The building was badly damaged during the
war. Also, it was not large enough to accommodate very
many patients by modern standards."

Summoning up her courage, Jordan asked the question
she most dreaded. "So the building was razed?"

"Oh, no!" Frau Probst laughed lightly. "You see, we
Viennese are very sentimental. I think many people would
have been very sad to see the old infirmary and its merciful

work completely forgotten. The building has been fully restored and is now used as a center for physical therapy.''

"What about the hospital's records, Frau Probst? Is there a chance they still exist?''

"Perhaps. It can do no harm to inquire,'' Frau Probst encouraged her. "I will give you the address, if you wish. The Institute for Physical Therapy is located near St. Stephen's Cathedral.''

Jordan jotted down the address, along with the directions for getting there, which Frau Probst helpfully provided. After thanking the young woman profusely, she again consulted the telephone directory and then dialed the number for the institute. Unlike Frau Probst, the receptionist spoke no English, but Jordan was able to muster enough German to obtain the name of the facility's director and make an appointment to see her at nine o'clock the following morning.

She was sorting through her files, sipping the now-lukewarm coffee the hotel had delivered an hour earlier, when the phone rang unexpectedly.

"Did I wake you?'' Nick's voice was even lower pitched than usual, as if to soften the intrusion.

"No.'' Jordan hesitated. In light of the misgivings she now harbored, she was at a loss for words. What, after all, did you say to a man who had been within a heartbeat of kissing you less than twelve hours ago, a man who might also be guilty of the vilest treachery? "I couldn't sleep,'' she added lamely.

"You're a hopeless workaholic, aren't you?'' Nick teased.

No, I just couldn't stop thinking about the tricks you might be pulling behind my back. "Yeah, I guess so.'' She laughed, an uneasy titter devoid of humor.

"Are you all right, Jordan?''

"Sure. I'm fine. Why?''

Nick hesitated a moment. "I don't know. You just don't sound like yourself."

"I'm tired. That's all." Jordan bit her lip. If she was going to hide her apprehension from a canny type like Nick Rostov, she was going to have to do a more convincing job of it than this. "You know, I think I will take your advice and take a nap. I'm really beat."

"That's more like it." Nick chuckled. "What time would you like to have dinner?"

"Oh, I don't know, Nick. I mean, I'm not at all hungry right now." In truth, her stomach had been howling for food since she had primed it with the coffee. She would risk severe malnutrition, however, before she would agree to have dinner with him that evening.

"Shall I ring you later, then?"

"Not tonight. I'll probably grab something light to eat and then turn in early."

"So you're going to sleep, eat and then sleep some more?" Nick's tone had acquired a testy bite.

Now that she thought about it, she hadn't offered him a very persuasive excuse. Then again, she didn't owe him any explanation for her actions, however bizarre. "That's right."

"Well, I guess my news will keep until tomorrow morning. Any chance of our having breakfast together?"

Jordan recognized her cue to demand, "What news?" and she steadfastly resisted it. "Probably not. I have an early appointment."

"I tracked down the Marienlazarett for you," Nick told her, with noticeable reluctance.

Jordan knew he must have hated showing that much of his hand, forfeiting such a large portion of his news to lure her out. "So have I," she said. In spite of the conversation's miserable progress, she couldn't help but smile as she deflated the remainder of his big-news balloons.

To his credit, Nick was quickly up and running again. "I'll be glad to help you with the language. Same terms as in Spitzdorf, of course," he was careful to add.

"I'll let you know" was Jordan's noncommittal reply. She feigned a muffled yawn into the receiver's mouthpiece. "Gee, I really do need that nap worse than I had thought."

"Okay. I'll talk with you later. Goodbye." The connection cut off with an irritable click.

The moment she had hung up, Jordan faced another onslaught of doubts—diametrically opposed to those she had confronted earlier. What if her suspicions about Nick were totally ill founded? What if he was the considerate, helpful man she had wanted to believe he was? What if he had spent half the day doing research for her only to have her put him off with transparently contrived ploys? *Then you, dear girl, look like an unmitigated jerk.*

The thought was not one she embraced readily. With only hunches and nebulous feelings to support her judgment, however, she could lose her mind trying to figure out Nick's angle. Right now, she had a more pressing conundrum to solve: how and why little Käthe Davidov had come to the Marienlazarett.

LIKE A BRISTLING MEDIEVAL pike, the Gothic tower of the Cathedral of St. Stephen soared above the Old Town to prick the heavy snow clouds hovering overhead. Jordan clutched the collar of her Burberry, bracing herself against the icy wind whipping across the plaza. After consulting her map, she had discovered that the physical therapy institute was only a short distance from her hotel. What she had envisioned as an invigorating walk, however, had turned into a race against frostbite, thanks to the bitter weather. Vow-

ing to follow Frau Probst's advice and take a tram back to
the hotel, Jordan turned into Schulerstrasse and hurried
toward the pale green building the museum employee had
described.

In contrast to its exterior, which had been restored to resemble the original eighteenth-century structure, the institute's lobby was filled with sleek modular furniture and
tropical plants. After announcing her arrival at the desk,
Jordan chafed her hands for a few minutes while the receptionist disappeared into a private office. She had succeeded
in thawing her fingers enough to sign the guest register by
the time the young woman returned. The receptionist
ushered Jordan into the office and then closed the door behind her.

"Dr. Hannelore Schelling. I am pleased to meet you." An
attractive, middle-aged woman, wearing a white coat over
a gray cashmere dress, rounded her desk to offer Jordan her
hand.

Jordan introduced herself and thanked the medical director for the interview. Dr. Schelling listened intently while
Jordan explained the purpose of her visit.

"I know hospital files are normally considered confidential. If that's a problem, however, I can present a letter from
my client's attorney, authorizing my access to records pertaining to Käthe Davidov." Jordan prepared to open her
briefcase, but Dr. Schelling shook her head and laughed
softly.

"I do not know if I should even call these boxes of paper
'records,' Miss MacKenzie. Much of the documentation was
destroyed when the Marienlazarett was struck by bombs
during the war. Only the files stored in an underground
shelter survived, but they have been poorly maintained over
the years."

"Where are the surviving files?"

Dr. Schelling pushed away from her desk. "If you like, I will show you."

Jordan followed the doctor out of the office to the service elevator. When they reached the basement, Dr. Schelling led the way past a boiler room and a storage chamber. At the end of the hall she fished a ring of keys from the pocket of her coat and unlocked an unmarked door. Flicking on the light, she wrinkled her nose at the untidy rows of crates and cabinets.

"Everything pertaining to the old infirmary is stored in these boxes." Dr. Schelling's capable-looking hand indicated a collection of cartons piled in one corner. "Several years ago, a university student researching epidemics was permitted to inspect the files. In truth, I do not know if he was able to bring much order to them. You are welcome to try."

"Thank you, Dr. Schelling." Jordan had already opened a folding chair and was hanging her coat over the back of it.

Dr. Schelling paused in the doorway and smiled. "Please let me know if you will be needing anything."

"Just time," Jordan told her, returning the smile.

And a new set of eyes that didn't feel as if someone had poured sand into them. And a nose that wasn't threatening to go on strike permanently after being assaulted by the accumulation of forty-odd years of dust and mildew. *And,* just in case some benevolent fairy godmother was listening, perhaps a shot of extrasensory perception or X-ray vision—Jordan wasn't particular—to save the hassle of digging through yet another crate that contained nothing of value.

Her fantasy wish list continued to grow as she methodically inspected the pathetic remains of the Marienlazarett's records. She interrupted her labor only once, to devour the cup of coffee and pastry that Dr. Schelling had kindly sent down to her. Secreted in the quiet, vaultlike room, Jordan lost track of time, was almost hypnotized by the seemingly endless succession of unfamiliar names.

She was returning yet another worthless box to the stack when a faint knock intruded on her dejected thoughts.

"Still hard at work, I see." Dr. Schelling peered around the door. "Have you had any luck?"

Jordan straightened her cramped shoulders and shook her head. "So far, no. And if Käthe Davidov's records aren't in those two boxes, I'm not going to have any."

Dr. Schelling consulted her watch. "The institute will be closing in about fifteen minutes. You may come back tomorrow or, if you prefer, you may continue your work tonight. In the latter case, I ask only that you remind Herr Pohl, our custodian, to lock this room when you leave."

"If you don't mind, I'd like to finish up tonight."

"That is fine. I wish you luck, Miss MacKenzie."

Jordan bade Dr. Schelling a good evening before turning back to her task. Both of the remaining boxes had suffered considerable water damage, suggesting that their contents might have been reduced to blobs of papier-mâché.

"Ugh!" Jordan muttered as she opened the box showing the least decay.

As she had feared, the files were in deplorable condition. Many of the documents were stuck together; water splotches had reduced the print of some to meaningless smears. Looking at the moldy-smelling mess, Jordan was tempted to replace the lid and simply call it quits. As long as there was a chance of finding a single readable document, however, she could never let herself take the easy way out.

She had finger-walked through fewer than half the documents when she encountered a rare chunk of alphabetized files. Her fatigue magically lifted as she progressed from the name Cziewslovski to Dahl.

"Dancek. Danner." Jordan read aloud as she moved through the files as fast as the decayed paper would permit. "Davidov. Davidov, Käthe," she repeated, almost too stunned to believe her good fortune. Taking advantage of the storage room's privacy, she let out a little whoop of joy. "I've found her! All right!"

Kneeling beside the box, Jordan carefully peeled the precious document from the two adjacent files sticking to it. Her eyes raced greedily down the page. As with the orphanage's file, much critical data had been omitted. No date or place of birth were given. In the space allotted for a description of Käthe's illness, someone had cryptically noted "typhus." In two important areas, however, the document yielded a mother lode of information. Käthe had been brought to the infirmary on December 5, 1920 by Jakov Davidov, a native of Kiev, Russia.

Jakov Davidov was an immigrant! Jordan rocked back on her heels, scarcely able to contain her excitement. Now at last she had something to work with: immigration records. She quickly fetched a notebook from her briefcase and recorded the information. Nick would be thrilled when she told him.... Jordan caught herself in time to check the thought that had sprung, uninvited, into her mind.

You've made a major discovery. Don't blow it now by fooling yourself into trusting Nick Rostov. He might be harmless, but you can't afford to take a chance. Jordan gave herself a stern lecture as she packed up her briefcase, collected her coat and headed for the elevator.

A penetrating cold hung in the basement's still air. Jordan shivered as she punched the elevator button a second time. Pulling on her coat, she frowned at the row of buttons that stubbornly refused to light. It was late, almost six o'clock by her watch. The custodian had probably turned off the elevators for the day. If she didn't want Dr. Schelling to find a human icicle in the institute's basement the next morning, she would have to take the stairs.

The stairwell was close and permeated by the nauseatingly clean smell peculiar to hospitals. On the first landing Jordan tried the door and was dismayed to find it locked.

"Damn!" she muttered. She jiggled the knob and then knocked on the door, but to no avail.

Surely Dr. Schelling had notified the custodian that someone else was still in the building. Trudging toward the next landing, she tormented herself with the image of an octogenarian watchman, dozing peacefully out of earshot. At the sound of a door closing somewhere above her, Jordan looked up. Slow, even footsteps carried through the empty shaft. Then silence.

"Herr Pohl?" Jordan jogged a few more steps and then repeated the custodian's name, this time more loudly. "Herr Pohl?"

No one answered.

Unless the man was stone-deaf, he must have heard her. Unless it wasn't Herr Pohl.

Jordan's fingers twitched on the stair rail, and she stood stock-still. Her eyes were frozen to the shadowy landing only a few feet above her, waiting for a movement, a sign, *anything*. An unnatural silence pervaded the stairwell.

Slowly, Jordan began to back down the stairs. Slowly, with a calm precision that sent cold fear washing through her, the footsteps above echoed in answer to her own.

Jordan turned suddenly to make a wild dash for the first-floor landing. She hammered her fist against the unyielding door.

"Help! For God's sake, somebody help me!" Her throat burned from the strain, but the words only bounced hollowly off the stairwell walls.

The footsteps were closer now, gaining on her. In desperation, Jordan made a break for the basement. She yanked open the heavy door and charged into the dimly lighted corridor. Her eyes darted into the shadows, frantically searching for a hiding place. She lunged into the boiler room just as the basement door slowly opened.

SOMETHING WAS WRONG with Jordan MacKenzie. Nick didn't delude himself that he knew her well enough to anticipate her every mood, but their last phone conversation contradicted almost everything he had come to expect from her. She had been abrupt to the point of rudeness, something she had avoided even before they had come to terms. Her healthy appetite had vanished and, most puzzling of all, she had professed absolutely no interest in hearing what he had learned about the Marienlazarett. Nick had no idea what had precipitated this 180-degree turn in Jordan, but he was going to do his best to find out before the day was over.

She had said she had an early appointment that morning, no doubt at the physical therapy institute. Nick had stopped briefly at Jordan's hotel around noon, tipping the doorman to watch his illegally parked Porsche while he confirmed that she had not returned. He then drove directly to the institute. The extension of Vienna's subway system beneath the plaza surrounding the Cathedral of St. Stephen had severely limited parking, and Nick wasted an infuriating amount of time driving in circles, finally settling for a spot blocks from his destination. He had arrived at the institute cold, irritated and out of breath. At least he had been able to determine that Jordan was indeed there, thanks to her signature on the guest roster.

Now that he had found her, the next step was less obvious. Even at her most cooperative, Jordan insisted on setting the parameters of his involvement in her investigation.

In light of their recent chilly exchange, Nick could imagine her indignation if he were to barge in on her research at the institute, uninvited and unannounced. The other alternative—and the only practical one, under the circumstances—was simply to wait her out.

Fortunately a small café was located diagonally across the street from the institute. The afternoon-coffee crowd had not yet materialized, and Nick was able to get a table with a good view of the institute's entrance. After checking his watch, he selected a newsmagazine from the café's reading rack and ordered coffee. By three-thirty, Nick had read the magazine from cover to cover, albeit with one eye trained on the green building across the street, and Jordan had still not appeared. As the streetlights winked on, he watched the facility's staff depart, their heavy coats buttoned over white uniforms.

It was now almost six o'clock. Frowning, Nick paid the café tab and headed across the street. Unless Jordan had taken to using back-alley exits, there was no way she could have left the building without his seeing her. What the devil was she doing in there, anyway?

Nick tried the front door and found it locked. Undaunted, he rattled the door and tapped on the glass. After several minutes of racket, a stooped little man in a workman's gray smock shuffled across the lobby. He shook his head at Nick and pointed to the office hours printed on the glass door. When Nick only continued to rap the glass, he grudgingly reached for his keys.

"Das Institut ist geschlossen." The custodian's finger underscored the closing time on the door to emphasize his point.

Adopting his thickest Viennese accent, Nick inquired about Jordan MacKenzie. After considerable resistance the custodian finally realized that the only way to get rid of Nick was to humor him. He fetched the sign-in roster and confirmed that Jordan was still in the building. Courtesy of Frau Dr. Schelling, she was authorized to remain in the basement archives as late as she pleased.

Nick was scrambling for a tactic to prevent the custodian from locking the door in his face when the fire alarm's shrill bell startled them both. Pushing past the custodian, Nick rushed into the building. As he ran into the stairwell, he could hear the older man calling after him, but Nick had only one thought: to find Jordan and get her out of danger.

"Jordan?" Nick shouted down the stairwell, taking the steps two at a time.

At the bottom of the stairs he cautiously tapped the door and was relieved to find it cool to the touch. Wherever the fire had started, it had not reached the basement. He couldn't smell any smoke, either, another good sign. Nick wrenched open the door.

"Jordan?" he screamed into the pitch-dark corridor.

Where the hell were the lights? Nick's hand was groping the wall when a staggering blow caught him in the midriff, knocking the wind out of him. As he sank back against the wall the lights suddenly blazed, revealing a figure in a black leather coat fleeing up the stairs. Nick was struggling to his feet when he saw a white-faced Jordan standing in one of the doorways, hand still poised on the light switch. He hesitated, but she immediately anticipated his question.

"I'm okay!" she cried. "He's getting away!"

Ignoring the pain singeing his middle, Nick ran up the stairs ahead of Jordan. He found the custodian doubled over on the first landing, apparently a victim of the same sort of ferocious attack.

"Help him!" Nick ordered Jordan.

Glancing over his shoulder, Nick was relieved to see her kneeling beside the injured man. If he overtook his quarry, he didn't want Jordan on hand. Whoever had punched him meant business, and if cornered, he wasn't likely to make exceptions for women.

Nick looked up to see the dark pant legs disappear through the opening to the roof. Then the trapdoor slammed shut with a grating crash. Not pausing to catch his breath, he forced open the heavy door. Following a trail of deep footprints in the snow, he dashed to the edge of the roof. The window cleaner's scaffold was still swaying lightly on its hinges, but the man in the black coat had vanished. In frustration, Nick peered down into the empty darkness that had swallowed up his attacker.

Chapter Six

The overnight snow had blanketed the Burggarten with a pristine-white down that glistened in the morning sun. As Nick waited for Daria in the small city park, he watched the snow frosting the statue of Emperor Franz Josef gradually submit to the bright rays. White clumps fell from the emperor's head and shoulders as noiselessly as feathers, pocking the drifts banked around the statue.

Nick heard Pedro bark before he spotted Daria, clinging to the taut leash that barely restrained the exuberant dog. The little animal covered the snowy ground in short leaps that sent sprays of white powder flying behind him.

"Here is your pet." Daria summarily presented Nick with her end of the leash. "I hope you aren't planning any trips for the rest of the week. I have some long rehearsals scheduled that are going to keep me tied up, and we both know that when Pedro gets lonely, he starts to eat shoes and pillows."

"Thanks for keeping him while I was in Spitzdorf." Nick gave his sister a sheepish smile. "I would have picked him up yesterday, but things didn't work out the way I had planned."

Daria adjusted her beret against a spirited gust of wind. "Something to do with the Radetsky music box, no doubt?"

Nick frowned, kicking at a chunk of icy snow that Pedro had just dug loose. "I'm almost certain." As they strolled through the park, he filled Daria in on the events of the past two days.

"Poor Jordan! Did she get a look at this brute who cornered her in the institute's basement?"

Nick shook his head. "After he chased her down the stairwell, she tried to hide in the boiler room. Judging from the wallop he gave me, she certainly took the wisest course of action. After she was sure he had gone into another room, she ran back to the hall, smashed open the fire alarm with her briefcase, and then turned out the lights. She told me later that she figured she knew her way around the basement better than he did, and the dark would improve her odds even more."

Daria whistled softly. "She sounds like one scrappy lady."

"Yeah." Nick caught his admiring smile just before it melted into a foolish grin. "Anyway, neither of us got a look at his face, thanks to the black ski mask he was wearing. But he was a big fellow, a bit taller than I am, I think. And strong." He pressed his sore middle with his free hand and grimaced ruefully.

"Do you think he's working for Gudrun Mayes-Cooper?"

Nick paused for a moment, giving Pedro's nose a chance to inspect an interesting smell. "I don't know, Daria. I told Jordan about the measures Gudrun employed to get the Gorky Madonna, and now she's convinced that Gudrun is behind both of these botched attacks. But—" He broke off to reel in Pedro.

"But what?" Daria prompted.

"It's only a hunch, mind you, but all this somehow smacks of even bigger stakes than acquiring a valuable artwork."

"Such as?"

Nick glanced over at the pretty, earnest face framed by the royal blue beret. "A title. A family fortune. The very fabric of someone's existence."

"You're talking about Radetsky?" Although the park was sparsely trafficked, Daria's voice dropped to a near whisper.

Nick nodded. "I know Grandmama was only a tiny thing when she last saw the music box, but you know what she's always insisted."

"That Pavel Radetsky had the box inscribed to her mother, calling her his beloved wife."

"That's right. Of course, contrary to what Grandmama believes, the Radetskys have always claimed that Pavel never married Olga Gallinin and never legitimized her children."

"A convenient way to dismiss any claims Olga's descendants might have on the Radetsky inheritance," Daria interjected with more than a tinge of bitterness. "Poor Grandmama! And then to lose her whole family as they fled Russia." She shook her head sadly before turning to Nick. "But assuming that Radetsky would want to interfere with the recovery of the music box, how would he know that Jordan has anything to do with it?"

"She told him, or rather she sent him a letter, requesting an interview. Which he'll never grant," Nick added with a cynical chuckle.

"I gather you haven't told Jordan about Grandmama's connection with the music box," Daria said slowly.

"No. And I won't until I know more about this mystery client of hers. So far, all I've been able to pry out of her is that the woman's name used to be Käthe Davidov. For all I know, Davidov could be the descendant of whoever betrayed Grandmama's family."

"It isn't a very flattering portrait to have of one's ancestor, someone who would abandon innocent people to certain death for the sake of money," Daria put in.

"No," Nick agreed. "But according to Grandmama, her mother bartered the music box to get them out of Russia. Whoever alerted the Bolshevik soldiers to their hiding place probably ended up with the music box."

They had halted on the corner facing the wall of the Hofburg, the still-imposing remnant of medieval Vienna's fortified center. Although the strong winter sun had dulled the nip in the air, Daria shivered at the light wind gusting across the street. "So what is your next move?"

"I think Jordan needs to meet the current Count Radetsky face-to-face."

Daria's dark, straight brows drew into a puzzled line. "A minute ago you seemed certain that Boris Radetsky would never agree to such a thing."

"Oh, he won't," Nick was quick to assure her. "I was thinking more of a social situation where she could bump into him casually. Say, at the Opera Ball. Of course, at this late date we'd need someone with connections to get tickets for us."

Daria stared at Nick in disbelief. "I don't believe it. My social-recluse brother is hinting for me to get him—and his *date*—tickets to the Opera Ball. I can't wait to tell Grandmama that you've finally decided to emerge from your cocoon." When she burst out laughing, Pedro excitedly joined in with a few sharp yelps.

"Be serious, Daria. I need your help. You're a dancer. You know hordes of people involved with the Philharmonic and the opera. And this is not an idle social excursion, by any means." Nick tried to look slightly offended. When Daria only continued to grin at him, he went on. "Well, will you?"

"On one condition."

Nick drew an impatient sigh. "Okay, I'm at your mercy. What are your terms?"

"That you relax and enjoy yourself for at least part of the evening. From the way you talk about Jordan, that shouldn't be such a chore."

Nick felt himself bristle at his sister's sly look. "I don't quite follow what you mean," he hedged. "Jordan is very attractive and personable, but ours is a business relationship."

Nick recognized the dreaded exasperated-sister look forming on Daria's face. "When are you going to realize that not every woman is like Inge? For heaven's sake, Nick, how long do you have to be divorced before you start to *live* again?"

"I'd rather you didn't bring up Inge right now." In spite of his affection for Daria, Nick's lips tightened.

"I'm sorry," Daria apologized. She hesitated for a few seconds, waiting for the air to clear as she always did whenever the conversation strayed to the sensitive subject of his ex-wife.

"That's okay," Nick conceded. Privately he realized that he would never have reacted so strongly if Daria had not hit close to the mark where his feelings about Jordan were concerned. Given his sister's overzealous interest in his social life, however, that was the last thing she needed to hear.

Daria pushed down the cuff of her glove and checked her watch. "I need to run, or I'll be late for my rehearsal."

Nick tightened his hold on the leash, reining in the lunging Pedro as Daria hurried across the street. "Don't forget the tickets!" he called after her.

Laughing, Daria threw him a jaunty wave before disappearing through one of the Hofburg's arches.

WHEN JORDAN HAD PACKED for her trip to research Kitty Ridgewood's European roots, she had tried to include everything she could conceivably need without burdening herself with excess baggage. Her packing list had included useful items ranging from a magnifying glass to insulated socks. At no time, however, had she thought her sojourn abroad would demand a floor-length evening gown. Then again, she had never dreamed a dashing, handsome man would invite her to the famed Vienna Opera Ball.

Since her discovery of Käthe Davidov's file among the Marienlazarett's records, Jordan had wasted no time launching an intensive search for information concerning Jakov Davidov's immigration to Austria. When she had phoned Kitty Ridgewood with news of the breakthrough, her client had been overjoyed, and Jordan was anxious to explore the lead to the maximum. After only three days in the state archives, she felt a little guilty at taking the afternoon off. Unless Cinderella's fairy godmother suddenly appeared in the archives' solemn halls and began waving her wand, however, she needed to buy a dress before the ball on Thursday. And this shopping expedition was in the line of duty, for Nick had assured her that the present Count Radetsky would be among the glittering event's revelers.

Jordan had not wandered far into the heart of Vienna's upscale shopping district before she spotted the right dress shop on Kärntnerstrasse. The store was straight out of one of her mother's daydreams, with a little showroom where you sat on moss green velvet chairs and sipped coffee while solicitous ladies showed you impossibly elegant confections.

With the same certainty that had guided her into the shop, Jordan recognized *the* dress the moment she saw it. It was an exquisite flow of ivory silk charmeuse with an equally stunning price tag. *Enough to buy a full set of steel-belted radials, with some left over.* Jordan could imagine her father clucking and shaking his head as she handed over her American Express card to one of the solicitous ladies. But then, her car had four brand-new tires, so why would she want to buy yet another set? Besides, she deserved a little celebration, Jordan told herself, clutching the big dress-shop box to her chest as she waited for the tram. She had made a major break in her investigation. She had escaped an attempted robbery and heaven-knew-what unscathed. And she could trust Nick Rostov.

His courageous attempt to overtake the thug stalking her in the basement of the physical therapy institute had banished her suspicion of him once and for all. Jordan now not only shared Nick's theory that Gudrun Mayes-Cooper was the prowler aboard the night train from Spitzdorf, she also suspected the ruthless art dealer had instigated the incident at the therapy center. If that was so, then Mayes-Cooper had definitely upped the ante.

The well-lighted pedestrian mall was bustling with shoppers and people hurrying home from work. In spite of the reassuringly normal atmosphere, however, Jordan fought to suppress the uneasy chill rippling through her. No one had appeared to be following her on her way to the physical therapy institute, either. Yet that awful man in the black ski mask had known she was there, had calculated the perfect time to catch her alone, had managed to enter the building unobserved.

During the tram ride back to the hotel, her mind kept wandering to Nick's story about Gudrun's pursuit of the Gorky Madonna and the resulting tragedy. Of course, she was no defecting spy, Jordan reminded herself. The Madonna's courier had met his unhappy fate for reasons that had nothing to do with the artwork. Gudrun had probably intended him no harm. Her mischief had simply exposed him to lethal enemies. Somehow, it was this last thought that Jordan found most disturbing.

SHE WAS DETERMINED TO PUT her worries aside, at least temporarily, the following evening as she prepared for the Opera Ball. After blowing her budget on the charmeuse gown—not to mention the silk pumps, elbow-length gloves and velvet cape she had picked up that afternoon—Jordan was *not* going to spoil the evening stewing over Gudrun Mayes-Cooper. Happily, Nick seemed more than ready to do his share of distracting.

Jordan had expected him to look smashing and handle things with style, but seeing him decked out in white tie was enough to stir the blood of a far more jaded woman. As Nick settled the cape over her shoulders and squired her to the limousine he had hired, Jordan felt as if she were being transported into a storybook fantasy.

Nick had apparently instructed the driver to take a roundabout route to the opera house, affording Jordan a glimpse of Vienna at its most charming. Settling into the limousine's buttery-soft leather seat, with Nick's fingers laced through hers, Jordan surrendered herself to the splendor of the old city. The dark surface of the Danube shimmering with reflected light, the stately equestrian statues of the Maria Theresa Memorial coated with a sugary glaze of ice and snow, the majesty of the spires and baroque cupolas rising from the Hofburg—all conspired to create a magical atmosphere.

The limousine pulled into an arcade where a liveried doorman assisted them from the car. Nick linked arms with Jordan and escorted her into the opera house. The lobby was overflowing with elegantly dressed people, forcing them to take a meandering route to the marble staircase leading to the gallery. Jordan was grateful for the slow pace, however, for it afforded her a better chance to take in her surroundings. As Nick led her up the red-carpeted stairs to the gallery overlooking the lobby, she gazed up at the crystal chandeliers and the frescoes decorating the vaulted ceilings.

Inside the great opera hall, the throng grew even denser. Jordan was beginning to wonder how anyone managed to dance, much less pick a single guest out of the crowd, when Nick squeezed her hand, pulling her within whispering range.

"See that tall fellow over there with the dark beard? The one trying to charm the woman in the bright blue dress."

Jordan nodded. "Is that our man Radetsky?"

Nick didn't take his eyes off the robust figure. "It is indeed."

Jordan watched Radetsky bend toward his companion's ear. When the woman burst into laughter, the count looked supremely pleased with himself. "He fancies himself quite a ladies' man, doesn't he?"

"Yes, which should make your job a cinch."

Jordan looked away from the flirtatious tableau to blink at Nick in unbelieving amazement. "*My* job? Now wait a minute, Nick. I'm willing to go the extra mile to get information for my client, but when it comes to falling all over some pompous character—"

"You don't think Radetsky is going to want to dance with me, do you?" Nick gave her back a reassuring pat. "Relax. After the dancing begins, I'll introduce you to some of Daria's friends. They'll want to show the lovely visiting American around, of course. All you need to do is make sure you wander close enough to the count to warrant an introduction. I guarantee you he'll take it from there."

"That's what I'm afraid of," Jordan muttered. Her grumbling was cut short as the lights dimmed and the

Vienna Philharmonic began their performance that tradi-
tionally precedes the Opera Ball. During the concert and the
short ballet that followed, she glanced over at Nick several
times, but his maddening, sphinxlike smile never wavered.

Of course, their reason for attending the ball in the first
place had been to meet Radetsky. She had no grounds to feel
cheated or miffed because Nick didn't regard the evening as
a strictly social opportunity. Still, Jordan couldn't quite
stifle the disappointment that had begun to nag her during
the debutantes' dance to *The Blue Danube,* which officially
opened the ball.

After the debs and their escorts had dispersed to mingle
with the crowd, Nick tapped Jordan's elbow. "Now's our
chance. Ready?"

"As ready as I'll ever be."

Jordan let Nick carve a path through the multitude. When
they reached a less congested alcove, a young woman immediately excused herself from her party and hurried to
meet them. Before Nick had even begun his introduction,
the woman's raven-dark hair and brilliant blue eyes identi-
fied her as his sister.

With a surreptitious wink to both of them, Daria took
Jordan's hand and led her back to the people chatting in the
alcove. "I've someone you must meet," Daria announced
in a voice just loud enough to get everyone's attention.

Jordan smiled and nodded politely as Nick's sister made
the introductions. The party was so large, Jordan soon
abandoned any hope of keeping track of names and con-
centrated on making appropriately lighthearted conversation. As Nick had predicted, a few of the party, most of
them young dancers, soon claimed her as their guest of
honor. While they were guiding her to another group of
friends, Jordan managed to catch Nick's eye across the
room. She gave him a here-goes-nothing smile before turn-

ing to one of her companions, a waif-thin ballerina named Bettina.

"Excuse me, but is that gentleman Count Radetsky?" Jordan was sure she sounded hopelessly phony, but the friendly young dancer didn't seem to notice.

"Yes, that is Count Boris Radetsky. You know of him, then? In America?"

Jordan tried to look nonchalant. "Oh, yes. I mean, well, you know, word travels." Damn Nick! If she'd known her role in the evening's caper called for serious method acting, she would have rehearsed in the privacy of her hotel room.

Not taking her eyes off Radetsky, Bettina inclined her head closer to Jordan. "He was divorced last year. A very— how do you say—*messy* affair. They say his wife caught him with an actress at the family hunting lodge."

Jordan was listening to Bettina's whispered account of the Radetskys' sensational breakup when the count suddenly turned in their direction. With the sixth sense of a man accustomed to fueling the gossip mill, he seemed able to tell immediately that they were talking about him. Before Jordan could discreetly look away, he caught her eye and smiled.

Jordan felt herself smiling back. *Oh, my God! He's walking this way! What on earth am I going to say? I'm not cut out for this Mata Hari stuff!* While her mind stumbled through a mine field of objections, her lips relentlessly held their inviting curve.

Radetsky glanced at Bettina just long enough to acknowledge her admiring gaze, but his attention was clearly focused on Jordan. He bowed slightly from the waist as he introduced himself. In mercifully clear German, Radetsky remarked that she must be new in Vienna, for such a beautiful lady would have surely attracted his notice earlier.

Still smiling, Jordan realized he was waiting for her to return the courtesy of an introduction. The thought that he might beat a quick retreat if he knew she was Jordan MacKenzie, the genealogist whose letter he had ignored, prompted her to think of a more ambiguous response.

"I've just arrived from the United States."

"To attend the Opera Ball, no doubt." Boris Radetsky gave her a knowing look, as if she had revealed a wealth of personal information in that single comment.

Boy, are you in for a surprise! "Among other things." Jordan allowed a touch of mischief to color the smile that was now permanently etched on her face.

Radetsky laughed, a low, bedroom chuckle. "May I have the pleasure of this dance, Miss . . . ?"

Jordan ignored the prompt and only nodded graciously. She let him take her hand and lead her onto the dance floor. The room was packed with hundreds of couples, whirling to the strains of a Strauss waltz, but Radetsky seemed unfazed by the crowd. He swept Jordan in assertively dramatic circles, clearing a swath among the more timid dancers.

"You are a marvelous dancer," Radetsky murmured, looking down into Jordan's face.

"It runs in my family." *At least one side of it.*

Radetsky gave her another of those suggestive laughs. "You are too modest, Miss...?" He feigned a hurt little-boy expression. "But come now, you will tell me your name, won't you?" he wheedled.

"MacKenzie. Jordan MacKenzie."

For the first time since they had taken to the dance floor, Radetsky missed a beat.

Jordan tugged lightly at her partner's hand. "Please, Count Radetsky, the dance isn't over yet."

Radetsky picked up to the beat, albeit with considerably less enthusiasm. "Very well, Miss MacKenzie. What do you want from me?" he asked through tightened lips.

"First of all, to finish this dance." Radetsky was so obviously accustomed to manipulating women, Jordan couldn't resist a little needling. "And I want a chance to ask you some questions about the Radetsky music box."

Radetsky's dark eyes roved the chandelier-lighted opera hall as if they were searching for the nearest escape route. "Ask your questions, then."

Jordan smiled sweetly, now thoroughly relishing her control. "Not here," she chided. "We're here to have fun, not discuss serious matters." Radetsky's perturbed expression cast doubts on how much fun he would be able to wrest from the remainder of the evening, but Jordan refused to feel guilty. "Can we make an appointment for later?"

"I will be leaving for my ski lodge tomorrow, and I have no idea when I will return to Vienna," Radetsky told her curtly.

Jordan refused to be put off. "Perhaps you could interrupt your skiing for an hour or so to meet with me."

"Very well," Radetsky reluctantly conceded. "I will see you at my chalet in Immel Saturday afternoon at half past three."

With perfect timing the final bars of the waltz signaled the end of the dance. Still holding Radetsky's hand, Jordan curtsied briefly, imitating the other women on the dance floor. "Thank you for the dance, Count Radetsky."

Radetsky looked as if he wanted to bolt, but his ingrained sense of etiquette forced him to bow stiffly. "Good evening, Miss MacKenzie."

"*Auf Wiedersehen*, Count Radetsky. Until Saturday," Jordan called gaily after his retreating figure.

Now that she had accomplished her mission with Radetsky, Jordan began to scan the hall in search of Nick. Bettina had mentioned that over three thousand people were in attendance, and to judge from the crowd pressing around her, that was a conservative estimate. She had succeeded in edging her way to an alcove when she felt someone snatch at her elbow.

"I had no idea you were such a terrific dancer." Nick smiled down at her as he neatly anchored her hand to the crook of his arm.

"For many years in my youth I was my mother's practice partner," Jordan informed him. "And, of course, I had a superb partner tonight."

Nick's throaty laugh carried below the music and chatter filling the hall. "See, what did I tell you? Old Boris just couldn't resist. Did you get to talk with him about the music box?"

"I broached the topic, after I had him trapped among those bijillion or so dancers. He's deigned to give me an interview on Saturday at his ski chalet in Immel, wherever that is."

"An easy drive from Vienna," Nick assured her. "Good work, Jordan." His hand closed over hers, giving it a warm squeeze. "That wasn't so bad now, was it?"

"No," Jordan admitted grudgingly. "I trust my assignment is complete now."

Nick regarded her in disbelief. "We've only just begun!"

Jordan pulled him to an abrupt halt, but before she could lodge a protest he turned to grasp her waist and lifted her hand to his shoulder. "To dance," he concluded.

For the first time in her life Jordan thanked her stars for the hours her mother had spent coercing her through foxtrots and waltzes in the family living room. As a rebellious tomboy, she had not realized that all those counted steps and repeated turns would someday lead into the arms of Nick Rostov. Now, however, she was heartily grateful.

As Jordan followed Nick's moves across the ballroom floor, an invisible shell seemed to encapsulate them, insulating them from everything but the romantic music, the sensuous rhythm of the dance and the reflection of each other in their eyes. After a time Jordan abandoned keeping count of the dances as one waltz flowed into yet another and Nick showed no inclination to release her from his arms. Looking up into Nick's handsome face, Jordan could not help but believe that he had fallen under the same magical spell as she.

Her head continued to spin for a moment when Nick at last led the way from the dance floor. Far from allowing the spell to break, he encircled her with his arm, protecting her from any unwanted intrusions of reality as he guided her out of the opera hall. Laughter and the sound of animated conversation carried from the rooms opening off the corridor. As they passed one large room, Jordan glimpsed richly dressed men and women gathered around gaming tables and a roulette wheel. Nick spirited her past the casino and into an alcove banked with vases overflowing with lavish white sprays.

"There's something I want to give you." Smiling, he pushed open one of the French doors opening off the alcove.

Jordan started at the sudden gust of cool air, but Nick pulled her closer to him, shielding her bare shoulders from the cold. A delicious warmth flowed through her as she molded to his embrace.

"I present to you the city of Vienna." Nick's hand swept the night air in a grand gesture.

Gazing out across the avenues and plazas that sparkled like a maze of jewels, Jordan laughed softly. "Is that all you wanted to give me? A mere city?"

"No."

Nick's fingers touched her cheek, then slowly drifted to the curve of her jaw. As he lifted her chin, a stillness fell around them, censoring out the sounds of the great city, the music swelling from the opera hall, everything except the exquisitely tender look in his eyes. Closing her own eyes, Jordan felt his mouth settle over hers. Impulse guided her hands to his neck while her lips returned the passion of his kiss, measure for measure. She murmured as his mouth wandered to her cheek, first nuzzling, then kissing a sensuous trail back to her lips. No man had ever kissed her like this. No man *could* kiss like this.

Suddenly a piercingly bright light exploded in the door of the alcove. Jordan started in Nick's arms, but as she looked up the strobe flared again, scalding them with its merciless glare. Jordan winced and recoiled from the camera aimed at them, but the man dressed in a waiter's uniform only fired another blinding volley before dashing away.

"What on earth do you suppose that was all about?" Jordan began, but Nick had already dropped her hand.

He rushed into the corridor to shout after the fleeing waiter. "I'll make you pay for this, Waxx! I swear I will, if it's the last thing I do!"

The waiter had disappeared from sight, but a vulgar laugh carried down the hall to mock Nick's threat.

Chapter Seven

"You are not feeling well, Nicolai Rostovitch?" Carefully replacing the porcelain teacup on its saucer, Maria Rachmanova cast a reproachful glance at the portion of rum cake Nick had scarcely touched.

"I'm fine, only a bit tired."

In truth, Nick had been so preoccupied that afternoon he had been tempted to beg off Rachmanova's invitation to tea. He knew, however, how much Grandmama looked forward to these uniquely Russian occasions, especially when she could share them with her grandchildren.

Rachmanova's teas were impressive, part solemn tradition, part theater. The retired prima donna blithely flouted the Viennese custom of afternoon coffee, clinging instead to her Russian tea and sweets. Seated among the heavy velvets and brocades that dominated her apartment, she dispensed steaming water from an antique samovar as if she were still Anatoly Kuzov's young ballerina, poised to sweep czarist Russia with her grace and skill.

With Rachmanova's sharp eyes trained on him, Nick made a show of finishing the rum cake before excusing himself. "Jordan and I plan to leave early tomorrow morning for Immel, and I still have a few things to take care of this evening."

"I am so pleased that Miss MacKenzie enjoyed attending the Opera Ball." Grandmama's blue eyes sparkled with girlish interest. "I hope her interview with Boris Radetsky will prove fruitful."

"So do I." Smiling at the two white-haired women, Nick thanked Rachmanova for her hospitality and then headed for the door before his grandmother could build another full-scale conversation around Jordan.

Thanks to Daria's advance work no doubt, Grandmama's absorption with the latest lead on the Radetsky music box had been temporarily superseded by Jordan MacKenzie's romantic potential. Experience had taught Nick the futility of trying to rein in his grandmother, especially where his personal life was concerned. Insisting that his alliance with Jordan was based solely on mutual business concerns would only have confirmed Grandmama's stubborn suspicions. Then, too, Nick was not all that certain where the boundaries of their relationship stood after those kisses on the balcony.

"I will show Nick out," Daria announced, gently waving their hostess back into her seat. Nick could hear her dancer's footsteps on the stairs behind him, light and precise. She caught his arm in the foyer of Rachmanova's building. "Something *is* bothering you, Nick. I hope you're not angry that I told Grandmama and Rachmanova about your taking Jordan to the Opera Ball."

Daria sounded so contrite, Nick hastened to reassure her. "No, it isn't that. It's something that happened at the ball," he admitted. He recounted the photographer's surprise attack in the alcove, omitting the fact that he and Jordan had been kissing. Nick hesitated, frowning up at the ornate molding skirting the foyer ceiling. "It was Bertie Waxx, Daria."

"You're sure?" Daria's classic brow furrowed in concern.

Nick nodded miserably. "He had disguised himself in a waiter's uniform, but I'd know that little weasel anywhere."

"Bertie Waxx is a tabloid reporter, Nick," Daria reminded him. "The yellow press thrives on prying into the lives of celebrities and aristocrats, and there are always plenty of both at the Opera Ball. Frankly, I would be surprised if he *didn't* find a way to sneak into the ball. You can be sure that you and Jordan are just one couple among many that he photographed last night. Given the competition in attendance at the ball, your picture probably won't even make it into the back pages of those sleazy papers that publish Waxx's stuff."

"I wouldn't have thought Inge's and my divorce would have been that interesting to the tabloids, either." Merely speaking the words left a bitter taste in Nick's mouth.

"Inge was touted as the world's top model." He could tell Daria was choosing her words, taking care to handle still-tender wounds as delicately as possible. "And then there was so much potential for scandal. I mean . . ."

"Go ahead and say it. My then-wife was having an affair with not one, but two of the wealthiest men in Europe. Hot gossip, I'll agree." Catching the pained expression in Daria's eyes, Nick blunted the angry edge in his voice. "I know all that's behind me—or should be. But I've locked horns with Waxx enough for him to have a personal vendetta against me. I'm afraid of the mess he might try to create now that he's seen me with a woman."

"I'm sure you have nothing to worry about." Daria was trying to sound encouraging. "After all, a photograph of you showing your date the Viennese skyline seems rather tame by Waxx's standards."

If that was true, I'm certain I wouldn't have a worry, either. Nick forced himself to nod agreement with Daria's optimistic prediction. As he emerged from the building into the blustery late-February wind, however, his mind refused to dismiss the new specter that had come to haunt it. A new ghost had joined the phantoms stalking him and Jordan MacKenzie: Bertie Waxx.

THE RICHTSBERGER HOF certainly wasn't the sort of place Inge Sorensen would have patronized. Not that the hotel was a dump, Bertie Waxx generously reminded himself. It was simply too middle-class, too ordinary for Inge's taste. Whoever Nick Rostov had gotten himself mixed up with this time apparently didn't share her predecessor's taste for ostentatious luxury, but that could mean anything. The redhead could be an heiress, traveling incognito, someone with heavy political connections, the *wife* of someone with heavy political connections. Bertie's mind raced excitedly ahead, tripping over and colliding with possibilities like a too-avid hurdler, as he slouched in the café chair, eyes glued to the hotel entrance directly across the street.

He had consumed so much coffee his nerves were thoroughly wired by the time the redhead emerged from her hotel. Bertie lurched in his seat, sloshing the remains of his last order onto the table. He watched the tall, slim woman walk to the end of the block and then pause.

"Blast!" Bertie muttered at the tram that rolled by to block his view.

He stood, but when the tram passed, the redhead was nowhere in sight. Had she gotten on the bloody tram? Staying in modest hotels was one thing, but using public transportation? As Bertie counted his change, he pondered the morning's bizarre revelations. Rostov's latest must want to keep a low profile at all costs, he concluded. Before he could uncover her story, however, he needed to find out who she was.

With this goal in mind, Bertie adjusted the wide lapels of his green-checked coat and sauntered into the lobby of the Richtsberger Hof. Like the professional he was, he took a few minutes to evaluate the scene. One look at the desk clerk told him he would have to seek assistance elsewhere. Bespectacled young men like that always took their jobs too seriously to volunteer information about guests. The waitresses idling just inside the tearoom door looked more promising, and Bertie decided to try his luck there.

As he wandered into the tearoom, one of the waitresses hastily folded the newspaper she had been scanning and tucked it behind the tray stand—not quickly enough, however, to conceal its front page from Bertie's sharp eyes. He had found a tabloid fan, he gleefully congratulated himself. Fate was smiling on his mission.

Bertie had not yet doffed his coat when the waitress arrived at his table. *"Guten Morgen, mein Herr,"* she greeted him. *"Sie wünschen?"*

As a man of the world, Bertie could converse in a half-dozen languages. He had never bothered much with incidentals like grammar and pronunciation, but so far such minor deficiencies had not stood in his way. Looking up into the waitress's bored young face, however, he sensed that a dash of foreign intrigue would enhance his position.

"Excuse me, luv, but do you speak English?"

"Yes." The waitress's nod was as uncertain as her reply.

Bertie's eyes narrowed sagely. "Ah, I would have thought as much. The minute I walked through the door, I said to myself. 'There's a young lady of accomplishment.'"

The waitress only frowned, and Bertie couldn't tell if she was resisting his line or merely having trouble understanding. Either way, he didn't want to push his luck. Best to get right down to business.

"I do quite a bit of traveling in my line of work. I must confess, I often miss hearing my mother tongue." Bertie fostered a sloppily sentimental smile. "But such is the nature of my work."

"What is your work?" the waitress asked, right on cue.

"I'm a journalist. Bertram 'Just-the-Facts' Waxx, at your service." He gave that revelation a few seconds to soak in. When her wan face remained blank, he went on. "Perhaps you have heard of some of the newspapers where my work has appeared. *The International Investigator, Inside Report, Eye on the World.*" He hesitated before playing his trump card. "*Aktuell-Edition.*"

At the mention of her own favorite tabloid, all traces of boredom vanished from the waitress's face.

"Ah, I see you are familiar with *Aktuell-Edition.*"

"Why, yes, I am."

Bertie glanced around the tearoom before leaning forward in his chair. "Can I trust you?" he asked in a dramatic whisper. He waited for the wide-eyed waitress to nod eagerly. "I am investigating a story here." He tapped the tabletop with his finger. "In this very hotel."

"Indeed!" The waitress matched his raspy whisper.

Bertie nodded solemnly. Then he beckoned her closer. "When the story breaks, it's going to be big, *big* news. But it's a difficult case. I could use some inside help."

The waitress peered around the room as suspiciously as he had. "What kind of help?"

Bertie cast a nervous glance over his shoulder. "There is a woman with shoulder-length reddish hair staying at this hotel. Do you know who I'm talking about?"

The young waitress smiled. "The hair. Yes, of course."

"Excellent." Bertie drew a deep breath, heavy with portent. "Now, if there was some way I could have a look at this woman's bill..."

The waitress drew back slightly. "That is against the rules."

Bertie eased a large-denomination bill out of his pocket and onto the table. The waitress looked at it for a long moment before slipping it into her apron.

"And I'll have a cup of tea while you're at it, luv," he called after her as she headed across the room.

The waitress was gone what seemed a very long time. Bertie was beginning to think she had gotten cold feet when she reappeared, tray in hand. This time she didn't linger at his table, but beneath his check for the tea he found a hotel bill for one Jordan MacKenzie.

Bertie whipped out a pen and notebook and began to record the pertinent information. Her room number was 407. She was a U.S. citizen, with an address in Silver Spring, Maryland. Except for a couple of coffees delivered to her room, she was doing her eating elsewhere. She had made two long-distance phone calls through the hotel switchboard. Bertie quickly jotted down the telephone numbers before signaling the waitress back to his table.

The pale young woman looked relieved to retrieve the bill, which Bertie palmed to her, along with enough change to cover the tea. "What did you learn?" she asked timidly.

Bertie smoothed his coat lapels into place and chuckled. "You'll read about it in the papers, luv."

"I HOPE YOU DIDN'T MIND my bringing him along." Nick diverted his eyes from the road long enough to cast a doubtful look at the wiry-haired mutt curled next to Jordan's feet. "I'm afraid Pedro was close to wearing out his welcome with Daria."

"I love dogs," Jordan assured him, reaching to stroke the lopsided ears. "But I'm curious. How in the world did an Austrian dog end up with the name Pedro?"

Nick chuckled. "Well, first of all, he isn't Austrian. He's Spanish."

"You got him in Spain?"

"On Formentera, to be exact. I had gone down to the island to... to get my head clear." Nick broke off. He frowned, expertly guiding the Porsche through a sharp curve in the mountain road. "It was right after my divorce." He sounded as if sharing that information required a great deal of effort. "To get back to Pedro's story, I found him while I was walking the beach one evening. He was pretty thin, so I think he was probably a stray who depended on tourists staying in the beach hotels for his survival. Anyway, we hit it right off, spent a lot of time together over the next few weeks. When I started packing to leave, it suddenly hit me that he was now my dog. So I got him a health certificate and brought him back to Vienna with me."

"Lucky Pedro," Jordan commented, but her mind was lingering on Nick's uneasy reference to his divorce.

In the short time they had known each other, their conversations had touched on an exceptional variety of topics, ranging from tastes in music and movies to childhood memories. She was struck now, however, by how little she knew about his recent personal life—as little as he knew about hers. Whatever her interest, Jordan sensed that she would learn the details of his failed marriage only when— and if—Nick decided to share them with her.

A sign in the crook of a curve, announcing the approach of Immel, reminded Jordan of their trip's purpose. If Spitzdorf was the paradigm for every snowy-village Christmas card she had ever received, then Immel was the quintessential alpine ski resort. The narrow streets of the village seemed to be trafficked exclusively by horse-drawn sleighs or high-priced sports cars. With equal uniformity, the pedestrians were dressed in either the traditional loden wool costume or fancy ski wear. Rising on both sides of the village were jagged peaks, glistening with snow. Shading her eyes against the glare, Jordan could just make out the thin line of a ski lift against the blindingly white background.

Leaving Pedro contentedly napping under an old down jacket in the Porsche, Nick and Jordan decided to have lunch in a small *Gasthaus*. The proprietor was happy both to recommend the *Gulasch* and to give them directions to Radetsky's chalet. They were finishing their coffee when Jordan made a suggestion she had been considering since the Opera Ball.

"Why don't you come with me to talk with the count?"

Nick's spoon poked the dollop of whipped cream beneath the coffee's dark surface. "What about Pedro? I had planned to take him for a walk while you met with Radetsky," he said after more consideration than the matter seemed to warrant.

"He's as warm as toast, bundled up in your old jacket, and probably won't wake for a couple of hours," Jordan countered.

Nick shrugged. "Radetsky granted you the interview."

Jordan watched Nick idly toy with his coffee spoon. For someone who had been badgering her for every fragment of information about the Radetsky music box, he was demonstrating surprisingly little interest in exploring this latest connection. "So did Dr. D'Antonelli and the physical therapy institute, and that certainly didn't discourage you from inviting yourself along."

The spoon rattled irritably as Nick dropped it onto the saucer. "Okay. I'll confess. Boris Radetsky and I don't get along. It all started with something that happened a long

time ago, and I won't bore you with the details. But I can
assure you I am not welcome in his chalet. Unless you want
to waste this trip, you need to meet him alone."

Jordan was surprised by this unexpected revelation, but
Nick was already pulling on his jacket, signaling an end to
the conversation. Following his lead, she collected her coat,
bag and briefcase while he settled the lunch tab. They
paused outside the *Gasthaus* while Nick unlocked the
Porsche and then wiggled the car keys from his key ring.

Jordan dubiously regarded the keys he handed her. "I
have no idea how long this meeting with Radetsky is going
to last. How am I going to find you afterward?"

Nick stooped to snap a leash onto Pedro's collar. "Come
back to the *Gasthaus* when you're finished. I asked the
proprietor about available rooms, in case we need to stay
over, and he's promised to hold a couple for us. At the very
least, we can have dinner here before heading back to
Vienna."

Jordan nodded before sliding behind the wheel of the
Porsche. She returned Nick's jaunty wave, but as she pulled
away from the curb she felt oddly out of joint. Nick's allu-
sion to bad blood between him and Radetsky had done
nothing to bolster her confidence. His reluctance to discuss
the matter had only fueled her uncertainty. What had happened to set the two men against each other? Common sense
suggested it had something to do with the music box, but
what? She continued to grapple with these frustrating
questions as she guided the Porsche along the narrow
mountain road.

The private road leading to Radetsky's chalet was even
more winding and snow banked than the public thorough-
fare. Jordan geared down, slowing to a crawl until she
reached the stone wall sealing off the count's private com-
pound from the rest of the world. As she lowered the car

window to press the intercom button, she peered through the wrought-iron gates. Two Mercedes sedans were parked in the courtyard, along with a large unhitched sleigh. Skis and poles were stacked near one of the arched doorways, along with a pair of carelessly discarded boots.

Jordan grimaced at the woman's static-clouded voice rasping over the intercom. She announced herself and then waited for the gates to swing open. To her consternation, several minutes passed and the gates remained obstinately locked. Perhaps the servant had not understood her. Resisting the uneasy feeling creeping over her, Jordan pressed the button again. Another anxiety-building wait intervened before a forceful masculine voice responded.

"The count bids me to extend his regrets, Miss Mac-Kenzie, but he will be unable to see you this afternoon."

A crack of static sent Jordan scrambling to catch Radetsky's spokesman before he cut off. "I will be happy to re-schedule for tomorrow, if that is more convenient for Count Radetsky."

The distant-sounding man answered without hesitation. "Tomorrow is out of the question. Due to a ski injury he suffered this morning, the count will be indisposed for an indefinite period of time. I am sorry, Miss MacKenzie, but Count Radetsky cannot receive visitors."

This time the intercom popped decisively. Jordan stared dejectedly at the now-silent speaker grid for a few moments. Although the chances of Radetsky's contacting her seemed remote, she wrote the name of her Vienna hotel on a business card and slid it into the letterbox below the intercom. However unintentionally, Nick had certainly gotten the best of today's wild-goose chase, she thought as she followed her own tire tracks cutting through the crusty snow. So much for their clever Opera Ball caper. Her mood continued to dim, matching the gloom descending over the wooded mountainside.

Although it was not quite four o'clock, the brief winter day had already begun to wane. Wrinkling her nose at the steady sleet pelting the windshield, Jordan flicked on the headlights. Thank God the Porsche handled so well, for the mountain road had gotten noticeably slicker since her ascent earlier that afternoon. Jordan frowned as the harsh beam of approaching headlights loomed in the rearview mirror. A tailgater was the last thing she needed under such hazardous driving conditions.

"Back off!" Jordan muttered to the unseen driver.

Her eyes darted to the speedometer needle and then back to the rearview mirror's reflected glare. They were approaching a straight stretch in the road. Surely this lunatic behind her would seize the chance to pass. As Jordan had hoped, the high beams veered to the left. She glanced over at the car that had pulled even with her, matching her speed.

"What are you waiting for, hotshot? Now's your big chance to pass."

Without warning, the sedan edged into Jordan's lane, narrowly missing the driver's side of the Porsche. Jordan gripped the wheel, holding the heavy sports car steady. With snow banked on the shoulder almost as high as the roof of Nick's car, she didn't have much margin for error. One careless move, and she would find herself marooned in a drift. At least she had that idiot driver out of the way.

To her consternation, the sedan now showed none of its previous appetite for speed. In fact, it had slowed to a tedious creep. Jordan strained to read the license plate, but the figures were spattered with mud. She had encountered a sociopathic driver once before, during a long drive across the Texas panhandle. That time, she had simply pulled into the first Denny's she spotted and drunk coffee until her tormentor had a sufficient lead on her. Unfortunately, the mountain road to Immel was devoid of even a suitable stopping place, much less a drive-in restaurant.

When the brake lights winked in front of her, Jordan sucked in her breath. She tapped the Porsche's brakes, struggling to widen the hairbreadth margin between the two cars. Whoever was driving the sedan was either crazy or he was deliberately trying to cause an accident. The image of a featureless face, cloaked in a black ski mask, leaped into her mind. What if that man was driving the sedan?

Jordan fled from the terrifying conclusion. She started when a horn sounded from behind her. Her eyes flew to the pair of headlight beams reflected in the rearview mirror. She wasn't alone on the road anymore. The driver behind her honked a second time, and the threatening sedan began to accelerate. Relief washed over Jordan as the sedan's taillights disappeared into the snowy fog.

She was still a little weak-kneed when she reached Zur Sonne, the *Gasthaus* where Nick had planned to meet her. Jordan dove for the first available parking place. Without bothering to button her coat, she snatched up her briefcase, locked the car and jogged to the well-lighted pension. She found Nick sipping hot chocolate in front of the common room's cozy fireplace with Pedro snoring at his feet. To judge by his alarmed expression when he saw her, she must have looked as harried as she felt.

"I hope it didn't go badly." Ushering her into a comfortable chair, Nick relieved her of the briefcase and coat.

"It didn't go at all." Jordan extended her still-sweaty palms over the blaze. Chafing her stiff fingers, she told Nick about the afternoon's increasingly disturbing succession of events.

"This guy driving the sedan, did you get a look at him?" Nick asked.

"You mean, was he wearing a black ski mask?" Jordan shook her head wearily. "No, but the net effect was the same. Someone tried to run me off the road today. And he would have succeeded if the other motorist hadn't come along. I guess I can thank my lucky stars that a witness always manages to show up in the nick of time. So far." She hadn't intended to sound so ominous, but the morbid afterthought cast a pall over the fireside, draining the cheer from the dancing flames.

Nick took both her hands in his and rubbed them gently. "There are a lot of people on the road who shouldn't be. This driver could have been just another one."

But he probably wasn't. Jordan knew that Nick believed that platitude no more than she did, but she managed a shaky smile. Being close to him, having him hold her hands, made her feel safe, and right now that was what she needed most—help in restoring her sense of personal security.

"I have a suggestion. I'm not too keen on driving back to Vienna tonight in this rotten weather. We have two rooms on hold here." Nick gave her hands an encouraging little shake. "Let's stay in Immel for the night. While Pedro and I were roaming around the village, we heard about a carnival procession that's scheduled for this evening. Do you know about our *Fasching* celebrations?"

Jordan shook her head, but she was already succumbing to Nick's soothing, low-pitched voice. He was obviously trying to distract her from a very real danger that had materialized that afternoon. His motives were so goodhearted—and his technique so effective—she had no urge to resist.

"*Fasching* is our Mardi Gras." Nick chuckled. "But here in Austria we make the festival last as long as possible. As much as a prelude to Lent, our carnival is also a way of chasing away the last dreary days of winter. I think you would enjoy watching the parade tonight. The *Gasthaus* proprietor assures me his hot spiced wine is the best in the village. And we could be back in Vienna early tomorrow, so you wouldn't lose much work time,'' he added.

"You've convinced me." Jordan smiled up into his face that was flushed from the firelight. After her frightening experience, she had not been looking forward to hitting the road again that night. Although she doubted the carnival would entirely supplant her concerns, spending the evening with Nick would go a long way toward reestablishing her equilibrium.

Nick seemed determined to free Jordan from as much worry as possible. Before dinner he asked the proprietor to store her briefcase in the establishment's safe, a precaution Jordan had routinely taken since the incident on the night train. After a delightful meal of roast pork with apples and dumplings, Nick whisked Jordan into the waiting open-air sleigh he had reserved on the sly. The cold mountain air nipped at their faces, driving them closer into each other's arms, as they rode through the village. The horses' harnesses were decorated with little bells that jingled merrily in the crisp night air.

"It's like Christmas," Jordan remarked, pointing to the evergreens strung with winking lights.

Nick only laughed, but his lips gently grazed a wisp of her bangs protruding from her knit beret. Jordan felt a sudden and surprisingly urgent surge of passion, as if her emotions had been simmering just below the boiling point ever since the Opera Ball.

When they reached the village square, the sleigh driver reined his horses to a halt long enough for Nick and Jordan to alight. The carnival procession had attracted a large crowd, but they managed to press their way through the throng until they had a clear view of the street. Nick posi-

tioned himself behind Jordan, arms lapped around her
neck, as the resonant clang of bells grew louder, signaling
the approach of the procession. Soon the narrow street was
filled with turning and bowing figures, some of them bran-
dishing torches. Their faces were concealed behind gro-
tesque wooden masks topped with headdresses fashioned
from twigs, leaves and flowers.

"The bells are supposed to drive out the evil spirits of
winter." Nick's warm breath stirred the hair curling around
her ear.

Jordan settled her hands over his wrists. "I suppose the
masks help, too." In spite of herself, she drew back as a
particularly demonic wooden face abruptly lurched in her
direction.

Lighten up, Jordan scolded herself fiercely. Granted, she
had had more than her share of hair-raising experiences in
the past few days, but that was no reason to jump at her own
shadow. And if a real threat did exist, the last thing she
needed was an undisciplined imagination to muddle her
judgment. In spite of her resolve, Jordan could not shake
the sinister associations the costumed figures elicited. Nick
apparently sensed her uneasiness.

"I don't know about you, but I'm ready for that hot
spiced wine." He playfully tugged at her shoulders.

"It is a bit nippy," Jordan agreed, turning her face up to
the sleet that had begun to pepper the revelers.

She eased comfortably into the crook of his arm as they
trudged back to the *Gasthaus.* By the time they reached Zur
Sonne, a layer of icy powder covered their coats and their
faces were blotched with rosy patches. Stamping the snow
from her damp boots, Jordan rubbed her wind-stung cheeks
vigorously.

"Let's change into some dry clothes before we have our
wine," Nick suggested.

Jordan nodded eagerly. She waited for him to pick up their keys at the desk, and then headed up the wooden stairs.

"I'm going to take Pedro out for a few minutes, so take your time," Nick told her.

"I'll meet you by the fireplace." Jordan smiled before slipping into her room.

She immediately stumbled over her garment bag, which the pension proprietor had deposited in front of the door. Jordan slapped the wall with one hand until she located the light switch, and flicked it on. The room was utterly charming, a bit drafty but decorated with carved wooden furniture, framed nineteenth-century prints and heavily embroidered drapes. As insurance against the draft, no doubt, a fluffy feather bed rested on the four-poster like a fat cumulus cloud fallen to earth.

Jordan swung the garment bag onto the bed, unzipped it and pulled out an embroidered rust turtleneck and black stirrup pants. She smiled at the sound of four frantic little paws racing down the hall outside, with more leisurely steps following them. Given Pedro's inquisitive nose, she would have time for a quick shower before he and Nick returned. Shucking her wet clothes, Jordan headed for the bathroom.

The bath was small but modern, with plenty of hot water and a wonderful hand-held spray. Jordan reveled in the jet of hot water that gradually thawed her cold-numbed feet and face. Soon the tiny cubicle was fogged with billowing steam. Jordan pushed the door slightly ajar to clear the air before beginning to towel her reddened skin. She stopped, towel looped over her shoulders, as something rustled in the bedroom.

Jordan slowly lowered the towel. The steam filled her throat, threatening to choke her, but she forced herself to listen. She had heard a noise. She was certain of it. She waited, hating the labored sound of her own breathing in the suffocatingly close little room.

There was only one way out of the bathroom—through the door. Jordan weighed her pitifully limited choices. She could wait or she could move. Knotting the large bath towel around her, she opted for the latter. Jordan touched the door lightly and was relieved when its hinges silently complied. She tiptoed cautiously, peering into the room.

It looked just as she had left it before her shower, garment bag dumped on the bed, handbag hooked over the back of a chair, wet clothes piled on the floor. Her eyes swept the room and then fell on the embroidered drapes. They stirred slightly and then fell, lifted by the draft seeping through the windows.

She felt so silly she almost burst out laughing. If she didn't get a handle on her nerves, she would start looking under her bed for monsters. She did need to do something about that draft. Even the plump feather bed would offer inadequate protection against the gusts leaking into the room.

Jordan walked to the drapes and pulled one panel aside. No wonder a gale was howling through the room. Someone had neglected to secure one of the glass-paned doors opening onto the balcony. Jordan was tugging at the ancient catch when she glanced down. All the blood drained from her face, but for a moment she could do nothing but stare at the pair of booted feet just visible beneath the drape's hem.

He knows I've seen him. Oh, my God! She stepped back and then wheeled. A scream swelled in her throat as a gloved hand closed over her mouth. Jordan swung one fist backward, but another hand stifled the blow in midair. Acting on pure instinct, she jerked her heel up and back and managed to catch her assailant right below the kneecap. Her bare foot couldn't have done much damage, but it was enough to throw him off guard for a second. His grip slackened, and Jordan lunged free.

"Help! Help!" She was screaming so loud her head felt as if it would burst.

Just as her hands closed over the doorknob, the hooded attacker grabbed her again. Jordan let out another blood-curdling scream as he hurled her back onto the floor. Grabbing a chair leg, she threw the piece of furniture into his path. She could hear rushed steps pounding up the stairs now, frantic barking, anxious voices in the hall.

The man in the black ski mask heard the steps, too. Jordan's stomach pitched as he reached inside his black leather coat, revealing a flash of blue steel. The intruder pivoted toward the door as it flew open.

"Look out!" Jordan yelled, diving behind the oversize wardrobe.

Nick quickly flattened himself against the hall wall. When Jordan dared look again, she saw the black-clad intruder disappear through the parted drapes.

"Are you hurt?" Nick grabbed her and pressed her to his chest.

Jordan managed to shake her head. As he moved toward the balcony, she snatched at his sleeve. "You can't go after him, Nick. I think he's armed."

"By the time the police get here, he'll be out of sight. I at least need to see where he's going." Nick had already straddled the balcony rail, prepared to drop to the ground.

The ice carpeting the balcony stung her bare feet as Jordan rushed to the rail. She watched Nick break his fall against a snow-crowned evergreen. He was regaining his footing when the chillingly innocuous sound of a silencer-dulled bullet chipped the air. Another silenced bullet discharged. Jordan's agonized cry cut through the still night as she watched Nick plummet face first into the snow.

Chapter Eight

"Nick!" Jordan's shriek rang in her ears.

Fear had numbed her senses, blanked out everything but the figure lying prone beside the cluster of shrubs. She was dimly aware of Pedro's hysterical yapping, of her hands on the ice-glazed rail, of the nettlelike sting of snow and broken evergreens against her bare skin as she landed heavily below the balcony. She was rising to her knees, trying to turn toward Nick, when an arm abruptly encircled her. She struck out as the arm shoved her onto the snow-covered ground.

"Be still!" Nick hissed, holding her flat beside him.

"My God, you're alive! I thought...I thought you had been hit," Jordan gasped through the wet snow sticking to her mouth.

Nick's arm flexed around her. "And I would have been, if I hadn't hit the ground when I heard that first shot."

Not daring to move a muscle, Jordan shifted her eyes toward the row of spruce and pine bordering the pension courtyard. "Do you think he's still out there?"

"After attracting so much attention, he probably wasn't inclined to hang around, but we're not taking any chances."

Jordan felt Nick's arm relax slightly as the undulating sound of a police-car siren drew near. They dared to sit up

only when three uniformed men charged into the courtyard.

"The fellow has a gun," Nick warned the policemen,
pointing toward the border of trees. "He fired at me from
right over there. That was the last I saw of him." He
watched the policemen run between the trees and then
turned to Jordan. "We need to get you inside."

Jordan glanced down at her bare legs and feet. In her state
of shock she had forgotten that she was still wearing only the
wet bath towel.

"It's all right." Nick closed his arms protectively around
her, guiding her toward the pension.

The proprietor, along with several goggle-eyed hotel
guests, had congregated in the door of the *Gasthaus*. They
stepped aside as Pedro barked sharply and then charged into
the courtyard. The little dog clearly sensed that something
was very wrong. Racing in a frenzied circle, he alternately
sniffed Jordan's and then Nick's feet to assure himself that
they were unharmed. He growled, digging at the churned
snow, as he inspected the spot where they had lain. When he
dashed toward the evergreen border, Nick called to him
sharply.

"Pedro, come here!"

To his credit, the *Gasthaus* proprietor stepped forward to
help. "I will see to your dog, Herr Rostov," he offered.

Nick nodded his thanks as he escorted Jordan past the
stunned onlookers and up the stairs. She was shivering almost uncontrollably now from the cold. Her legs were stiff,
her knees almost too locked to negotiate the few wide stairs
leading to the pension's second level. She let Nick lead her
into his room and bundle her into the big feather bed.

"I'm going to fetch some clothes from your room. I'll
only be gone a second, but I'll leave the doors open, okay?"

Jordan nodded shakily. Her teeth had begun to chatter, and she fought to control the trembling spasms seizing her limbs.

As he had promised, Nick quickly returned with an armload of warm clothing and Pedro at his heels. He glanced toward the hall where the sound of authoritative masculine voices was drawing closer. "I'll talk with the police while you get dressed." He gave her an encouraging smile before stepping into the hall and drawing the door closed behind him.

Still huddled in the feather bed, Jordan pulled on the fleecy wool socks. Her numb hands felt clumsy, fumbling with sleeves and pant legs. Her brain didn't seem to be functioning much better, either. Jordan took a deep breath and tried to reconstruct the night's terrifying events in an orderly fashion. She didn't want to forget anything that might be of value to the police, but her mind shrank from the memory of the masked attacker and his deadly weapon.

When Nick knocked on the door, Jordan joined him in the hall. A pleasant-looking young man with curly brown hair introduced himself as Herr Boehm of the local police force. Before beginning his questioning, he took pains to assure Jordan that the area was now secure. Herr Boehm and his colleagues had followed the intruder's footprints in the snow to a nearby side street. The prints had abruptly disappeared at the curb, directly in front of deep tire ruts which, the policeman surmised, the escape vehicle had left in its wake.

"I suppose you have no way of knowing where he went?" Jordan asked.

"Not at the moment," Herr Boehm replied cautiously. "We will, however, conduct a thorough investigation. Because of the carnival, a great many people will be in the streets quite late tonight. There is an excellent chance that someone may have noticed a fast or reckless driver.''

But not a calm, collected one, Jordan thought with a sinking heart. A jittery criminal would have fled the second he realized the room he had broken into was occupied. Her assailant, however, had been brazen enough to hide and then try to strong-arm her. By the same token, Jordan felt certain he had made his getaway in a cool, calculating fashion. The odds that he had attracted any attention in the process were practically nil.

Despite her pessimism, Jordan painstakingly recreated the terrifying incident for the policeman. She racked her brain for the least detail she could recall about the man's appearance. Except for his approximate height and type of physique, however, his head-to-toe black garb had successfully obscured any telling characteristics.

"I believe his eyes were blue," she added as an afterthought. "But I can't really be certain."

"I understand, Fräulein MacKenzie," Herr Boehm kindly reassured her.

After Jordan had signed her statement, she inquired about the next stage of the investigation.

"Since this fellow wore gloves, we will probably find no fingerprints. We have, however, discovered one bit of evidence that may prove useful. During our search of the *Gasthaus* courtyard, we found an empty shell casing."

"That could be matched to the gun the man fired?" Nick asked.

The policeman nodded. "That is correct." He smiled cordially at both of them before glancing at his report. "Very well. I have telephone numbers where you may be reached, if necessary." He handed each of them a business card. "Should you have any questions or information, please do not hesitate to contact me."

Jordan and Nick thanked Herr Boehm. After he had disappeared down the stairs, they turned to each other.

"How do you feel?" Nick asked.

Jordan clutched the back of her neck, squeezing the aching muscles. "Too tired to stand on my feet another minute. Too nervous to sleep. I don't know. I guess I feel thoroughly messed up. What about you?"

"Much the same. But I suppose we should try to get some rest." Nick hesitated. "If you like, you're welcome to spend the rest of the night in my room. There's an extra folding bed in the closet," he was quick to add.

The frightening experience they had shared blunted the self-consciousness Jordan would ordinarily have felt accepting his offer. "I wasn't looking forward to spending the night staring up at the ceiling in that room, listening to every squeak and rustle," she confessed, following him into the little pension room.

"Then you can spend the night staring up at the ceiling in my room." Nick managed a weary chuckle.

While Nick secured the door and checked the room's windows and balcony doors, Jordan pulled the metal folding bed out of the closet. Pedro trotted between the two of them, overseeing the operation.

"Everything is locked up tight," Nick told her, summarily seizing the extra pillow she had been fluffing. "You take the four-poster." Anticipating her protest, he shook his head emphatically. "Please don't make me argue, Jordan. I'm too tired."

Jordan smiled at Nick's comically unchivalrous method of settling their sleeping arrangements in her favor. She could tell that their brush with danger had been as draining for him as for her, and she appreciated his effort to lighten the tension with humor. Most of all, she was grateful for his simply being there, comforting her that she didn't have to

face the night's terrifying memories alone. While she
changed into a nightgown in the bath, she could hear him
rearranging furniture and putting away things in the room.
Just the sound of him going about such mundane tasks reassured her that, for the next few hours at least, the world
had returned to normal.

When she returned to the bedroom she found Nick
dressed in sweats, sitting on the side of the folding cot. He
waited until she had climbed into the big four-poster before
turning out the light. Jordan heard the cot's flimsy sup-
ports squeak as Nick tried to accommodate his rangy frame
to its narrow dimensions.

"Good night, Nick."

"Good night." In the dark room, Nick's voice sounded
warm, familiar.

Jordan lay beneath the covers of the thick feather bed,
listening to his faintly audible breathing. He had taken
charge so readily, handled the aftermath of the terrifying
attack with such clearheaded thinking, it was hard to believe he had almost been killed. When she had seen him lying facedown in the snow, raw, agonized emotion had
governed her reaction. Until now, Jordan had not allowed
herself to fully explore the most terrible possibility. What if
the gunman's bullet had found its mark? What if he had
only continued to lie there in the snow, silent and unmov-
ing? What if Nick had been taken from the world, from *her*
world, forever?

The thought was unbearable. Jordan realized how much
he had come to mean to her, how much she cared for him.
Slowly, a tiny bead of hot salt water found its way between
her tightly closed lids. She pressed her lips together, fighting to stifle a sob. When she heard Nick stir, she hastily
dabbed her damp face with the hem of the quilt.

"Jordan?" Nick's shadowy silhouette loomed beside the bed. His hand gently smoothed her brow. "It's all right, darling. Go ahead and let yourself cry. You've been through so much, I don't see how you've held back so long."

"It isn't that." Jordan swallowed with difficulty, struggling to recover her voice. "You were almost killed tonight. Nick, I don't know what I would have done—" She broke off.

"But I wasn't. I'm here, and we're both safe." Sliding his arm around her shoulders, Nick eased onto the bed beside her. "We're going to come out of this all right, darling. I promise." He tenderly kissed her moist eyelids. Then he pressed her face to his chest, rocking her gently as if she were a child awakened from a nightmare. "I promise," he repeated.

Jordan slipped her hand into his and held it tight. By what power Nick made such promises she had no idea. But for tonight she needed to believe that together they could overcome the threat shadowing their lives.

THE INSISTENT CLICK of Pedro's claws, pacing the hardwood floor, awakened Jordan just as the dawn was beginning to seep between the embroidered drapes. She sat up slowly, taking care to work her fingers free of Nick's slackened grasp without waking him. He must have spent the whole night sitting half-propped on the pillow next to her, holding her hand. His sleeping face, the traces of stress still etched on its handsome features, elicited a fresh wave of tender feelings in her.

Swinging her legs over the side of the bed, Jordan pressed her finger to her lips and shook her head at Pedro. She dressed as quietly as possible while the little dog looked on, tail wagging in anticipation. When Pedro saw her pick up the leash, he could no longer contain himself. He bounded around the room and then scurried beneath the folding cot. When he emerged, he held something clasped between his teeth. The object rattled noisily across the wood floor as Pedro first tossed and then pursued it.

"Shh!" Jordan cautioned the playful dog.

Pedro trotted back to Jordan, plaything in mouth, and rolled on his side at her feet.

"Whatever you're chasing is making entirely too much racket," Jordan whispered, kneeling beside the dog.

When she scratched Pedro's stomach, his jaws released the prize. Jordan watched the gold-colored cylinder roll a few inches before coming to rest beside her foot. Sitting back on her heels, she picked up the spent casing.

"Where did you get this?" she murmured, stroking the dog's head with her free hand.

Jordan's mind flashed back to the previous evening. Herr Boehm had found only one spent casing, but she distinctly remembered hearing the gunman fire two shots. When Pedro had charged into the courtyard, he must have picked up one of the casings and carried it back to the room without anyone's noticing.

"Jordan?" Nick's voice from the bed sounded slightly alarmed, if groggy.

"I'm here." She stood up and smiled at him. "I was going to sneak out quietly and take Pedro for a walk before you woke up."

Nick stretched his stiff shoulder muscles. "Pedro doesn't know the meaning of the word *quietly*." He shook his head and then patted the bed, allowing the dog to hop up beside him.

"Maybe not. But he's an excellent sleuth." Bracing one knee on the bed, Jordan reached to drop the casing onto Nick's lap.

Nick whistled under his breath. "He found this thing?"

Jordan nodded. "Apparently. Aren't you proud of him?"

"Yes, and I imagine Herr Boehm will be, too."

"I don't see any point in giving it to the police. They already have one for their investigation."

Nick eyed the metal cylinder dubiously. "I suppose you're right. What are you doing, starting a souvenir collection?" He deposited the casing into Jordan's outstretched hand.

Jordan gave him a wry look, but then she sobered. "I'd like to start a little investigation of my own. I don't doubt the police will do a thorough job, but they might overlook some possibilities that we wouldn't. Connections with Gudrun Mayes-Cooper, for instance."

Nick frowned down at the rumpled feather bed. "After last night I'm beginning to doubt Gudrun's involvement. She's a ruthless person, but she's never employed lethal violence to get her way, so far as I know."

"If not Gudrun, then who?" Jordan pressed him.

Nick drew a deep sigh before answering. "I don't know," he finally admitted.

Jordan regarded him closely, not liking the hesitant ring of his answer. "Gudrun may have nothing to do with the trigger-happy brute last night," she conceded, "but there's certainly no harm in learning everything we can in the meantime. I'm going to air express this spent casing to my dad. He's retired from the FBI, but he still has friends who can get him a firearms technologist's report on it."

"It can't hurt," Nick agreed. "We have so few clues as it is."

In fact, they had almost nothing that would qualify as a real, substantial clue. That discouraging thought continued to nag Jordan during the drive back to Vienna. They took turns at the wheel, ostensibly to allow each other some much-needed nap time. Even her disjointed dreams, however, were tainted with the images of sinister featureless faces.

When they reached the city, Nick drove directly to Jordan's hotel. He double-parked in front of the Richtsberger Hof long enough for Jordan and Pedro to climb out.

"Wait for me in the lobby. I'll bring your bag and briefcase around as soon as I find a parking place."

"Great." Jordan tugged at Pedro's leash, pulling him away from the curb, as Nick shifted into gear.

The area around the hotel was quieter than usual, its sidewalks populated only by a few winter tourists and Sunday-afternoon strollers. Yielding to Pedro's determined encouragement, Jordan decided to take him for a short walk. As always, the little mixed-breed's nose quickly occupied itself with gathering data. Jordan let him take his time while she idly gazed into the windows of the shops they passed. Except for a news kiosk catering to hotel customers and tourists, none of the businesses was open on Sunday. When they reached the kiosk, Jordan looped the leash around her wrist and dug her wallet out of her handbag. She could use a bit of news from home, anything to take her mind off the craziness of the past week. Jordan had selected an American fashion magazine and the latest issue of *Time* when a British tabloid caught her eye.

Ordinarily, Jordan confined her tabloid reading to extended waits in supermarket lines. The provocative headline and the even more startling picture accompanying it, however, eclipsed any breaking story *Time* might offer. Lifting the cheap daily from its slot, Jordan stared at the boldface letters.

Playboy back in action
His Latest Conquest?

the headline proclaimed. Right below it, for all the world to see, was a photograph of Jordan and Nick wrapped in each other's arms, lips joined in a passionate kiss.

Jordan hastily scanned the columns. She was relieved to find herself described only as a "mysterious beauty." Where Nick was concerned, however, the article offered snippets of information that seemed to have nothing to do with the Nick Rostov she knew. He had never said anything about his career as a "jet-set daredevil ski champ." And who was this "supermodel Inge Sorensen"? According to the tabloid, Nick and she had engaged in a "torrid romance."

Resisting the futile impulse to buy every copy in the slot, Jordan tried to avoid the clerk's eyes as she paid for the tabloid and the magazines. Folding the offensive photo inside the paper, she hurried Pedro back to the hotel.

Nick was waiting for them in the lobby. "Pedro must have wanted to stretch his legs," he commented, ushering them into the elevator.

Jordan gave him an incredulous glance. *Playboy?* She tried to reconcile the obnoxious label with the intelligent, sincere man she knew. Or thought she knew. Memories from the past night—his touch, his tender words, his embrace and, most painful of all, her own emotions—rose in her mind to torment her. She felt upset, foolish, angry, confused, hurt and stupid all at once.

"Is something wrong?" Nick asked, giving her a puzzled look.

Jordan shook her head, averting her eyes to the successively lighted floor numbers. She waited until they were inside her room to produce the tabloid.

"What does this mean?"

Nick stared at the headline for a few seconds and then cursed under his breath. "Where did you get this?" His voice was hoarse with anger.

"At a newsstand, where everyone else can get it. But before you ask any more questions, you need to answer mine."

Running his fingers through his hair, Nick strode to the window. "Those papers thrive on distortion," he said, keeping his back to her.

"I've always felt that way, too. But why would someone want to put a picture of us on the cover of one of these rags? I mean, I'm not Elizabeth Taylor or Cher." She tried to keep her voice even.

Nick pushed away from the window. "It's all because of my divorce and a reprehensible subhuman named Bertie Waxx, the guy who photographed us at the Opera Ball." He hesitated, glancing around the hotel room as if he were looking for a misplaced cue card.

Jordan nodded encouragingly. "I remember your saying he was a paparazzo who regularly crashed society affairs."

"Bertie Waxx has made a profession of prying into people's personal lives. Occasionally he finds something juicy enough to sell to a scandal sheet. When he doesn't, his imagination makes up the difference. That's what happened when he decided to create a sensation about my divorce from Inge. I guess I gave him a little more help than he needed, did some stupid things. But I never deserved the label of playboy." He sighed heavily. "Oh, God, I don't even know where to start."

"Wherever you feel most comfortable," Jordan suggested gently. Whatever his story might be, Nick's obvious distress had softened her accusative stance.

Nick sank down onto the side of the bed, folding his hands in front of him. "You see, Jordan, I came to my current profession by the sheerest stroke of luck. I spent most of my college years on the ski slopes, not in the classroom. I had no real direction, and after graduation I simply kept doing the one thing I could do reasonably well—ski. I was on the competitive circuit, won a few championships, not thinking beyond the next slalom. All that came to an end when I took a very bad fall in Chamonix. They managed to patch up my knee, but not well enough for a professional skier. Overnight I went from being a hot competitor to a spectator on the sidelines. I was finished.''

"That must have been very traumatic. I'm sorry," Jordan began, but Nick shook his head.

"I'm not. Sooner or later I would have had to give up racing, and then what? As it was, I was leading a fairly aimless life. Thank God I was never unthinking enough to get into the drug scene, but the company I kept and a few of our escapades furnished Bertie Waxx with a filler item or two. It's amazing how interesting Waxx can make a rowdy party—with a few well-known people on hand—sound. At any rate, I was a washed-up skier bumming around the Balearic Islands when I met Vittorio. When he learned that I was interested in Russian icons—something, I might add, that I had come by only because of my heritage—he encouraged me to study further.''

Nick's shoulders rose in an indifferent shrug. "I had nothing better to do, so I took his advice. I had to work really hard, a new experience for me, and for a long time I was just another obscure specialist, earning little notice and even less money.''

"But you obviously did manage to build a reputation for yourself in the art world," Jordan interposed.

"Yes," Nick conceded. "But deep down inside, I guess I still missed the glamour of the ski circuit. I honestly can't think of another reason why I fell for Inge.''

"The supermodel?''

"Bertie is still using that moniker for her?" Nick shook his head in disgust. "According to the people who make such proclamations, she was *the* face the year we met. I had enjoyed some modest successes in my new profession, but nothing to equal my old giant slalom daredevil stuff. I'm ashamed to admit it, but I guess I was terribly flattered when Inge showed an interest in me. Soon we were going to all the 'in' spots together, the resorts, the casinos, the big galas, and Bertie was tagging along, documenting the whole thing. I got up the courage to propose on New Year's Eve after an all-night party in Paris, and she accepted. From there it was downhill."

"You two weren't really in love?" Jordan posed the question carefully.

"We didn't even know each other." As Nick stared at his folded hands, a sad look drifted across his face. "I kept trying to persuade myself that we were just going through some rough spots. I didn't want to admit what a big mistake I'd made. In the meantime, Inge continued with her life, just as she had before we were married. Bertie's papers kept me informed as to her latest companion of choice. During the divorce he never missed a chance to broadcast the details of her affairs. When it was all over, I simply wanted to run away. But apparently you can't hide from Bertie Waxx."

He looked up at Jordan, his clear blue eyes pleading for understanding. "Perhaps I should have told you about this sooner, but it's all so difficult to talk about. You must believe me, Jordan, I never wanted to involve you in this mess."

Jordan took his hands. "I understand, Nick. From what you've told me, it seems that Bertie Waxx is really more interested in Inge than in you. Sooner or later another fashion model will have an unpleasant divorce, and Waxx will move on to greener pastures."

Nick turned his hands palms up and squeezed her wrists. "I hope you're right." He smiled, with obvious effort, and then withdrew his hands from her clasp. "Well, I'd better go home. I've neglected some research for an acquisition I'm arranging for a German museum, and this was to be the afternoon I made up for lost time."

"If it makes you feel any better, I'm going to use the rest of the day for paperwork on my other cases," Jordan said as she followed him to the door. "I'll touch base tomorrow."

After Nick had departed, however, Jordan's mind balked at poring over the photocopied nineteenth-century property title transfers of a Scottish immigrant clan. Her thoughts kept gravitating to the tabloid's explosive headline and Nick's account of his turbulent life. After she had read the tabloid article in its entirety, its transparent bid for sensationalism lent credence to Nick's insistence that he had been maligned. Then, too, she was unaccustomed to seeing herself portrayed as a wild-living downhill racer's latest heartthrob, to say the least. Despite her efforts to put aside the distasteful tabloid story, a disjointed feeling lingered with Jordan throughout the afternoon.

At three o'clock she reached for the phone to call her father. Even on Sunday, Dad was an incurable early riser. By now he would have had several cups of black coffee and read through the sports section.

"Hello?"

"Hi, Dad! It's me, Jordan. I hope I didn't disturb you."

"Jordan! No, of course, I'm up and at 'em. Your mom's still sleeping in, though. It's great to hear from you, baby. How are things going?"

Someone who didn't know Jack MacKenzie would probably have described his voice as gruff, but to Jordan, the husky baritone always sounded warm and loving. "Okay. Listen, I have a favor to ask. It's kind of unusual, though."

"Anything for my girl," her dad assured her.

Jordan screwed her courage to the sticking point. "I'd like to have a firearms technologist examine a spent casing I'm going to send you."

For several long moments the only sound on the line was the shadow of another long-distance conversation, seeping through the static.

At last Jack MacKenzie cleared his throat. "May I ask how this casing happened to come into your possession and exactly why you want it analyzed?"

Jordan had never lied to her father, but she sensed that a thorough account of the casing's history would have him on the next plane out of Dulles International to Vienna. "A friend's dog found it. He thought it might have something to do with some shots that were fired earlier." That *was* true, she insisted to herself, if you were willing to split hairs.

"Huh." She could see her dad stroking the Sunday-morning stubble on his chin as he mulled over the cryptic information. "You know, honey, I've always maintained you had a right to a life of your own. I've never meddled in your business, have I?"

"No, Dad."

"All right." Her father paused. "Is this anything the police ought to know about?"

"They do already. Trust me, Dad. There's nothing you need to worry about." Jordan knew she was going out on a limb with that one, but the occasion seemed to warrant it. "It would mean a lot to me and my friend if you could give us a little help."

Her father sighed as only parents can. "Okay. Express it to me, and I'll see what I can do."

"Thanks so much, Dad! I'll talk with you and Mom later this week. Please give her my love."

"Sure. And, Jordan..." Her father hesitated. "Do your old man a favor, and take care of yourself, okay?"

"I promise, Dad." As Jordan hung up the phone, she hoped it would be one she could keep.

BERTIE WAXX HAD BEEN ABLE to ascertain two things about the long-distance numbers Jordan MacKenzie had dialed from her hotel room. They were in the United States, and they were business numbers. Since returning to his hotel late Friday evening, Bertie had tried both numbers at least a dozen times without getting an answer. The residence of someone Nick Rostov's girlfriend deemed worthy to phone would have been equipped with an answering machine, a maid or both. No, the two numbers no doubt belonged to businesses that were closed for the weekend.

Bertie's theory was borne out when he renewed his efforts on Monday.

"Genealogical Research, Inc. May I help you?"

Bertie chuckled to himself, conjuring a sharp-nosed, spinsterish image to go with the secretary's crisp voice. "With whom do I have the pleasure of speaking?"

"Molly Bledsoe. Now may I ask with whom *I* have the pleasure of speaking?"

A cheeky old bird, thought Bertie. "My name is Reginald Mundley, Miss Bledsoe. I am an acquaintance of Jordan MacKenzie."

"I'm sorry, Mr. Mundley, but Ms. MacKenzie is out of the office."

So! MacKenzie worked for, or more likely owned, this genealogical-whatever company. Miss Cast-iron Bledsoe had let that one out of the bag more quickly than even Bertie could have hoped. "Yes, of course. Now I remember dear Jordan mentioning a trip to Europe or something of the sort. How is that going, anyway?"

"Well," the secretary told him in a tone that left an icy frost on the receiver. No doubt Bledsoe was one of those watchdog types who considered protecting the boss's privacy her sacred duty. You could put that kind on the rack and not wring a word out of her. "Would you care to leave a message?"

"No, luv. I'll catch her later."

Merrily humming to himself, Bertie rang off and dialed the other number.

"This is Kitty Ridgewood."

For once, Bertie's unshakable aplomb deserted him. *Kitty Ridgewood?* Yes, he had heard correctly. He had just dialed a number that sailed merrily past all the nasty secretaries and brutish bodyguards, over the electronically monitored walls and security systems, around the restraining orders and legal injunctions to connect him directly with the most successful cosmetics huckster in the history of the world.

"Hello? Who is this?" Ridgewood sounded as impatient and shrewish as he had always portrayed her in his stories.

Smiling broadly to himself, Bertie hung up the phone without saying a word.

Chapter Nine

"It's time you told Jordan the whole story, Nick."

Daria leaned back in her seat, propping her feet on the rung of the free café chair. With her dancer's leggings and tights protruding below the hem of her trench coat, she looked more like a slightly Bohemian teenager than the world-class ballerina she was.

"About Radetsky, you mean?" Nick shifted in his chair as if his posture could somehow evade the uncomfortable truth.

Daria's nod was uncompromising. "From what you've told me during the past hour, I don't think you have any choice. If Bertie Waxx really has picked up the scent, then you can be sure he's going to bring out the issue of Radetsky's contested title. Wouldn't you rather have the chance to tell Jordan about Grandmama's mother losing the music box that was her single proof, after Pavel Radetsky's death, that she was his wife? You can be certain Waxx isn't going to waste valuable column space developing fine points." She took a sip of coffee, giving her words a chance to soak in. "Secondly, you really owe it to Jordan to share your suspicions about Radetsky with her."

Nick squirmed an inch or two to the other side of the café chair. "At this point I don't have a shred of proof that

Radetsky is behind this character stalking Jordan, only a hunch."

Daria was undeterred. "Fine. That's as much proof as you had connecting Gudrun Mayes-Cooper with the earlier incidents. As I see it, your suspicion has simply shifted from one distasteful person to another. But let's suppose for a moment that you *are* right about Radetsky. Is it fair to Jordan to say nothing and allow her to deal further with a man who may actually be a threat to her?" She shook her head disapprovingly before going on. "And I think there's another compelling reason for you to talk candidly with Jordan."

Nick looked up from the empty coffee cup he was cradling between his palms. "Yet another?"

"The most important." The wrought-iron chair scraped against the marble floor as Daria leaned across the table. "You care about her, Nick."

Nick opened his mouth and then closed it again before he could parry his sister's argument with a glib remark. Yes, he did care about Jordan, more than he had been willing to admit even to himself. Not that he made a practice of self-deception. The relationship between them had simply evolved so naturally, he was hard-pressed to put his finger on the exact point where "enjoyed" had become "attracted to," where "like" had evolved into... Nick blinked, sobered by the short yet immensely powerful word that had leaped into his mind with startling force.

"You're right, Daria," he said simply. "We're having dinner together tonight, and I'll tell her then."

Daria smiled. His dear sister, bless her, understood him so well he didn't need to go into a lot of soul-searching detail trying to define his feelings for Jordan. And by not forcing him to explain his complicated emotions, she had made it easier for him to accept them himself. Love, after all, might be a devil to understand, but it was nothing to be ashamed of.

THE PRATER WAS A LONELY place at this time of year. The bitter wind blowing off the Danube had cleared the sprawling park of all but the heartiest strollers. Arvidsen liked the emptiness. His profession had given him an appreciation for solitude.

He chose a telephone kiosk not far from the *Riesenrad,* the giant Ferris wheel that towered over the barren landscape like a monstrous juggernaut. His client was expecting him, would be watching the silent telephone, palms clammy with dread. The uncertain voice that answered told Arvidsen that he had been right.

"This is Brenner," Arvidsen replied.

His client was distraught almost to the point of incoherence. Arvidsen listened without comment to the now-familiar injunctions for discretion, caution, secrecy. He let the agitated voice exhaust itself before he spoke. Then he tersely related the details of his latest operation.

"You used a gun?" The voice dropped to an almost inaudible whisper, as if it were sharing an obscenity.

"Does that shock you?" Arvidsen baited his client with a low, sarcastic laugh. He watched the vapor shadow of his breath expand on the kiosk's glass panel.

He could hear his client swallow, dry mouthed and tense. "If you act too rashly, we may never know this woman's secrets. The dead do not speak, Herr Brenner."

Arvidsen recognized the bravado, the flimsy gambit to cover cowardice in the face of violence, and his contempt for his client burgeoned. "Indeed they do not. I am glad you understand the necessity of a gun."

"Herr Brenner, may I remind you that *I* am paying for your services." It was the reprimand of someone accustomed to ordering servants about, and its ridiculous self-importance tried Arvidsen's patience. "I will not have—"

Arvidsen cut the wearisome tirade short. "You hired me to do a job."

That reminder always silenced his client, and today was no exception. It was strange, Arvidsen mused, how quickly one got to know people well under these circumstances. Once they stepped outside their normal boundaries, he was all they had, and they clung to him as much as they hated him.

"Very well. Do what you must do. She must be stopped." His client's voice hardened, dull and heavy as lead. "At all costs."

THE HUSHED CHAMBERS of the state archives seemed incongruously welcoming to Jordan when she returned on Monday to continue her search for Jakov Davidov's immigration records. Something about the endless rows of neat shelves, the carefully labeled files of microfiche, the overweening order maintained with precise numbers and letters reassured her. Such an institution made no allowances for the ambiguities and uncertainty that plagued the world outside. In these halls there was no place for a madman armed with a gun.

Given her frame of mind, she was almost dismayed when Davidov's name appeared on the microfiche viewer, signaling an end to her time in the secure haven of the archives. The breakthrough was a major one, however, for it provided concrete information about Jakov Davidov's fateful odyssey across Europe. According to the police registration records, Davidov had spent scarcely six weeks in Austria before emigrating to the Netherlands on January 9, 1921. At the time he would have been twenty-five years old. The record listed no dependents. His profession was described simply as *Arbeiter,* a worker.

She would make immediate arrangements to visit Amsterdam and try to pick up Davidov's trail in Holland. As she rode the tram back to her hotel that afternoon, Jordan considered the next step of her investigation and the puzzling questions she hoped it would answer. Everything she had learned about Käthe and Jakov Davidov's circumstances flew in the face of the two links Kitty had given her. If Davidov had been a common laborer, how had his child come to possess a fourteen-carat gold necklace and a photograph of an artwork commissioned by the czar? She supposed he could have found those things during their journey from Russia. In turbulent times, a lot of property passed helter-skelter through many hands. Whatever the case, Jordan could only follow Davidov's tracks and see where they might lead.

Nick was excited at the news of her discovery. In fact, he seemed exceptionally animated that evening when he picked her up at the hotel and drove them to an exclusive restaurant on Gersthofstrasse. Or was he nervous? Jordan couldn't decide, but Nick seemed to be making more small talk than usual. Then again, perhaps she was just tired. Scrolling through miles of microfiche for hours on end didn't exactly make her the ideal dinner companion. Before they left the hotel, they had made a pact not to discuss the awful experience they had shared Saturday evening. Nonetheless, the memories preyed on their minds, and Nick's nonstop, upbeat conversation could be an effort to distract them. Whatever the case, Jordan was genuinely happy to see him—and he her, if the tender looks and occasional brush of the hand he gave her were any indication.

"So when do you plan to leave for Amsterdam?" Nick asked when they had finished the excellent meal and were waiting for the dessert menu. His eyes roved the dining room, moving skittishly among the stylish art nouveau furnishings.

"As soon as possible. Probably tomorrow. I'll be sure to keep in touch," Jordan added quickly.

Nick nodded, suddenly looking down at the table. "Of course. Uh, Jordan, there are a few things I'd like to discuss with you before you go to Amsterdam." He idly fingered the engraved silver saltcellar.

"Sure." Jordan waited for him to go on, but the arrival of the waiter, bearing two dessert menus, interrupted their conversation.

Jordan slid her chair back from the table. "If you'll please excuse me, I'm not in the mood for high-level decision making. Just order two of whatever you have, okay? Remember, I like anything that's fattening."

Nick smiled and nodded his agreement as Jordan picked up her handbag and walked across the dining room. The restaurant's powder room was as exquisitely decorated as the rest of the place, replete with mirrors bordered by gold-leaf frames and delicate frosted-glass wall sconces. Even the attendant's chair was upholstered in sumptuous peach-colored velvet.

After applying lipstick, Jordan rummaged through her handbag for the customary tip for the attendant. The woman had wandered off to fetch supplies, but Jordan politely deposited a few coins in the china dish next to her chair. She was zipping her coin purse when her eye fell on a folded paper, not quite concealed by the chair's flounced skirt. The sight of the word *Radetsky* was enough to overcome any inhibitions she had about stealing a look at the attendant's paper.

Giving the door a quick, precautionary glance, Jordan opened the copy of *Aktuell-Edition* on the counter. She had gotten so much practice reading German in the state archives, she had little trouble translating the headline. Lost Treasure, Found Love it proclaimed. And beneath that line, Rival Radetsky Heir Romances Mystery Lady. The crowning insult was the photograph of Nick and her kissing at the Opera Ball, an even more tantalizing shot than the one that had appeared in the British tabloid.

As Jordan's eyes galloped down the page, she could scarcely believe what she was reading. In breathless, superlative-ridden prose, the article described how Nick and Boris Radetsky were embroiled in a feud over the family title. Nick insisted he was Pavel Radetsky's heir. The two men were sworn foes, each determined to possess a vast fortune and centuries-old title. Jordan reread each word carefully, hoping that her command of the language had—for once, happily—failed her. To her dismay, however, she realized that her translation had been letter-perfect. Why, in the many hours Nick and she had spent discussing the music box, had he never even alluded to his relation to the Radetsky family? Her stomach began to churn in earnest.

As if wrestling with Nick's disturbing omission were not enough, the first reference to herself Jordan spotted turned her hands to ice. Once again she was described as a "mysterious beauty." This time, however, the author had gone further, identifying her as a close friend of Kitty Ridgewood. A wave of panic swept over Jordan, and she took immediate steps to bridle it, with mixed success.

This was a European paper, she reminded herself, and a bad one at that. The chances of Kitty Ridgewood ever seeing it were so remote as to be nigh impossible. And even if the ridiculous story made it into the U.S. tabloids, Kitty hadn't struck her as the sort of person who would gobble up papers filled with Elvis sightings and women giving birth to aliens. The arguments Jordan offered herself were logical—and utterly unconvincing.

At the sound of approaching steps, Jordan hastily folded the paper and stuffed it under the prissy little chair just as the attendant pushed through the door. The woman regarded her warily, and when Jordan faced the mirror she could see why. The color had drained from her face, leaving two blotches of blusher glowing garishly on each cheek, and her eyes were wide and staring. She looked sick—exactly the way she felt.

Somehow, Kitty Ridgewood would learn about this story, and she would be enraged at having her name exploded in the yellow press. Kitty would fire her. Nick Rostov had lied about his motives for pursuing the Radetsky music box. He had ingratiated himself with her only as a means of garnering a contested inheritance and vanquishing an old enemy. Worse still was the way he had gone about it. He had manipulated her, convinced her that he was on her side, that he genuinely cared about her, when nothing could be further from the truth.

At this last bitter realization, Jordan's eyes began to sting. Angrily snatching a tissue from her handbag, she dabbed at her smeared mascara. If she was crying, it was only because she was absolutely furious. She swallowed the lump in her throat before turning to the attendant. Depositing a generous tip into the china dish, she told the woman she wasn't feeling well and asked her to fetch her coat from the cloakroom.

While she waited for the attendant to return, Jordan plotted her strategy. For a moment she toyed with the idea of confronting Nick, and almost immediately discarded it. Her repulsion at the lies he was certain to offer in his defense outweighed any satisfaction she would get from putting him on the spot. No, she wanted to get Nick Rostov out of her life as quickly and directly as possible.

She could easily slip out of the restaurant without attracting his attention. Plenty of taxis would be cruising the fashionable area at this hour. Once she was back at the hotel, she would settle her bill, throw her things into her garment bag and head for the train station. There had to be a train going in the direction of Amsterdam sometime that evening, and Jordan planned to be on it.

The attendant helped Jordan into her coat, patting the collar into place in a motherly fashion. As Jordan followed the heavily carpeted corridor to the restaurant foyer, she glimpsed Nick, back turned toward her, watching two dishes of ice cream melt while he awaited her return. *Serves you right, you sneaking, deceitful jerk,* she thought fiercely.

To her consternation, not a single taxi was waiting in the standing zone outside the restaurant. Jordan noticed the doorman loitering near the restaurant door, talking with a man in a green-checked coat. She was about to ask the doorman's assistance when she got a better look at his companion. Although she had caught only the most fleeting glimpse of the bogus waiter who had photographed them at the Opera Ball, the doughy features and slicked-back hair had stuck in her mind. Any lingering uncertainty vanished when Bertie Waxx flashed her a vulgar smile and reached for one of the cameras dangling around his neck.

For a brief, terrifying moment, Jordan questioned her own sanity. This had to be a nightmare, first discovering the awful tabloid story in the powder room and now finding Bertie Waxx lurking outside the restaurant. But she wasn't dreaming. This was inescapable, hell-on-earth reality, and she was going to have to deal with it.

Recklessly dashing from the curb, Jordan hailed a passing cab and hurled herself into the back seat. She was about to give the driver directions when she caught sight of Waxx clambering into a taxi right behind her.

"Where are you going, madam?" the driver asked in the careful English of one accustomed to reassuring tourists.

"Anywhere. I don't care. Just drive," Jordan ordered.

The cab driver looked a little frightened as he studied her in the rearview mirror, but he dutifully pulled away from the curb. When the cab behind them followed suit, Jordan realized she was going to have to be creative if she hoped to elude Bertie Waxx. Sitting on the edge of the seat, she alternately checked the tailing cab's progress and gave her driver orders to turn into various side streets. Once she thought they had lost Waxx's cab when a signal light changed abruptly, but the vehicle zigzagged through traffic and managed to overtake them at the next intersection. Deliverance came at last in the form of a tram that cut off Waxx's view for a precious few seconds, just enough time for Jordan's cabbie to turn into an alley. After they had driven several blocks with no sign of the pursuing taxi, Jordan instructed the cab driver to take her to the Richtsberger Hof.

Inside the hotel, Jordan went directly to the front desk. While the concierge fetched her briefcase from the safe, she settled her bill.

"I hope your stay with us has been a pleasant one," the concierge told her as he handed her the briefcase and a note from her room slot.

"Very pleasant, thank you," Jordan assured him with a grim face that contradicted her assertion.

In the elevator she read the note the concierge had given her. Gudrun Mayes-Cooper was soliciting another meeting. "Tomorrow for tea, perhaps?" the affectedly feminine handwriting asked. When she reached her floor, Jordan crumpled the note in disgust and pitched it into the waste can between the two elevators.

Never one to waste time dallying over practical tasks, Jordan swept through her hotel room, emptying drawers and stuffing clothes into her garment bag. When she pulled the ivory silk evening gown out of the wardrobe her lips began to tremble, but she quickly snuffed such uncalled-for emotions. Unceremoniously wadding the dress into a ball, she crammed it into the bottom of her bag, along with the velvet cape, and jerked the zipper closed. Jordan took only a second to check the empty bathroom cabinet before heading out of the room.

She was juggling the bulging garment bag, trying to punch the elevator button with the corner of her briefcase, when she felt a presence behind her. Before Jordan could turn, however, a muscular arm coiled around her neck, almost wrenching her off her feet.

Jordan tried to scream, but the death grip stanched her cry in her throat. With the insidious power of a boa constrictor, the arm tightened its hold. Jordan's heels dug futilely into the carpeting as the man dragged her toward the stairwell. Her hands flailed at the air, trying to find an ear, a nose, a jaw, anything she could punch, claw or gouge. The pressure against her windpipe was beginning to make her nauseous. *Don't faint. For God's sake, hang on. If you don't, you're dead.*

Jordan's breath was coming in weak gasps, her head swimming dangerously, when the doors of one of the elevators suddenly opened. Stars burst in front of her eyes as the autodrive of a camera buzzed, firing a series of blinding strobes. For one infinitely precious nanosecond, her assailant's grasp slackened, but it was enough time for Jordan to pull free. She heaved her briefcase over her head, smashing its hard edge into his face. Just then the other elevator opened its doors. Jordan shoved her luggage into the car and lunged after it.

She was sagging against the wall of the car, trying to catch her breath, when a hand suddenly thrust between the closing doors. Jordan hoisted the briefcase and began to hammer the intruding fingers. The sounds of what could only be curses in an unfamiliar language competed with the relentless whir of a camera's autodriven shutter. Tears of frustration were streaming down Jordan's face when the battered hand abruptly withdrew from between the doors. Just before the doors sealed, she heard a Cockney-accented voice yelp, "Don't hurt me!"

Jordan was still coughing, clasping her bruised throat, when the car jarred to a halt in the lobby. She staggered to the front desk, dragging her garment bag behind her, and motioned to the startled-looking desk clerk.

"You need to call the police. A man just tried to strangle me on the fourth floor. I think he may have attacked another guest, as well."

The clerk's eyes widened in full-blown alarm as he reached for the phone. He gestured frantically for his colleague to see to Jordan, but she brushed him away. She stopped short when she spotted Nick Rostov charging through the front doors.

"Where the devil have you been, Jordan? When you didn't return to the table, I was worried out of my mind." Nick frowned, regarding her anxiously. "My God, your neck is bruised! What's happened to you?"

"You can save your pious concern, Count Wanna-Be Radetsky." Jordan fixed him with a cold stare.

"What are you talking about?" Nick demanded, but the color had drained from his face, signaling her accusation had made a direct hit.

Jordan gave him a derisive snort, shaking her head in contempt. "I don't believe this. You just can't let go of the act, can you?" She attempted to stalk past him, but he moved to block her path. "Out of my way, Nick."

"Not until we've talked this through," he insisted. His attempt to detain her was abruptly short-circuited, however, by the arrival of a half-dozen uniformed police officers. The policemen stormed through the hotel doors, giving Jordan the chance she needed to push past Nick and make her escape to the street.

Feeling as if he had taken a wrong turn somewhere and ended up in a madhouse, Nick watched the policemen fan out across the lobby. With the clerk shouting excitedly after them, the squad quickly took control of the elevators, stairs and doors, effectively shutting off all exits. Nick found himself herded to one side of the lobby, along with several other stunned bystanders. Damn Jordan! If she hadn't managed to bolt through the door, she would have been penned up here with him, and he would have had a chance to sort through the misunderstanding. *Count Wanna-Be Radetsky.* The pejorative rang in his head, taunting him with its harsh accusation. In the hour since she had laughingly asked him to order dessert for her, Jordan had learned something about his complicated heritage that had made her look at him as if he had crawled out of a sewer.

While two of the police officers made the rounds, questioning the people assembled in the lobby, Nick speculated about how Jordan could have heard of his connection with Radetsky. A likely conjecture sprang to mind when he saw Bertie Waxx, glassy eyed and rumpled, stagger out of one of the elevators.

"Fortunately, the bloke's hand was hurt rather badly," Nick overheard Waxx tell the policeman escorting him. "I managed to keep my wits about me and retreat into the lift before he could pry the doors apart. I am disturbed that this fiend is still at large," Waxx concluded reproachfully, straightening his wrinkled green-checked coat.

After offering Waxx the stock assurance that he had provided information vital to apprehending the criminal, the policeman seemed relieved to abandon the ruffled-looking tabloid reporter. For his part, Nick was only too glad to have his turn with Waxx.

"You slimy little miscreant, what did you tell Jordan MacKenzie?" Nick loomed over Waxx, flexing his hands to still their urge to wring the scrawny neck.

"I don't know what you're talking about, Rostov," Bertie told him smugly.

Nick's eyes traveled to the two cameras still slung around Waxx's neck. "Up to your old tricks, aren't you, Bertie?"

When Nick reached for one of the cameras, Waxx wagged his finger. "Now, now, Nicky. Let's not do anything the coppers wouldn't approve of. They frown on camera bashing, you know. And just look how *many* are in this hotel!"

Nick deftly lifted first one, then the other Nikon from Bertie's neck. While Waxx looked on in helpless horror, he removed the film from each camera before returning it to its owner. After pocketing the film, Nick pretended to adjust the camera straps around Waxx's neck. "There. Good as new." Then his face darkened. "I don't know what you've been up to with Jordan, Waxx, but I'm warning you. The next time we meet, you'd better make sure the police are around to protect you."

Chapter Ten

A drizzling rain darkened the narrow streets and canals of Amsterdam, blurring the lines between sky and earth and water to a vaporous, dull gray. Riding the tram through the center of town, Jordan promised herself that if the oppressive weather ever lifted, her spirits would improve, as well. As it was, she felt as cheerless as the bleak clouds that had hovered over the city since her arrival two days earlier.

Turning away from the droplet-spattered window, Jordan tried to concentrate on the recent positive developments in her investigation. The Dutch Bureau of Statistics was a modern wonder, its staff uniformly efficient and helpful. Assuming Jakov Davidov had not unexpectedly veered in another direction in transit from Vienna, she should be able to pinpoint his arrival in the country through well-cataloged immigration records—if not here, then in Rotterdam or The Hague. Then other bureaucratic fingerprints—identification papers, marriage licenses, tax receipts, property titles, a death certificate—would accumulate to complete the picture. With a little luck, she might even be able to phone Kitty Ridgewood with definitive information about her father before the next week was out.

One person she would not be phoning was Nick Rostov. The thought blundered into her consciousness before she could censor it, lingering long enough to stoke the flames of bitterness back to life. Despite her best efforts, Jordan had not yet been able to put her anger to rest. During the long train ride to Amsterdam, she had spent the night huddled in a compartment by herself, alone with her unhappy thoughts. At first she had attempted to convince herself that she was so furious with Nick because she had not actually confronted him with the facts, vented her emotions and gotten the festering resentment out of her system. Jordan was too honest, however, to ignore the real source of her miserable feelings: she was angry at herself for being duped.

Had she not listened so willingly to Nick's pat explanations, responded so eagerly to his phony charm, wanted so badly to believe that their purposes coincided on any number of levels, he would never have been able to deceive her so successfully. It was this participation in her own deception that rankled most deeply with Jordan. Not only had she been fooled, but she had aided the process every step of way—just as she had with Christopher.

That dismal reminder weighed on her as she climbed off the tram and dashed through the pelting rain to the office building where she planned to spend the day. Inside the lobby, Jordan folded her wet umbrella into its case and took a deep breath. Unlike the damp, decaying world outside, the place smelled like a library—clean, dry and permanently preserved against temporal ravages.

Seated in the little carrel she had reserved for the duration of her research, Jordan tried to block out everything but the leather-bound volumes, the spools of microfilm, the muted sounds of pages turning and an occasional throat being cleared. To her great annoyance, however, her mind kept wandering, so much so that she let the name "Davidov" roll past on the microfilm and had to scroll back to it.

Jakov made it to Holland, to Amsterdam, no less! The moment she brought the fine-printed name into focus, excitement eclipsed her gloom. Only five days after leaving Vienna, Jakov Davidov's entry into Holland had been duly recorded, complete with a local address. Best of all, the file listed the name of his employer, Th. Stern and Sons. Jordan regarded this added fillip of information in puzzlement. To have been so down on his luck in Vienna, Kitty's father had certainly found work quickly in Amsterdam. What sort of job had he performed for the Dutch company? If the firm was still in business, perhaps she could find out.

Jordan knew it was a long shot, but she asked the archivist if she could see the telephone directory. There were numerous listings for Sterns, so many that Jordan was beginning to think she was pressing her luck too far when her finger glided over an entry for Th. Stern and Sons Diamond Exchange. By an enormous stroke of good fortune for his survivors, Jakov Davidov had landed employment with a family business that was still operating under the same name. Jordan quickly noted the address and phone number of the company before returning the directory to the central desk.

On her way to the stairs Jordan first checked her watch and then her tourist's pocket map of Amsterdam. She wasn't that far from what the map described as the diamond district. If she hurried she could probably reach the Sterns' place of business before the midday lunch break and at least make an appointment to talk with the right people. Jordan was hurrying around the second-floor landing when she spotted a curly dark head over the side of the rail.

When Nick reached the landing he paused, keeping a respectful frontier between them. *Dueling distance,* Jordan thought, fixing him with an ice-cold glare.

"What do you think you're doing here?" she demanded under her breath.

"Excuse me, but I was under the impression this building was open to the public," Nick shot back in a less-subdued tone. He caught himself and lowered his voice. "This seemed a likely place to look for you. I want to talk with you, Jordan, and see if we can't iron things out."

"There's nothing to discuss, Nick. If you want to challenge Boris Radetsky over his stupid music box, you're going to have to do it on your own," Jordan informed him.

"Damn it, Jordan! Will you listen?" Nick snapped.

To Jordan's delight, a middle-aged man appeared in the doorway of the adjacent hall to frown reproachfully at Nick. "Sir, please! People are working," he lectured in clipped English.

Nick glanced irritably from the man to Jordan, as if he were uncertain which nemesis to take on first. "Jordan, I'm asking you one more time to sit down with me and discuss this misunderstanding like two adults."

"And I'm telling you one *last* time, that I'm not going to let you lie to me anymore."

"I've never lied to you," Nick insisted, his voice rising along with his vexation.

"Not telling the truth is the same thing as lying in my book," Jordan shot back. "You were perfectly happy to let me go on believing that your interest in the Radetsky music box was purely professional, that your name cropped up in the tabloids only because of Inge. You never once mentioned that you and Radetsky were battling it out for an inheritance." With every degree her anger rose, Jordan came closer to sputtering, and she abruptly broke off.

"We're not battling it out!"

"Oh, no? Then why wouldn't you come with me to meet Boris Radetsky at his chalet in Immel?" Jordan countered.

"I told you he and I didn't get along. I mean, it isn't just Boris and I, it's the whole family and... Oh, it's all so complicated! I can't simply explain it to you standing here in the middle of a stairwell." He threw up his hands in exasperation.

"Don't even try, then. You used me, Nick, because you thought I was a means of getting at Radetsky. Oh, God, when I think of how you manipulated me into pulling that idiotic caper with him at the Opera Ball, as if I were some... some..." Eyes still blazing, Jordan turned as the gray-haired guardian of silence once more appeared in the doorway.

"Sir! Madam! May I remind you?"

"I'm very sorry," Jordan apologized to the man.

Thrusting her briefcase to one side like a fender, she plowed past Nick and down the stairs. She took the steep steps as fast as her pumps would permit, expecting him to follow her. When she reached the ground floor, however, Nick was nowhere in sight.

Perhaps he had recognized a lost cause and reconciled himself to pursuing the Radetsky music box, the Radetsky title, the Radetsky fortune and the Radetsky whatever else on his own. She had not been unreasonable, she assured herself as she slid open the umbrella and headed along the canal. Once she had determined Christopher's true marital status, she had broken that relationship off for good. In fact, she had seen him only once after confirming the damning truth, and then just long enough to sever ties. Watching the fat drops of rain dribble off the edge of the umbrella, Jordan wondered if that unpleasant encounter on the landing would be the last time she ever saw Nick Rostov.

Several of the shops facing the canal had already locked their doors for the midday break, prompting Jordan to consult her watch. Her annoyance flared anew when she realized how much time she had squandered sparring with Nick on the landing. Even if she took the tram, the diamond exchange would be closed by the time she reached it. Although she had no appetite, Jordan decided the most practical course of action was to emulate the locals and have lunch. She selected a small café and ordered a *brodje* and a bottle of mineral water. As she picked at the delicious sandwich, she watched the pattering rain gather momentum outside the café window. By the time she ventured into the street again, the shower had metamorphosed into a full-scale downpour.

When Jordan at last spotted the large black-and-white letters identifying Th. Stern and Sons, she had cursed both the pocket map for its grossly misleading scale that had deceived her into walking across half the city and herself for wearing thin leather pumps in such nasty weather. She took a few minutes inside the entrance to the diamond dealer's showroom to sponge her coat and shoes with a crumpled tissue before ringing the buzzer for service.

A young woman with fashionably short black hair soon appeared behind the glass window and said something in Dutch. Before Jordan could ask if she spoke English, the woman read the visitor's puzzled expression and quickly shifted into her second language. "May I help you, madam?"

"I hope so." Jordan produced one of her business cards and slid it through the narrow opening under the glass window. "I'm researching the family tree of an American client, and I believe a relative of my client was once employed here. Would someone be able to give me information about a man who worked for this company in the 1920s?"

The young woman seemed surprised by the unusual request, but she offered to consult the person who currently handled the company's bookkeeping and records. She disappeared into a back room, out of sight of the glass window. When she returned, an attractive woman with a silvery pageboy accompanied her. The steel-reinforced door separating the company's inner sanctum from the entrance area beeped momentarily as the woman joined Jordan in the foyer.

"I am Esther Rabin, Miss MacKenzie." The woman offered her hand, along with a warm smile. "Anna tells me you are looking for a gentleman who worked here many years ago?"

Jordan nodded and repeated her explanation. "The man's name was Jakov Davidov," she concluded. "Do you think you might be able to locate his personnel records?" Her face fell when Esther chuckled and shook her head.

"Nineteen twenty-one was a very long time ago, when I was just a baby. To be honest with you, I do not even know if we kept such records in those days. Our business was very small then, and things did not have to be written down just so. But," Esther Rabin added, "I will never forget Jakov."

"You knew him?" Jordan gasped, not believing her good fortune.

"Oh, yes." The pleasant-faced woman smiled. "You see, my name was Stern before I married. This was my father's company. He was from Russia and had been poor early in his life. Jakov was from Russia and was very poor. So Papa wanted to help him. He taught Jakov to cut diamonds although he was much older than any of the other apprentices, and he gave him a place to live—" Esther pointed to the ceiling "—with us in our apartment over the workshop." She shook her head wistfully. "Poor man! He died very young, I think, of tuberculosis. Of course, then he seemed old to us children, but he could not have been even thirty-five." Esther fell silent, a sad expression smoothing the laugh lines feathering the corners of her mouth and eyes.

"That's a shame," Jordan concurred. "Do you remember his ever talking about his daughter?"

Esther looked puzzled. "Jakov Davidov was very fond of children, but he did not have any of his own, Miss Mac-Kenzie. And he never married."

"Not here, but perhaps in Russia?"

Esther shook her head emphatically. "No, I am certain he would have said something about such an important thing. He talked a great deal about his life in Russia."

"He never mentioned a girl named Käthe?" Jordan persisted.

Esther frowned for a moment. Then her deep-set hazel eyes widened. "That would be little Katya, of course!" she exclaimed, pressing her hand to her cheek. "She was the sorrow of the poor man's life, Miss MacKenzie, little Katya was."

"Why?" Jordan pressed eagerly.

"Such a terrible thing! He had to leave her behind in a hospital in Vienna. I believe the child had contracted typhus or some other dreadful disease, and the authorities refused to let her cross the border. Jakov had no money, and he could not find work in Vienna. It was after the war, you know, and many people were without work. He believed life would be better in Amsterdam, and he was right. But he could not bring little Katya with him." Esther's hands rose and fell in a gesture of despair. "A very sad story."

Jordan nodded her agreement. "What a cruel twist of fate, to be forced to abandon your own child through no fault of your own."

"But Katya was not his child, Miss MacKenzie," Esther corrected.

"She wasn't?" Jordan asked in surprise.

"No, no! Jakov found her during his journey from Russia. A little lost babe," Esther added poignantly.

"Did he ever tell you about how he found Katya or where?"

"Perhaps he may have said something, but I don't recall. I was small myself, and as you can guess, that was many years ago. The memories fade with time." She gave a throaty laugh. "I will tell you something, Miss MacKenzie. If you would like, you are welcome to look at what Jakov left behind. Since he had no family, after he was gone my mother placed his things in a trunk. It seemed so heartless, I suppose, simply to toss them away."

"You have the trunk here?"

"No, it is stored at our home. Do you know Heerwijl?" When Jordan shook her head, Esther shrugged lightly. "It is just on the outskirts of the city, very easy to find. I will be leaving work tomorrow at midday. That is my children's way of making me retire, to send me home early." She laughed. "Is it possible for you to meet me at three o'clock?"

"At your convenience, Mrs. Rabin," Jordan replied gratefully.

"Let us say three o'clock, then."

Esther took one of the company's brochures from the stack next to the reception window. On the back of the pamphlet she jotted her home address and directions for reaching it by bus as well as on the highway. She looked pleased to be of help when she handed it to Jordan. She held the door open, giving Jordan a chance to open her umbrella.

"Thank you so much, Mrs. Rabin! I'll look forward to seeing you again tomorrow afternoon."

The woman smiled and nodded before ducking back into the building, pulling the door securely shut behind her. After the pleasant and fruitful meeting with Esther Rabin, the rain-drenched streets seemed even less hospitable. The approaching dusk had darkened the sky to an oppressive slate color. Dense fog shrouded the canal, giving the passing barges the appearance of eerie ghost ships. Jordan quickened her pace as she crossed a narrow bridge spanning the canal.

She had walked several blocks before she realized she must have taken a wrong turn in the unfamiliar area. Huddled beneath her umbrella, Jordan consulted the pocket map and discovered that she had mistakenly wandered into the map's C-5 sector, almost a whole quadrant removed from the tramline running to her hotel. Repocketing the now-soggy map, Jordan began to retrace her steps.

Getting lost in a strange city was a trying experience at best, but choosing this sort of neighborhood in which to do it bordered on the foolhardy. At some point the staid warehouselike fronts of the diamond trading establishments had given way to abandoned buildings, seedy bars and grimy picture windows with lingerie-clad women lounging in them. Jordan hunched down inside her coat and ignored the two men dressed in nail-studded black leather who called to her from a doorway.

The streetlights had begun to flicker on. Far from brightening the landscape, however, they lent a sinister gothic atmosphere to the narrow streets. Jordan nervously glanced over her shoulder and tried not to think about old Jack the Ripper movies while she thumbed through the map's moist, flabby pages. To her dismay she realized that she should have crossed the canal two blocks sooner, a maneuver that would require her to backtrack past the two skinheads loitering in the doorway.

Biting her lip in irritation, Jordan surveyed the darkening street and decided to keep walking until she reached the next bridge. The last thing she needed in this deserted place was to attract two hooligans' attention. Not bothering to refold the map, Jordan shoved it into her pocket and set off at a fast clip. Her heels beat an urgent rhythm against the wet cobblestones, one that grew more clipped at the sound of other, heavier steps behind her. Not daring to look behind her, Jordan hoisted the briefcase under her arm and lengthened her strides. The punks following her probably constituted no threat, just a nuisance. They would grow bored with plodding through the rain and turn to an easier target to harass.

Despite these self-assurances, Jordan began to look for a bar or a café, any public place where she could get off the street for a few minutes and discourage the rowdies. When none appeared, she took the next-best option. Quickly glancing over her shoulder, Jordan turned into an alley. She ran an obstacle course between overflowing garbage cans and malodorous piles of trash to dash into the next street. Flattening herself against the side of the building, Jordan peeked down the alley and was relieved to see the two leatherboys saunter past.

Her relief at outwitting the hooligans was short-lived, however. This was no place for anyone to enjoy a leisurely evening stroll. The sooner she got to the tramline, the better. Jordan was about to retrace her steps when she noticed a shadow falling across the far end of the alley. Had she actually seen someone dressed in black or was her imagination playing unkind tricks on her? Whatever the case, prudence demanded that she give her perceptions the benefit of the doubt. This street appeared to run parallel to the one connected to it by the alley. If she followed it, she would reach her destination—she hoped.

The even fall of footsteps behind her flooded her system with adrenaline. Jordan tried to reason with herself and quell the panic threatening to seize her. Simply because someone was walking behind her didn't necessarily mean she was being followed. But it could. This last thought spurred her to abandon any pretext of normalcy, throw down the umbrella and break into a full run. When the footsteps followed suit, Jordan's worst fears were realized.

Her pursuer was gaining on her. The realization taunted her straining leg muscles and lungs. She kept her eyes focused on the lights of a barge approaching on the canal. If she could only keep up her pace, maybe she could reach the barge and signal for help before... Her mind refused to consider the chilling alternative.

Jordan slipped on the wet cobblestones as she turned onto a bridge.

"Ho! Help me!" she cried, jumping up and down and waving to the barge. "Help me!" She choked on the words as the barge glided beneath the bridge, impervious to her pleas.

She could see the person following her. He was taking his time now, hugging the row of buildings, a dark silhouette in the streetlights' anemic glow. His companion must have lost interest, Jordan thought and then froze. *This wasn't one of the punks.*

For a moment the horrific realization paralyzed her limbs, anchored her to the spot like a prehistoric creature petrified in time.

"Hey!" A shout that carried across the water jolted her into action.

Jordan pivoted, but just as she started to sprint across the bridge she heard a sickening sound, a dull, muffled thump like a dart embedding itself in a bale of straw. Acting on instinct, Jordan sprawled on the bridge as another bullet whined just inches from her, ricocheting off the bridge rail. Daring only to move her eyes, she scanned the shadowy row of buildings. She couldn't see him, which meant he probably couldn't see her. Maybe he thought his first shot had hit her. In that case, he would want to make sure.

Pressing herself against the slimy-wet cobbles, Jordan listened to the measured steps approaching along the canal. He was going to find her soon. Standing and running was out of the question. Even if she lay stock-still, he would probably want to put another bullet into her for good measure. With the silencer he had no reason to economize. Jordan's eyes darted to the narrow gap beneath the bridge railing. The space was so tight it would be difficult to squeeze through, but it was her only escape route.

One. Two. Jordan mentally counted. *Three!* With a sudden burst of energy she scooted beneath the rail and into the murky water. For a second a blind panic gripped her as the icy, oily water engulfed her. She fought to hang on to her wits, to be calm, to keep thinking. The briefcase acted as a float, pulling her to the surface. In desperation, Jordan let it go. The gunman would be stalking the bridge now, waiting for her to break the water's surface. Although her lungs were threatening to burst, she needed to stay submerged, out of sight.

She could hear churning now in the water, and the sound raised a new fear, that of being swept beneath a passing barge. Relying on her distorted hearing, Jordan pulled in the direction of what she believed to be the shore. The water frothed around her as the craft plowed past. Her head was beginning to feel like a helium balloon. Her lungs cried for air. On the verge of passing out, Jordan risked breaching the surface. Gasping for breath and shaking uncontrollably from the frigid water, she realized that she had surfaced almost directly beneath the bridge. She clung to the pilings, filling her aching lungs as she listened for signs of movement above her.

She could see her briefcase, floating in a pool of light. She was sure he had spotted it, too. Jordan could hear him pacing along the rail overhead, trying to figure out how to retrieve it, no doubt. Her heart sank when the lapping water carried the briefcase a few feet closer to her hiding place. It was close to the embankment now. All he had to do was shinny down to the water's edge and reach for it. And when he did, he would see her.

Her overtaxed lungs rebelled as she sucked in a deep breath and prepared to submerge. His feet were scuffling against the slick stones, grappling for footing on the embankment. Jordan forced herself to wait, trying to control her shaking and conserve her precious breath until the last moment. A bulky shadow loomed on the shore. She watched the shadow waver, regain its balance and then crouch.

"Stop!"

The damp air amplified the shout. Jordan saw the shadow leap to its feet, fire two quick shots at an unseen target and then scramble up the embankment. Other voices on the shore and the sound of running feet now mingled with the chug of an approaching barge. Yet another shot sounded from directly above her, signaling that the gunman was now on the bridge. A wave of panic washed over Jordan as she turned and saw the barge enter under the bridge from the other side and bear down on her. She suddenly realized she had lost almost all feeling in her arms and legs in the icy water and could hardly hold on to the piling.

As the huge black silhouette of the barge glided by her almost close enough to touch, the gunman sprang over the side of the bridge, falling into a crouch on top of the barge cabin. As the barge continued moving slowly away from the bridge, the man in the black leather coat turned on his knees. Jordan saw his hand rise, level at her, take aim just before she plunged below the water.

She felt the barge's wake dragging her into the canal and her numb fingers grappled clumsily for a hold on the pilings' slime-covered stones. She could hear another boat, this one motorized, cutting through the water. If she drifted away from the shore, she would be hit. If she surfaced, he would kill her. Fear battered Jordan's mind while her lungs battled to conserve their dwindling oxygen supply.

When she felt a pair of arms close around her, she was too exhausted to struggle. She was going to drown, anyway. What difference did it make that he had her now? Her hands flailed helplessly without coordination, slapping at the empty air.

"Jordan! Jordan!" The voice was as insistent as the tight grasp encircling her chest. "It's all right, darling. He's gone. You're safe."

"Nick?" Jordan choked out his name. When they reached the embankment she collapsed onto the wet stones, still heaving for breath.

Nick smoothed her hair back from her face. "I'm here. It's okay."

"How..." Jordan gagged on the foul water and then recovered herself. "How did you know I was here?" With what seemed to require enormous exertion, she turned to face him.

The hazy streetlight illuminated his smile. "The way I always do. I followed you."

Before he could go on, a uniformed man edged down the embankment and helped them both onto the shore. Shivering, Jordan gratefully accepted the blanket the policeman offered her and followed him to a waiting police car. Her teeth were chattering so furiously she had trouble recounting the gunman's pursuit, but she managed to give a detailed description of the attack, during the drive to the hospital.

At the infirmary, Jordan was immediately treated for hypothermia. After submitting to a routine examination and a cautionary antibiotic injection, she insisted on being released the moment her dried clothes were returned to her. She was so exhausted she only wanted to get away from bright lights and people in uniforms and have some time to herself. She found Nick waiting for her in the hospital lobby.

"I've got something for you." His smile was uncharacteristically shy as he held out her briefcase.

Jordan regarded the water-soaked brown leather case. "Well, at least it matches the rest of my outfit." Her hand swept the front of her ruined suit. She took the briefcase, giving him an awkward smile of her own. "Thanks."

Nick stuffed his hands into his coat pockets and surveyed the lobby. "I'm holding a cab outside." He removed one hand from its hiding place to gesture self-consciously. "I thought I could drop you off at your hotel, if that's all right."

Jordan looked down at the coat folded over her arm. "Fine. I'm staying at the Imperial." She waited until they were inside the dark cab to voice what was really on her mind. "I'm sorry. For the way I acted today. And last Monday."

Nick shook his head. "I'm the one who should be apologizing. I should have told you about my connection with the Radetsky clan long ago, but I was afraid you would run scared if you sensed a potential bombshell that might affect your client."

Jordan chuckled, the first time in what seemed decades. "So you let me read about it in a tabloid instead."

Nick turned to look her in the face. "So that's how you found out about my family's contention with Radetsky!"

"Courtesy of our own Bertie Waxx. I guess I overreacted, but I'd sensed earlier that you were holding something back. You'd avoided telling me that you and Radetsky didn't get along, and when you did you were very hesitant to explain why. I wanted to believe you hadn't tried to deceive me, but I wasn't getting much support from the evidence. If I may ask, how did this rift with the Radetskys start in the first place?"

Nick drew a long breath. "I suppose with the music box. You see, Jordan, Count Pavel Radetsky was my grandmother's father. Her mother was a famous ballerina, Olga Gallinin, who had met Radetsky shortly after joining the Kuzov dance troupe in Kiev. He was dashing, worldly and handsome. She was young, beautiful and very vulnerable."

Nick smiled, a little sadly. "It is really no surprise that they became lovers. Then came the revolution. Pavel was killed defending the czar, no one knows exactly where, leaving Olga to fend for herself and their two children. My grandmother has always insisted that Pavel married Olga before his death, in a private ceremony. Unfortunately, the revolution swallowed up any witnesses to that event. According to my grandmother, her mother still had one vestige of proof, however, in the music box which Pavel had had engraved to her as his 'beloved wife.'"

"And when the music box disappeared, so did the proof," Jordan provided.

"Exactly. Once they reached the West, where they had already built up substantial investments, the Radetskys naturally insisted that Pavel and Olga were never legally married. My grandmother had no means of countering their assertions."

"So you believe the Radetsky clan secretly has possession of the music box?" Jordan guessed.

To her surprise, Nick shook his head. "No, although I'm convinced they would love to know who does. As far as the fate of the Radetsky music box is concerned—" his shoulders rose in a despairing shrug "—it's anyone's guess what became of it. Grandmama claims her mother used the valuable item to bargain their safe passage out of Russia. Something went terribly wrong, however, although Grandmama was too young to know exactly what. Of her family, she was the only one to reach the West safely, thanks to the dancemaster Kuzov. Her mother and sister were discovered by soldiers and killed. And the Radetsky music box vanished."

"What a tragic story! It's hard to believe one family could suffer so many reversals of fortune."

Nick sighed, averting his gaze out the window. "You're probably going to find *this* incredible, too, but I had resolved to tell you the whole story that night at dinner. Unfortunately, you disappeared before I had the chance. Then when I finally caught up with you in the hotel, I could tell something awful had happened."

"That dreadful man slipped up behind me and grabbed me while I was waiting for the elevator on my floor. I got away from him, but he managed to trail me here. I'm certain he was the person who shot at me by the canal tonight."

"So am I. I guess we should be glad we didn't settle our misunderstanding earlier this morning, or I might not have been on hand when you needed help tonight."

Jordan regarded him with sheepish amazement. "You'd been following me since I left the bureau?"

"More or less. At first I was so angry—mostly with myself—that I didn't know what to do. But then I realized I couldn't simply leave things the way they were. I had no idea where you were staying, but luckily I spotted you coming out of the café. I figured you would be even less willing to talk standing out in the pouring rain, so I had no choice but to follow you. Then you disappeared into that diamond dealership for a long time."

"That was a very worthwhile lead, by the way," Jordan put in, lapsing into their old, comfortable way of talking.

Nick nodded approvingly before he went on. "When you finally reappeared, I thought you would return to your hotel, but instead you headed for that hellhole red-light district."

"I *thought* I was going to my hotel," Jordan was embarrassed to inform him.

"I was trying to overtake you when I spotted the guy in the black leather coat. I was in quite a quandary. I wanted to warn you, but I was afraid to attract any attention for fear he'd shoot us both. You gave me a real scare when you ducked into that alley. I couldn't find you for a moment, and I almost assumed the worst. That's when I headed for a kiosk and called the police. By then, that thug had gotten way ahead of me, and when I finally caught up with him he'd already drawn his gun. I yelled, right before you fell. At that point I didn't know if you'd been hit."

"I was playing possum."

"Yeah, but you certainly had me scared. When the gunman realized there were two of us, I think he panicked a little bit, too. Still, two unarmed people don't even the odds against one man with a gun, and I don't know what would have happened if the police hadn't arrived when they did."

Jordan shivered involuntarily. "At least we didn't find out." She adjusted her shoulders beneath Nick's arm as it slid around them. "How does he keep tracking me down, Nick? It's as if he knows my exact itinerary."

A frown deepened the shadows on Nick's handsome face. "How many people did you tell that you were going to Amsterdam?"

"None. That's just it. I haven't even phoned my secretary at home, and yet this horrible man seems always to know my plans."

"Some people are extraordinarily skilled in surveillance," Nick suggested, but he sounded less than satisfied with the explanation.

"I wonder if he knows where I am now?" Jordan mused gloomily.

Nick abruptly loosened his hold on her shoulders to lean forward. "I don't know, but we're not going to take any chances. I want you to stay the night in my hotel, just to be on the safe side, okay?" When Jordan nodded, Nick instructed the cabbie to alter his route.

Reliving the evening's troubling incidents, even with Nick, had been a strain for Jordan. She was happy to close her eyes, rest her head securely against his shoulder and share the remainder of the drive in silence. When they reached the hotel, Nick whisked her out of the cab and through the lobby with a minimum of fuss. In the room he summarily relieved her of her briefcase and coat and ordered her into the bath.

"Fill the tub with hot water and soak until you feel warm and relaxed."

Jordan did as she was told. Although she usually selected stodgy, tourist-class lodgings in convenient locations, she was glad that Nick had checked into a luxury hotel. After taking a dip in the canal, she appreciated the ample selection of shampoo, bath salts and quality soap provided in the bath. She was wrapped in a thick Turkish towel, combing out her hair, when Nick tapped at the door.

"See if you can wear this."

He reached through the discreetly cracked door to offer a large white sweatshirt.

"Just my size," Jordan teased.

She slipped the fleecy shirt over her head and shook out her hair before joining Nick in the room.

He looked up from a well-stocked silver tray resting on the dresser. "I ordered a little something to eat. If you're in Amsterdam, you ought to take advantage of the chocolate."

Pulling up a chair, Nick beckoned Jordan to sit before handing her a cup of steaming cocoa and a plate of small sandwiches.

As she munched the delicious snack, Jordan reflected on the ricochet pattern that had characterized their relationship. She supposed the dramatic events they had shared had something to do with the matter. After all, she had lived thirty-two years without ever having to call the police. Yet in the short time since she had met Nick Rostov, she had tussled with a prowler on a train, been cornered in a dark basement, had a near-disastrous chase on an icy mountain road and survived two shootings. Even an activity as ordinary as enjoying a late-night snack together now seemed an extraordinary and rare luxury. Jordan wondered wistfully if they would ever have the chance to get to know each other simply as two normal people.

"You were hungry," Nick commented, helping himself to another sandwich.

Jordan nodded eagerly. "You know me. I eat—"

"When you're frustrated. You told me that in Milan, the first time we had coffee." Nick chuckled as if he were especially fond of the memory.

"Did I? Well, it's true. Nothing's changed." She caught herself, brought up short by the clear realization that one very important aspect of her life had changed drastically. "I guess a few things have changed," she amended, dropping her voice.

"For me, too." The plate clinked lightly against the silver chocolate service as Nick replaced it on the tray.

Jordan suddenly felt very awkward. Here she was in a strange hotel room, dressed in a baggy sweatshirt, both hands occupied with cup and plate. When Nick walked toward her, she balanced the cup on the plate and moved to stand. She sank back into the chair as he took the dinnerware and carelessly shoved it onto the tray. Despite her fatigue, Jordan's pulse accelerated when he took her hand.

"I followed you to Amsterdam because I thought I wanted to set the record straight about my relationship with Radetsky." Jordan thought she detected a tremor pass through the hand closed around hers. "After I saw you fall on that bridge tonight, when I thought you might have been shot, I realized something infinitely more important was at stake." Nick swallowed hard. "I had to face a possibility that I had been too cowardly to consider—how I would feel if I had to give you up. It was almost unbearable," he confessed in a voice choked with emotion.

Jordan lifted her free hand to touch his face lightly. "I know what you're feeling. You don't have to explain."

Nick apparently took her at her word, for he said nothing else. He only leaned forward to cup her chin in his hand, lifting her mouth to meet his lips. The kisses they had shared at the Opera Ball had been electric, exciting, charged with newly fired passion. Tonight, however, their joined lips spoke a deeper language, one formed by a personal vocabulary of shared thoughts and experiences, inflected by a newfound trust.

Jordan closed her eyes, freeing her other senses to respond to the pressure of Nick's mouth. She murmured softly as his lips ventured to her cheek, then to her temple, exploring the sensitive skin of her earlobe. When his mouth drifted back to hers, she parted her lips. Jordan nibbled first his lip and then his tongue, subtly varying the pressure and tenor of her responses to harmonize with his.

When his hand covered her cheek, she shifted her mouth to nuzzle his palm lightly. Then her own hands began to skim the curving outline of his shoulders, her fingers tracing the striations of well-defined muscle beneath his shirt. Her hands' progress was arrested when Nick clasped them, pulling them together in front of her. Holding them cradled like a precious bouquet in his hands, Nick looked down into her eyes. For a moment he held her in his gaze, a tiny reflection in a shimmering dark sea. For a moment her whole being was captured in the depths of his eyes, becoming a part of him as he was of her.

"I want you, Jordan, more than I've ever wanted anything, more than I ever thought possible."

"And I want you, Nick." Jordan heard her own soft voice, was surprised by its sureness.

Still holding her hands, Nick pulled her to her feet, guiding her toward him. Then he freed her hands, allowing them to follow their impulses. Her fingers slid first to his shoulders and then down his chest, releasing the trail of buttons in their path. As she cushioned her face against the soft mat of hair covering his chest, Nick abandoned his remaining clothing, guiding her hands to aid in the task. Then his hands began a delightful exploration of their own, dipping into the heated recesses of the sweatshirt. When his fingertips skirted the tops of her breasts, a delicious sensation coursed through her.

Like a cool plunge, the air fanned her flushed skin as he lifted the sweatshirt over her head. Jordan felt his hands travel down her body as he sank to his knees. Her head fell back, her whole body surrendering to the exquisite magic his lips worked on her breasts. As his mouth began its slow, achingly sensuous journey down her middle, Jordan moaned instinctively, rising to his touch. Tingling waves broke over, inundating her with an ecstatic pleasure. She swayed, letting the potency of his mouth carry her beyond the petty confines of the hotel room, above the snares and dangers of the world outside, to a rapturous height known only to the two of them.

When he eased back onto the bed, his hands carried her with him, lifting her hips to mold her body against his. Jordan slid her legs around him, letting the rhythm of his desire dictate her own. She was now driven by a force more powerful even than her own need for satiation—her desire to give to him as he had given to her. Feeling his heaving sides beneath her hands, his body's quivering response to their union, Jordan experienced a satisfaction as intense as any physical release. In an insight as simple as it was profound, she recognized the essence underlying true love—the joy in bringing happiness to another.

Love. Nestled in Nick's embrace, Jordan countenanced the word she had avoided for so long. Turning her face against his shoulder, she felt his hand gently drift through her hair, letting it fall in fine strands across the pillow. Then she heard him whisper, "My Jordan." Closing her eyes, Jordan let her lips caress him tenderly as they drifted off into a shared dream.

Chapter Eleven

Jordan tugged sleepily at the quilted duvet, pulling it over her exposed ear to help block out a faint rustling somewhere in the background. She pressed her face into the pillow, resisting the day's intrusion on her senses. When the bed sagged to one side, she took her time rolling over.

"Good morning, darling." Nick leaned across the rumpled cover to kiss the tip of her nose.

Wriggling her arms from beneath the heavy duvet, Jordan lapped them around his neck, barring any possibility of retreat for the moment. She returned his greeting with a kiss on his chin, then another, more prolonged one on the lips. Nick smiled as he sat back on the edge of the bed beside her.

"How long have you been up?" she asked, reaching to cover a yawn with the back of her hand.

Nick rubbed the beginnings of a beard shadowing his chiseled jaw. "It depends on when you start counting. I got up about two hours ago to chase away the maid and then came right back to bed. The next time I woke, I ordered coffee and breakfast for us. Care for some?"

When Jordan nodded agreeably, he pushed up from the bed to fetch a tray full of rolls, cheese, sliced ham and fruit. Propping herself on the fat pillows, Jordan distributed generous servings onto two plates while Nick poured coffee. There might be no way to avoid facing the day, but snuggling next to Nick over a leisurely breakfast certainly smoothed the transition.

"It must be at least ten o'clock," Jordan commented, smoothing a dollop of jam onto a chunk of buttery roll.

"Guess again." Nick chuckled over the rim of his coffee cup. "It's almost noon."

Jordan straightened herself so abruptly she almost upset the coffee cup balanced on her knee. "Good Lord! I've got to get moving. I have an appointment at three."

Nick reached to steady the perilously rocking cup. "Take it easy. We'll get you there on time. Where is this appointment?"

Jordan told him about Esther Rabin's invitation to her home in the suburbs. When she moved to scoot out from under the cover, Nick caught her knees, playfully anchoring both her legs to the bed.

"Finish your breakfast," he told her. "I only need a few minutes to shower and get dressed. Then while you do all that, I'll rent a car for us. This place sounds as if it's only a short distance out of the city."

Jordan grinned as he jostled her legs gently before heading for the bath. Accustomed as she was to handling everything herself, a give-and-take partnership was a novel concept to her, but it definitely had its advantages. Sampling a slice of cheese, Jordan let her mind drift back to the previous night and the pleasures they had shared. Although she still carried an inner afterglow from the physical closeness, equally pleasurable was the intimacy they enjoyed on other levels. Liberated from the wariness that had overshadowed their association for too long, they could talk freely now about their aspirations, their fears, their personal lives, their work. Jordan caught herself as her eye fell on the edge of a splotched brown leather briefcase.

After guarding the briefcase with her life for the past week, she had almost forgotten about its unfortunate swim in the canal. How its contents had fared was anyone's guess, but now was as good a time as any to find out. Especially with Nick in the shower, she thought, a little guiltily. After rhapsodizing to herself over their newly discovered intimacy, Jordan realized that in one area, at least, she could not be perfectly candid with him—where Kitty Ridgewood's identity was concerned.

Scurrying out of bed, Jordan swung the pathetic-looking briefcase onto the luggage stand, adjusted the combination lock and snapped it open. She sighed with relief to find that, save for a little seepage staining the lining, the briefcase's interior was remarkably undamaged. Glancing quickly at the closed bathroom door, Jordan opened the manila envelope to check the sepia-toned photograph and the gold locket and found them still perfectly dry and intact. She had secured the briefcase and tucked it away in the closet by the time Nick emerged from the bath, toweling his hair.

Under the shower's brisk jet, Jordan wrestled with a new and potentially more troubling problem in reconciling her alliance with Nick and her loyalty to her client. She had been deeply moved by Nick's account of his grandmother's misfortune. After losing both her parents and her sister, she had been robbed of the single legacy that would have established her legitimacy—the music box. Although Jordan had never met Nick's grandmother, she could easily imagine the bitterness she must feel toward the betrayer who had taken the valuable art object and then abandoned Olga and her children to a cruel fate. If hatred was ever justified, then it certainly was in such a case, Jordan conceded.

How this elderly woman would feel about the descendants of the betrayer was a question less easily answered. Would she absolve the children from the sins of the father?

Or would she be vindictive? The latter alternative offered a
host of possibilities for generating bad publicity for Kitty
Ridgewood. Despite her desire for candor with Nick, Jordan realized that she would have to keep Kitty's identity to
herself until she knew more about her background.

As she dressed after her shower, Jordan wrinkled her nose
at the stiff, wrinkled clothes that reeked of dried canal water. Thanking providence once more for Nick's ready assistance, she waited in an inconspicuous corner of the hotel
lobby while he fetched a car from a nearby rental agency and
then drove back to the hotel to pick up her and his luggage.
They then drove straight to Jordan's hotel. By the time she
had changed into clean clothes, collected her garment bag
and paid her bill, Nick had found Heerwijl on the map provided by the car rental company.

During the night the rain had mercifully abated, making
traffic conditions less tedious than they would have been in
a heavy downpour. During the short drive into the suburbs, Jordan filled Nick in on the information Esther Rabin had given her about Jakov Davidov. As Esther had
promised, the town of Heerwijl was situated on the cusp of
greater Amsterdam, a neat collection of white houses with
red-tile roofs and well-tended gardens clustered on the flat
landscape. The Rabins' house stood at the end of a quiet
cul-de-sac.

Esther had obviously not forgotten the appointment, for
she opened the front door almost immediately after Jordan
pressed the buzzer.

"Please come in, Miss MacKenzie." She smiled graciously as Jordan introduced Nick, welcoming them both
into the comforting warmth of the tiled foyer.

"Come, I will show you Jakov's trunk." Adjusting the
sleeves of her navy blue cardigan, Esther beckoned them to
follow her through the cozy living room. Jordan and Nick

waited while she unlocked a door and then led them into the garage. "I would offer to take your coats, but you may find that you need them here," she warned, pulling her sweater snugly across her chest.

Esther guided them around a Mercedes station wagon and then gestured toward a small wooden trunk, bound by tarnished brass fittings. "So. That is it." She stepped back, regarding the old trunk a little sadly. "Please let me know if I may be of help."

After thanking Mrs. Rabin, Jordan crouched beside the trunk and lifted its lid. For a moment she only stared at the collection of worn and faded items, the touching remnant of one man's life. As she began to sort through his modest possessions, Jordan felt as if she were violating Jakov Davidov's privacy. There were a few articles of clothing, a blue-striped shirt, a pair of faded black pants, a vest. Jordan placed the folded clothes in a neat pile before digging deeper into the trunk. She found a shaving brush and a folded straight razor wrapped in brittle, yellowed newspaper. His prayer shawl had been carefully packed away, along with a book printed in Hebrew. Jordan silently thanked Esther's conscientious mother when she opened a flat, newspaper-wrapped bundle and discovered a cache of papers and folded documents.

"Wonderful!" she murmured under her breath.

She had to restrain her eager fingers to avoid damaging the fragile paper as she unfolded the first sheet. A quick glance told her that it was Jakov's Dutch identification document, containing the basic information she had gleaned in the statistics office. The next document appeared older, stained and laced with deep wrinkles. When Jordan opened it, she blinked and then frowned.

"What's wrong?" Nick asked. Since she had opened the trunk, he had been standing a respectful distance behind her, obviously still mindful of her client's dictum regarding confidentiality.

Grimacing, Jordan shook her head and then handed the paper to Nick. "It's in Russian, isn't it?"

"It sure is," Nick said slowly, his eyes wandering over the faded Cyrillic letters. "I guess you *really* need a translator now, huh?"

Jordan sat back on her heels. "You're on."

Nick propped his hip against the hood of the Mercedes and studied the document. "This is Jakov Davidov's official identification paper issued by the last czar's government. He was born on April 15, 1896 in a place called Zelnov in the Ukraine." He lifted the paper closer to his face. "His father's name was Itzhak but I can't make out the mother's."

"That's okay," Jordan assured him. "What about this?" She handed him a small handwritten note.

Nick turned the paper right side up and then smiled. "It's a bill of sale for two goats and a cart. The ink is pretty badly smeared, but it looks as if the transaction took place sometime in 1916."

"Does it say where?" Jordan asked.

Nick's mouth twisted to one side as he labored over the smudgy writing. "Zelnov, I think."

"What we've learned so far would indicate that Jakov spent most of his life in Zelnov before his immigration. Or at least, he came back to his birthplace around 1916," she amended, cautioning herself not to jump to conclusions.

Nick carefully folded the note. "I think your first assumption is probably correct. A poor man from a small village wouldn't have had much mobility in those days. Find anything else interesting?"

Jordan glanced over another official-looking document before passing it to Nick. "I think this is another ID. At least, it looks like the one you just translated."

"It is," Nick assured her. "For a fellow named Yuri Grushkin."

"I wonder how Davidov ended up with someone else's ID," Jordan mused.

"Wait a minute." Not looking up from the paper, Nick began to smile. "I think I've figured out a likely answer to your question. I believe Jakov and Yuri were one and the same man. The birth dates are identical on both documents, as well as the height and color of hair and eyes. One significant difference is that Grushkin's place of residence is listed as Kiev."

Jordan rose onto her knees, craning for a look at the mystifying document. "Why would Davidov want two sets of papers? From what Mrs. Rabin has told me about him, he certainly doesn't sound like a criminal type."

Nick shook his head. "Jakov wasn't doing anything except trying to better his lot in life. As a Jew in czarist Russia, his options were very limited. My guess is he obtained the set of false papers with the hope that he could find work outside his village. Apparently his strategy succeeded well enough to get him to Kiev."

"Here's the last item." Jordan gave Nick another tattered, handwritten note. She watched him squint over the difficult script, his face growing increasingly sober. When he said nothing after a few minutes, she prompted him. "Can you decipher the writing?"

Nick's eyes did not move from the paper. "Yes, it's very clear," he said in a strangely hushed voice.

"Is something wrong, Nick?" Jordan stood, joining him beside the station wagon. Frowning, she gestured toward the ragged paper. "What is this thing, anyway?"

"It's a travel pass issued to Grushkin and approved by a Comrade Bukin of the Red Army on October 23, 1920. The pass authorizes Grushkin to drive a child named Natalie from Kiev to the town of Vinnica." He swallowed audibly. "The pass was requested by Anatoly Kuzov."

"Kuzov?" Jordan repeated, trying to remember where she had heard the name.

"My great-grandmother danced for Kuzov's ballet company in Kiev." For a long moment Nick only stared at the rakes and trowels suspended on the garage wall. When he looked at Jordan again, his face betrayed his intense emotions. "My grandmother's name is Natalie."

Jordan's eyes widened, darting first to the paper and then back to Nick. "You believe the child Grushkin—or rather, *our* Davidov—was driving to Vinnica was your grandmother?"

Nick nodded very slowly, as if he were in a daze. "Jordan," he said in a strangely flat voice, without looking at her. "What is your client's name?"

Jordan bit her lip, folding her arms across her chest. "Oh, Nick, please don't ask me that," she began.

"No, I mean what is the name of the child you researched at the orphanage and in the Marienlazarett?"

"Käthe Davidov, but you know that already. According to Mrs. Rabin, Jakov referred to the little girl as 'Katya.'"

"And that's what my grandmother always called her little sister, short for Ekaterina."

The garage became very still as they both grappled with the stunning and unavoidable conclusion. Without speaking, Jordan reached for her briefcase. Lifting it onto the car, she opened it and pulled out the manila envelope. She slid the sepia-toned photograph in front of Nick.

Nick took a deep, uneven breath. "It's her. If you had ever seen my grandmother, you would have recognized her as the girl in this picture." His voice caught, and he broke off.

Turning away from the picture, Jordan leaned back against the Mercedes and shook her head. "My God, your grandmother and Kitty Ridgewood are sisters!"

"*The* Kitty Ridgewood is your client?" Nick gasped in amazement. "No wonder you were sworn to secrecy."

Jordan chuckled, relieving some of the tension the dramatic discovery had created. "My client and your great-aunt."

"After all these years who would have thought..." Nick fell silent, looking once more at the small piece of paper that contained the earth-shattering revelation.

"There are still some loose ends to tie up. Does your grandmother remember very much about her sister? The last time she saw her, for instance?" •

"To be honest, I think the pain of losing her mother and Katya forced Grandmama to suppress a lot, but now that we have this link—" Nick lifted the travel pass "—I wouldn't hesitate to question her closely. She will be so happy."

"So will Kitty," Jordan added.

Nick's face suddenly dimmed. "Could I ask you to wait a couple of days before you contact Kitty Ridgewood? I'd like the chance to investigate this pass more thoroughly."

"You think Jakov Davidov, alias Yuri Grushkin, is the betrayer who got the music box?" Although Jordan felt liable to make the suggestion, she hated incriminating the indigent immigrant with whom she had come to sympathize. She was relieved when Nick immediately shook his head.

"No, I don't. I mean, he could have gotten possession of the music box, I suppose. But his impoverished circumstances in Vienna and then here certainly don't support the theory. I'm wondering why Kuzov obtained a pass only for my grandmother and the coachman. Why not for Olga and Katya as well?''

"Maybe they were going to travel separately at a later date, to avoid attracting suspicion," Jordan suggested.

"Anyone with aristocratic connections traveling anywhere was the object of suspicion in Red-occupied territory," Nick countered. "Natalie was no safer traveling alone than with her mother and sister. I've thought of another, very disturbing possibility," he went on. "Perhaps Kuzov found bribing so many Red officials to be too expensive. He managed to save himself and several of his dancers. And my grandmother, for which I will be eternally thankful. But at some point he may have run out of gold, jewelry and artworks to barter."

"You believe he may have taken the music box from Olga, promising to use it to obtain a pass for her, and then reneged." Jordan was appalled by the thought.

Nick's handsome face hardened. "In such times, anything is possible. Kuzov had the reputation of being an autocratic, self-absorbed man. He viewed himself as furthering a divine mission for the sake of dance. Immigrating to the West was merely an extension of that purpose. Or at least that's the impression I've gotten from reading his diaries. He talks far more about bringing his art to the West than about bringing human beings to freedom."

Jordan thought for a moment. "Do the diaries cover the period when he emigrated from Russia?"

"Oh, yes. Kuzov portrays himself as being very self-sacrificing for the sake of his troupe. Or at least Rachmanova's translation paints such a picture of him." Noticing Jordan's brow furrowing in confusion, he went on. "Maria Rachmanova is a retired Kuzov dancer who translated his diaries into German and English. She regards herself as the keeper of the flame, and I wouldn't put her above purging any material that might have cast Kuzov in an unflattering light. I shouldn't speak unkindly of her, though, for she was a friend of my great-grandmother's and still keeps in close touch with Grandmama.''

''People can sometimes justify difficult things to protect those they admire and love,'' Jordan reminded him.

Nick shoved himself away from the station wagon. ''Well, there's one way to find out.'' He gave Jordan a conspiratorial smile that wasn't entirely humorous. ''Get our hands on the original diaries and compare for ourselves.''

LUCK CONTINUED TO FAVOR Jordan and Nick when they reached Schiphol Airport and were able to book the last two seats on an evening flight to Vienna. With the next important step of their investigation centered in the Austrian capital, neither of them had relished wasting an additional evening in an Amsterdam hotel. Then, too, Jordan was eager to leave behind the scene of her last and most threatening encounter with the phantom gunman. Seated next to Nick in the dimly lighted cabin of the aircraft, she consoled herself that for a time at least she had eluded the man stalking her. No one, not even Molly Bledsoe, had the faintest idea where she was, and she vowed to take extra precautions to cover her tracks in Vienna.

Nick had apparently been thinking along the same lines. During the drive from the Vienna airport into the city, he made a suggestion that was both practical and appealing.

''Why don't you stay with me for the next few days? Check into your old hotel, just as if you were picking up where you left off. Collect your mail and phone messages regularly. Then just quietly disappear. At the very least, it would make it harder for someone to monitor your day-to-day activities.''

Nick looked happy when Jordan agreed, in part, she flattered herself, because he had come to rely on her company and missed her when they were apart. At least, that was the way she felt about him.

Following the plan Nick had laid out, they drove to the Richtsberger Hof. The concierge's automatic welcoming smile was tinged with a trace of alarm, no doubt inspired by the bizarre circumstances surrounding her departure from the hotel. He took special pains to mention that the police were eager to question her. Jordan nodded politely, signed the register and then returned to Nick's waiting car.

Given Nick's socially prominent background and profession, Jordan had expected his apartment to be expensively decorated, with an ample display of valuable paintings. When she stepped through the door of the spacious flat, she was startled to find it sparsely furnished, albeit with a few quality pieces, and devoid of all but a handful of well-chosen artworks, mostly modern sculpture. Although any of the furnishings would easily have passed in an *Architectural Digest* spread, the place had a comfortable, lived-in feel to it.

"I only have one house rule, and it is strictly to protect the innocent," Nick told her as he rearranged the guest-room closet to accommodate the contents of her garment bag. "No shoes shall be left lying around at any time, lest Pedro devour them. You have a temporary reprieve, but I'm picking the little monster up from Daria this evening, so be forewarned."

Jordan laughed, but she obediently placed her two pairs of pumps in the bottom of the closet and then closed the door securely. While Nick opened a bottle of wine, she changed into jeans and a sweater. When she joined him in the living room, she adjusted the blinds for privacy before accepting the glass of white wine.

"Just in case Bertie Waxx is anywhere in the neighborhood," she told him with a wry smile.

Nick carefully twisted the wine bottle to catch the drip. "Bertie is persistent, but I think he may be willing to leave us in peace for a while." His low chuckle sounded wicked. "I don't imagine he'll be quick to forget how I ripped the film out of his camera the night you stormed out of the Richtsberger Hof."

Jordan sat bolt upright on the sofa. "You mean he didn't give the film to the police?"

Nick regarded her with a puzzled expression. "No. At least, not these two rolls."

Jordan slapped the sofa cushion in frustration. "He took pictures of the man who attacked me, Nick! If you'd only known, you could have saved the film."

Without saying a word, Nick walked to the foyer closet. When he returned he dropped two rolls of 35-mm film into her lap. "As a matter of fact, I did just that. I must confess my first impulse was to expose both rolls right before his beady eyes. With so many police about, however, I wasn't sure how they might regard my destroying what was, technically speaking, Bertie's property. So I simply pocketed the film. No wonder he didn't run to the police and raise a stink when I emptied his cameras. The little weasel had every intention of withholding evidence for the sake of his wretched tabloid shots."

Jordan handled the rolls of film as if they were lumps of gold. "I wish there was some way we could get a look at these pictures before we give the film to the police. I think I would feel much safer if I could recognize the person who's been stalking me."

"If you don't mind spending an hour or so cooped up with a lot of chemicals in the bathroom, we can develop the film and make prints without leaving the comfort of home.

In my line of work, I often need to photograph potential acquisitions. When I have the time I like to do my own printing, so I have all the necessary darkroom equipment.''

Jordan was already on her feet. "Let's do it."

While Jordan cleared the bathroom counter, Nick wheeled a cart loaded with a printer, trays and brown glass chemical bottles out of a closet. They filled the trays with solution and connected the safety light before sealing the door with a blackout sheet. Jordan hovered beside Nick as he hung the strips of developed film to dry from the shower-curtain rod.

"Some of these shots look pretty cloudy," Nick remarked ruefully, echoing Jordan's thoughts. "That's what happens when you tear film out of a camera without re-winding it properly first."

"What about this one?" Jordan carefully grasped the sprocketed border of the film, holding it up for a closer look.

Nick squinted at the frame. "It looks like someone with a hammerlock around your neck."

"That's what we're looking for," Jordan assured him. "That hulk almost strangled me."

As soon as the film was dry, they set about making prints. Despite the sealed room's snug temperature, a shiver rippled through Jordan as the attacker's face gradually emerged onto the white photographic paper. As Nick plunged the print into the fixer bath, she studied the hard, boxy features of her assailant's face. It was a countenance chipped from granite, cold, passionless and unrelieved by any human sympathy.

"So this is what he looks like, up close, without the mask," she murmured under her breath.

Nick's hand rested lightly on the back of her neck, giving it a supportive squeeze. "Before we pass this film on to the police, let's make an extra set of prints for ourselves. We need to study this face until it's etched in our memory. I wonder who he is."

An idea suddenly occurred to Jordan, and she glanced up at Nick. "My dad might be able to help in that department. I need to phone him about that spent casing I sent him, anyway. Bertie managed to get a few pictures of this guy alone, after I got away from him. I'd like to fax one to Dad and see what he comes up with."

"It's worth a shot," Nick conceded.

Jordan cut a reproving look at him, feigning a frown. "Please. I'd prefer you didn't use that expression."

Nick laughed as he removed the blackout blanket from the door and showed Jordan to the telephone on his desk. After consulting her watch, she calculated that her parents would just be finishing lunch.

The phone rang several times, indicating that they were probably still lingering around the table. When her father answered, he sounded as if he had tried to swallow the last of his sandwich too quickly and was having a hard time of it.

"I'm sorry if I interrupted your lunch," Jordan apologized.

"Don't worry about that! I'm relieved to hear from you." He cleared his throat, recovering himself. "Today's your mom's bridge day, you know, so I'm batchin' it. I don't enjoy eating alone that much, reminds me of all those greasy burgers I used to gulp on the run at the Bureau."

Jordan chose the opportunity to sidle into the subject prompting her call. "Speaking of the Bureau, did you get the spent casing I sent you?"

"Yeah, sure did." Her father chuckled, more a short grunt than a laugh. "Jordan, that thing was fired from a gun—how should I put this—that in our experience has been

very popular with hit men, did you know that?" Not giving her a chance to answer, he went on, his voice rising as his
words gained momentum. "Now I know some would argue
that this weapon is fine for target practice, but that's not its
main selling point to the folks who turn up in the Bureau's
records. Honey, I don't know who this friend of yours is
that you're trying to help out, but I sure don't like the ideas
this casing has given me."

"Please don't worry about me, Dad," Jordan told him in
a calm voice calculated to soothe him.

"I'm trying not to, but you're not making it very easy,"
Jack MacKenzie complained gruffly. "Okay, I'll send you
a copy of the analysis. Where should I mail it?"

"Uh, just a minute." Cradling the phone beneath her
chin, Jordan shuffled through some mail lying on the desk.
Holding up a newsmagazine, she read Nick's address from
the label. "If you need to get in touch with me, here's a
phone number where you can leave a message, too." She
gave him Nick's number.

"Okay, baby. Anything else I can do for you?" he asked
rhetorically.

"As a matter of fact," Jordan began, winning a groan
from her father, "I have picture I'd like to fax to you."

"Something tells me this isn't a snapshot of the Alps."

"No," Jordan conceded. "I'd like for you to find out
whatever you can about the man in the picture—if he has a
criminal record, anything of that sort."

"Jordan . . ."

"Trust me, Dad," Jordan pleaded.

A heavy sigh rasped into the phone. "All right. Fax it.
But I'm warning you, Jordan, if you ask for any more favors like this, I'm going to fly over there and see what the
hell is going on for myself."

Chapter Twelve

The moment the frosty-looking blonde stalked into the restaurant of the Sacher Hotel, Bertie knew Gudrun Mayes-Cooper had arrived on the scene. She looked exactly the way he had pictured her during their brief telephone chat, a long-legged model-type with eyes like razor blades. Bertie watched her consult with the maître d' and then turn toward his table. The cool violet eyes narrowed, slashing at him across the crowded room, as he threw up a hand and waved to her.

"Have a seat, Miss Mayes-Cooper. So glad you could join me."

Bertie made a pretense of rising in his seat to gesture toward the vacant chair. He proffered a hand, relishing the finicky way she clasped it, as if she were fishing something unmentionable out of her soup. As she slid onto the chair, Bertie could see she was taking him in, disapproving, no doubt, of quite a bit she saw.

"Shall we order a bite?" Bertie beckoned to the waiter before shaking out the napkin and tucking it into his collar.

"No, thank you." Gudrun's expensive stockings rasped impatiently as she crossed her legs beneath the tablecloth skirt.

Bertie made her wait while he ordered tea and then looked over the pastry cart. As soon as the waiter was out of hearing range, however, Gudrun dropped any pretense of sociability.

"I didn't come here for tea, Mr. Waxx, and I'd appreciate your getting to the point."

Bertie sliced off a substantial chunk of the *Sachertorte* he had ordered and popped it into his mouth. "The point is, Miss Mayes-Cooper, that you and I—" he gestured with his fork toward her and then toward himself "—have an area of common concern where we might be able to offer each other valuable assistance. I am referring, of course, to our mutual interest in Miss Jordan MacKenzie."

The stony violet eyes stared at him. "What do you mean?"

Bertie carefully scraped his fork across the dessert plate, scooping up the last of the torte's rich chocolate glaze. "Come now, Miss Mayes-Cooper. When I rang you up yesterday, you seemed rather keen on getting in touch with Miss MacKenzie. Do I recall your asking me if I was a friend of Miss MacKenzie's who might arrange a meeting for you? Something about a very special work of art she has an inside track on, I believe it was."

Gudrun's eyes darkened to a lethal shade of purple, and he could tell she would have given half her privileged life for the chance to retract those few overeager comments she had made on the phone. "As I told you yesterday, I have no idea how you got my name or the name of my hotel. *And* I resent your idle speculation."

Bertie put aside the empty dessert plate and turned his attention to the tea. As he spooned sugar into his cup, he clucked under his breath. "What a shame! And I thought we could work together."

Gudrun regarded him with the instinctive distrust of the habitually dishonest. "To what end?"

Bertie topped off the cup of tea with a splash of milk. He stirred the concoction rapidly, creating a little vortex in the pale beige liquid. "Why, to further your quest for this precious treasure, of course!"

"I appreciate your deep love of art, Mr. Waxx, but I need to see what I'm buying." Gudrun gave him a brief, acid smile.

"Miss Mayes-Cooper!" The spoon rattled against Bertie's saucer as he gasped in professed shock. "However did you get the impression I was suggesting the vulgar exchange of funds?"

"Everyone is selling something, Mr. Waxx," she informed him with the authority of one who knew firsthand. "What are you offering me and what is your price?"

"The opportunity to substitute, shall we say, for Miss MacKenzie at a meeting with *the* Count Radetsky." She was a canny one, but Bertie was too quick to miss the eager quiver that flitted across his opponent's face. In that fleeting, unguarded instant, Bertie knew he had her. "Five hundred pounds and the information is yours."

"That is a ridiculous amount of money. How do I know this information isn't completely worthless?"

Bertie lowered his voice to heighten the import of his words. "I have an inside source on Miss MacKenzie, a person whose reliability has already been demonstrated to you." He poked the table with his finger, underscoring the sentence's finale. "You were wondering how I acquired your name. Well..." He settled back in his chair, allowing himself a smug smile.

Gudrun pretended to think for a moment, but Bertie could see she was impressed. "I'll give you two hundred pounds, and not a twopence more," she finally said.

"*Two* hundred?" Bertie repeated, feigning amazement. "Surely you can't be serious!"

"Three hundred, and that's my last offer." Gudrun's perfect lips drew into a sour little purse. "One hundred fifty up front, and one hundred fifty *after* the meeting."

Bertie prefaced his acceptance with the obligatory frowning and head shaking. "Very well. Three hundred it is."

Gudrun abruptly leaned across the table, coming closer to him than she had since her arrival. "Listen carefully, Mr. Waxx. I am warning you. If something runs afoul with this arrangement, you will be very sorry indeed."

"You've nothing to worry about, luv." Bertie smiled in satisfaction. "You have my word as a gentleman."

"I CAN'T HELP IT, NICK. I still feel like a common thief, sneaking into someone's house on the pretext of having tea and then pocketing a couple of books while the hostess isn't looking."

Daria shrugged the large leather bag from her shoulder onto the hood of Nick's car, making no secret of her distaste. Frowning, she sorted through the assorted tights, leotards and ballet slippers, finally pulling two worn leather-bound volumes from the jumble of clothing. She thrust the books into Nick's hands. "Here. I hope you're satisfied."

"You didn't steal anything, Daria," Nick assured his sister. "We simply borrowed two of Kuzov's diaries. And at any rate, Rachmanova will never notice that two of the volumes are missing unless she suddenly gets the urge to count all thirty-two of his diaries."

Daria's eyes widened in alarm at the dreadful possibility. "Just make sure you have them back to me early tomorrow morning. I deliberately left my gloves beneath a chair in Rachmanova's sitting room, so I have an excuse to stop by her apartment on my way to rehearsal." She sighed uneasily. "I only hope I can find a way to return the books to their proper place on the shelf without her noticing."

"Have a coughing fit and then ask her for a glass of water. While she's in the kitchen, pop them back into place," Nick suggested helpfully.

Daria rejected the ploy with a withering glance. "This isn't funny, Nick."

"No, it isn't," he agreed, sobering. "You know me well enough to realize that I would never have asked such a favor if I didn't have a very good reason. As I told you when Jordan and I picked up Pedro last night, we uncovered some information in Amsterdam that makes examining Kuzov's journals imperative. I simply can't go into detail right now."

"That's another thing that bothers me, all this hinting at earthshaking discoveries and hush-hush secrecy," Daria interrupted to complain.

Nick reached to take his sister's hand and gave it a firm squeeze. "Trust me, Daria. I'll tell you everything very soon."

With that promise, Nick managed to wrest a conservative smile from his sister. As he drove along Schottenring to his apartment, however, he could only wish that the diaries' contents would prove as conclusive as he and Jordan hoped. Regardless of what the diaries revealed about Kuzov, Nick would be able to share the happy news of Katya's survival with Daria and, most importantly, Grandmama.

Jordan had planned to contact Kitty Ridgewood late that afternoon, as soon as she could reasonably expect to find her California-based client in her office. Once Kitty was on her way to Vienna, they would break the news to Grandmama.

Neither Nick nor Jordan wanted to delay reuniting the sisters a moment longer than necessary. At the same time,

Nick realized that the reunion would unavoidably resurrect a host of suppressed memories for his grandmother, many of them sad. If Rachmanova was shielding Kuzov, the threat of Grandmama recalling a damning bit of evidence would prompt her to double her guard, perhaps even destroy an incriminating volume. Tonight was their one and only chance to examine the diaries, and they needed to make good use of it.

Jordan had apparently been thinking along the same lines, for when Nick reached his apartment he found her waiting on the sofa with Pedro, armed with a notepad and his copy of the translation of Kuzov's journal, ready for action.

"Any luck contacting Kitty?" Nick asked as he hung his jacket in the foyer closet.

Jordan shook her head. "No, she wasn't in her office. I spoke with Gloria Bowing, her secretary, and requested that Kitty get in touch with me as soon as possible. Gloria has a tendency to be a little high-handed, anyway, but she was positively hostile today. I guess she was offended that I wouldn't go into detail with her on the phone, but I won't entrust this information to anyone but Kitty personally."

"I wouldn't, either," Nick concurred, dropping onto the sofa between Jordan and the napping dog.

Jordan absently tapped a pencil against the notepad. "You don't suppose Kitty has gotten wind of any of Bertie Waxx's stories?" she asked at length.

Nick studied the cracked leather spine of one of the diaries. "I seriously doubt it." When that comment failed to dispel Jordan's pensive expression, he shook her knee gently. "Come on. We have some serious reading to do."

Tedious would have been a more accurate description, Nick reflected as the late afternoon wore into evening and the evening into night. While he read aloud from the original, Jordan followed in the translation, cross-checking for discrepancies and omissions. Although they had targeted a relatively brief period in Kuzov's life, the year immediately preceding his flight from Russia and the months following his arrival in the West, the dancemaster's difficult script made deciphering the original a slow, painstaking process.

Nick was certain that no one but an obsessive admirer like Rachmanova would have had the patience to translate all thirty-two volumes of the journal. As if his nearly illegible handwriting were not torture enough, Kuzov had been a long-winded journalist, given to rambling philosophizing and self-important asides about his aristocratic acquaintances. Even Jordan's forbearance, honed by years of poring over official fine print, was severely tested.

"It seems that a lot of the material did end up on the cutting-room floor," Jordan commented when they paused around midnight to brew a pot of extra-strong coffee.

"I imagine few publishers are interested in bringing out a book that outweighs the average reader," Nick remarked dryly, lifting the saturated coffee filter from the carafe and dumping it into the kitchen waste can. "I have to hand it to Rachmanova. She did a marvelous job of plowing through all this guff and making it fit into two volumes you can pick up without a forklift."

Jordan wrinkled her nose over the potent steam rising from the coffee carafe she held. "So far, the out-takes seem pretty harmless, at least as far as our interests are concerned."

"We're not through yet," Nick reminded her grimly. Hooking his finger through the handles of two mugs, he led the way back to the sofa.

They had emptied the eight-cup carafe before the Bolsheviks had officially closed Kuzov's ballet school. Pale pink slivers of dawn had begun to slip between the blinds by the time he had hatched his plan for fleeing to the West. It was past ten in the morning when Kuzov at last reached the turbulent city of 1920 Vienna. Nick and Jordan had followed his odyssey faithfully—without discovering even the most veiled hint of any ill will toward Olga Gallinin.

"Rachmanova chose to leave out a great deal, but only to keep Kuzov from looking like a fool," Nick concluded, wearily closing the second volume.

"He must have been an unbearably pompous man," Jordan agreed. "But I think he truly admired and cared about your great-grandmother. You know, she's about the *only* person who escaped his criticism. If you were to believe Kuzov, every other ballet company was a bunch of klutzes trained by tasteless imbeciles. He even made fun of his own supporters." She laughed, covering her mouth as her chuckle distorted into a yawn. "Remember those snide comments about Countess what-was-her-name? The one he described as a dim-witted peacock incapable of the finer emotions?"

"Something like that." Nick stifled his own yawn.

"And the countess was one of his most generous patrons! I imagine his aristocratic supporters would have been shocked if they had been privy to the unflattering portraits he painted of them in his journal."

Nick's shoulders rose in an indifferent shrug. "Kuzov wasn't particularly generous where human frailty was concerned. He even poked some fun at Rachmanova. Poor thing, it must have hurt her when she read those remarks about her peasant's knees and 'strained grace.'"

"Kuzov was an unlikable man, but that doesn't necessarily make him a ruthless one. Maybe he simply didn't record his darkest thoughts, but somehow I don't get the impression he betrayed your great-grandmother. After all, he wrote pages about bringing her to the West and making her the prima donna of the century," Jordan reminded Nick.

"I'm inclined to agree with you. Well, since our work is done, I suppose I'd better return these volumes to Daria." Nick pushed himself up from the sofa with effort. Rounding the back of the sofa, he leaned to kiss the top of Jordan's head. "While I'm out I have a few errands to run, need to pick up some food and laundry. Why don't you get a little sleep? When I get back we'll have lunch and then pay Grandmama a visit this afternoon."

"You're not going to sleep?" Jordan looked as aghast as her drooping eyelids would permit.

"Eventually." Nick ruffled her hair before heading to the coat closet. "'Bye," Jordan heard him call from the foyer.

Jordan cast an envious glance at Pedro, who lay peacefully snoring in one of the armchairs. She groaned as she roused herself from the sofa and carried the empty mugs and carafe to the kitchen. It was still too early to phone anyone in the United States. She would take Nick's advice and crawl into bed for a couple of hours.

Jordan had showered and was groggily rummaging through her clothes in search of a nightgown when the telephone rang. Dragging her bathrobe behind her, she went to the desk and picked up.

"Hello?" she said, hoping that the caller would speak slowly enough for her to understand.

"Jordan! Thank God, I've found you!" Molly Bledsoe exclaimed. "Where in heaven's name have you been?"

"Oh, all over the place." Jordan ran a hand through her hair, trying to collect her thoughts. She had been unprepared to hear Molly's excited voice, much less offer a recap of her recent misadventures. "I should have checked in with you sooner, but things have been incredibly hectic."

"You had me worried out of my mind! Why haven't you returned my messages? I must have left a dozen at that hotel over the past couple of days!" Molly scolded. "I didn't hear a peep from you for almost a week. Finally I called the last number I had for you, at the Vienna hotel, but you never called me back." Molly paused to draw a much-needed breath. "Well, I said to myself, that simply isn't like Jordan. I knew something had to be wrong, so that's when I decided to call your folks."

"You called my parents?" Jordan asked in dismay.

"Of course I did! I didn't consult a psychic to get this telephone number," Molly informed her a little tartly. "Have you seen Kitty Ridgewood?" she demanded.

"Seen? What do you mean?" Jordan asked.

"What I mean is that she is on her way to Europe to find you, and let me tell you, she is one mad lady. Now you know, Jordan, you've had some trying clients over the years. And in all the time I've worked for you, I've been diplomatic and patient in dealing with them, haven't I?"

"Yes, you have, Molly," Jordan managed to put in.

"But I have *never* had anyone talk to me the way this Ridgewood woman carried on yesterday." Molly's voice was thick with offense. "Honestly, I think she must be nuts. She kept raving about your flitting all over the Continent with a jet-set playboy, throwing her name around and getting your picture in sleazy tabloids. I kept trying to tell her she must have someone else confused with you. If Ridgewood would have quit spouting nonsense long enough, maybe I could have convinced her she was mistaken. Imagine *you* cavorting with a Russian ski champ! Is that ridiculous, or what?"

"It's pretty ridiculous, all right." Jordan mustered a weak laugh.

"At least I've been able to warn you now, so you're prepared to deal with her," Molly congratulated herself.

"Now," she went on briskly, "do you have something to write with?"

"Yes, I think so." Jordan fumbled among the debris on Nick's desk and found a blank envelope and a felt-tip pen.

"Good. A Count Boris Radetsky phoned the office two days ago." Molly spoke slowly, pronouncing the count's name syllable by syllable. "He said you had contacted him about some research, and he was desperate to get in touch with you. At that point I had no idea where you were, but of course I didn't tell him that. Anyway, he wanted to arrange a meeting for one o'clock this afternoon. I told him I'd give you the message. I don't suppose you happened to pick it up at the hotel?"

"No," Jordan confessed.

"I suspected as much." Molly sighed heavily. "All right, here are the directions to his country estate."

"Country estate?"

"That's what I thought, but he said not to worry. According to Count Radetsky, it's just on the outskirts of Vienna, about a forty-five-minute drive. You're to meet him at the gate—you'll recognize it by the winged angels on either side—and he'll drive you the rest of the way to the estate itself."

Jordan jotted the directions Molly gave her on the envelope. "Thanks, Molly. I'm sorry I didn't touch base with you sooner," she added.

"So am I," Molly concurred gruffly. "Now you'd better step on it. If I've got these time zones straight in my mind, you don't have a minute to spare. You don't want to keep a count waiting!"

Especially one who had proved so reluctant to talk so far, Jordan added to herself as she hung up the phone and dashed back to the closet. Nick had taken her Burberry to the cleaners yesterday, thereby severely limiting her wardrobe choices. Still, the count couldn't object too strongly to casual dress if he had chosen his country estate as the site of their meeting. Jordan phoned a taxi before pulling on a pair of black wool slacks with a coordinating geometric-print sweater and hurriedly applying a smattering of makeup. After dashing off a brief note to Nick explaining her absence, she threw on her quilted jacket and headed downstairs.

Fortunately, the cab driver was familiar with the outlying areas beyond Vienna's urban core. He drove confidently, weaving through the traffic clogging Eichenstrasse until they had reached the highway. Jordan compulsively checked her watch as the snowy landscape sped past the window. Even with the cabbie clocking 130 kilometers per hour, she was already late. They had exited the highway now and were following a deserted two-lane, bordered on either side by dense forest. Jordan inched to the edge of the seat, anxiously scanning the impenetrable hedge looming to her right. When she spotted an arched gate flanked by winged cherubs, she signaled the cabbie to stop.

Jordan paid the driver and then climbed out of the cab. The iron gate was secured by a slack chain, but the snow-covered driveway was imprinted with fresh tire tracks. Through the trees Jordan could barely glimpse the roofline of a baroque residence. Radetsky, however, was nowhere to be seen. He had no doubt tired of waiting for her and driven back to the house.

For a moment Jordan toyed with the idea of retreating to the cab and simply returning to Vienna. How receptive Radetsky would be to her tardy arrival was anyone's guess. Still, Molly had said he was desperate to get in touch with her. Jordan decided that at the very worst he would refuse to see her, in which case she could wheedle one of the ser-

vants into letting her use the phone to summon a taxi back
to the estate's gate.

After dismissing the cabbie, Jordan returned to the gate.
Although the chain effectively barred automotive traffic, it
allowed enough purchase for her to slip easily between the
two hinged gates. Apparently others had already chosen that
route, as evidenced by several sets of footprints pocking the
snow. Jordan was thankful for her warm boots as she
trudged along the driveway leading to the house. It was a
longer walk than she had anticipated, certainly not the sort
of activity she craved in her sleep-deprived state. When some
of the tracks veered off into the woods, Jordan decided to
follow what appeared to be a shortcut to the house.

As she went farther into the forest, she struggled to keep
sight of the house's towering chimneys. In some spots the
terrain sloped, entirely cutting off her view. The snow was
much deeper, too, blanketing hidden snares of coiled vines
and underbrush. Jordan paused for a moment to scan the
silent forest. Perhaps the best plan was to backtrack and
continue along the road. At least she would be spared the
irritation of wading through snowdrifts and stumbling over
buried logs.

Jordan was turning when she noticed a length of red fabric extending from behind a low cluster of bushes. Picking
her way through the treacherous ground cover, she ducked
to avoid a low branch. Her head scraped the limb, releasing
its burden of snow onto her. Jordan was rubbing the wet
powder from her eyes as she approached the circle of
bushes. It took her a few minutes to recognize the red cloth
as a wool muffler. When her vision cleared she saw another, much thinner ribbon of red running parallel to the
muffler. The ribbon glistened, its edges fading to a sickly
pink in the snow. A drumming filled Jordan's ears as she
stepped closer to the bushes. Her eyes followed the red

trickle to its delta, watched it gradually expand into a bright crimson pool buoying a woman's motionless head. A scream caught in Jordan's throat, frozen in mute horror, as she gazed down at the lifeless woman, into the empty, staring eyes of Gudrun Mayes-Cooper.

PEDRO HAD MISSED his morning walk, and he was growing impatient. As he unlocked the door, Nick could hear the little dog whining and pacing inside the apartment.

"Come on, Pete. Let's try not to wake Jordan, okay?"

Nick deposited the laundry and bag of groceries on the foyer floor. Grabbing the leash from its hook inside the closet, he followed the jubilant animal down the corridor to the stairs.

He circled the block, allowing Pedro a reasonable session of sniffing and digging in the snow. Although his pet was accustomed to lengthier walks, Nick felt justified in reining him in early today. After plodding through Kuzov's diaries all night, he wanted nothing more than to crawl into bed and close his eyes. The thought that Jordan would be waiting for him in that bed injected a spurt of energy into his step as he chased Pedro up the stairs.

Nick's face fell when he peeked around the bedroom door and found the duvet and pillows undisturbed. He had checked the kitchen and the guest room before he noticed the note propped beside the phone. Nick frowned over the hastily scribbled message. If only he had gotten home sooner, he could have driven her to the estate. He would have kept his distance, of course, out of Radetsky's sight, but at least Jordan would not have been alone.

As Nick put away the groceries and hung Jordan's restored Burberry in the closet, he tried to rationalize away his concerns. Radetsky was a distasteful man, but he had never demonstrated any homicidal tendencies. And if he wanted to harm Jordan, the last place he would choose to do it would be on his own property. Despite these logical arguments, Nick continued to worry. He started when the phone rang unexpectedly.

"Hello?" The slightly gruff American voice sounded uncertain as to how it should react to Nick's German greeting. "Uh, do you speak English?"

"Yes. May I help you?"

A relieved sigh carried over the line. "I don't know. Maybe I dialed wrong, but I'm trying to get in touch with a woman named Jordan MacKenzie."

"Jordan isn't here right now. Can I give her a message?"

"You can tell her that her dad called." The man cleared his throat. "Uh, listen, who am I talking with, anyway?"

"I'm Nick Rostov." Now it was Nick's turn to scramble for the right words. In the thirty seconds he had talked with Jordan's father, he had gained the distinct impression that Mr. MacKenzie would not deal kindly with anyone who trifled with his daughter, and Nick wanted to banish any suspicions on that count. "I'm a friend of Jordan's."

"Oh." Jordan's father hesitated, obviously mulling over this last bit of information. "Yeah, she said something about a friend who could take messages. Uh, you wouldn't happen to be the friend she's had me do all this . . . research for, would you?" he asked warily.

"Not exactly," Nick hedged. "But she did mention something about faxing a picture to you. She'll be very eager to hear what you have learned."

"Yeah, well, that's why I'm calling. I guess you can just tell her I'll express the profile to her overnight. But say—" Mr. MacKenzie broke off. "Would you kind of keep an eye on her, you know, look out for her?" he asked hesitantly.

"Of course I will," Nick promised. "Is there any reason she should worry about something?"

Jordan's father drew a deep breath rippling with tension. "I don't know. I mean, I have no idea what the hell's going on over there. First, my daughter sends me the spent casing from a .22-caliber handgun. Next thing I know, I've got a faxed picture of a guy who's wanted for the assassination of an African diplomat in Paris last year."

"The man in the picture is an assassin?"

"Actually, that's a pretty dignified term for him. I'd choose hired killer, if you asked me. Arvidsen—that's his name, Dirk Arvidsen—has been a soldier of fortune for most of his adult life. He made one stab at respectability a few years ago, working as a personal bodyguard for some Russian fellow in Paris, but he just couldn't stay on the right side of the law."

"You said Arvidsen worked for a Russian?" Nick interrupted.

"Uh-huh. Let's see if I can find the info." Mr. Mac-Kenzie's voice grew muffled for a second. "Yeah, here it is, says Arvidsen was the private bodyguard of Sergei Bestimynov, a Russian impresario now residing in Paris."

"Excuse me, Mr. MacKenzie, but I've just noticed the time. I'm afraid I'm late for an appointment." Nick fought to bridle the urgency creeping into his voice.

"I won't keep you, then. Don't forget to tell my little girl I called, okay?"

"I certainly won't," Nick promised before throwing the receiver onto the cradle and dashing for the door.

He pulled on his jacket as he ran down the stairs, taking the steps two and three at a time. *Arvidsen worked for a Russian émigré. That's how Radetsky found him.* The awful thought pounded inside his head like an incurable headache as he jumped into the Porsche and tore out of the garage.

Vienna's traffic could be crushing, but fortunately the brunt of rush hour was still in the offing. Nick drove as recklessly as he dared, cutting in front of and around anything that got in his way. When he reached the highway, he pulled into the fast lane and pressed the accelerator to the floor. On the winding rural road leading to the Radetsky estate, he reluctantly reduced his speed. If he spun out on a curve and broke his neck, he wouldn't be of much use to Jordan, he reminded himself. When he spotted the winged cherubs guarding the estate's gate, he swerved off the road and abruptly braked.

Cursing Radetsky, Nick stooped to slip beneath the chain securing the gate. His breath formed gray puffs of vapor in the cold air as he paused to take in his surroundings. There were car tracks on the driveway, some of which could have been made by Jordan's taxi, but someone had since locked the gate. *Trapping her.* Nick's mind progressed to the sinister conclusion. Whatever the case, he didn't need to let Radetsky or any of his watchdogs see him strolling up the driveway to the house. If he cut through the woods, he would have good cover for at least part of the way. As he got closer to the house, he could decide what to do next.

Nick had pushed into the forest only a short way when he was struck by the almost unearthly stillness of the place. Nothing stirred, not an animal or even a hardy winter bird. It was as if everything were hiding, waiting for something to happen. Suddenly a piercing crack cut through the cold, damp air. Nick froze for a split second, frantically looking around him. When the second shot rang out, he threw himself facedown onto the snowy ground.

SHE WAS BREATHING so heavily he would surely be able to hear her. Flattening herself behind the small stand of spruce, Jordan pressed the back of her hand against her mouth to muffle her nervous gulps of air. Where was he? She had not been able to place the direction from which the shots had been fired, had reacted on pure instinct when the first angry crack had shattered the quiet.

She glanced at Gudrun's outstretched hand, still visible from behind the bushes shrouding her corpse, and her stomach heaved. *Get control of yourself. There's nothing you can do for her now. All you can do is save yourself.* Jordan forced herself to look away, to concentrate on her own situation.

Her eyes darted among the trees, searching for a movement, a flash of clothing, any sign of the gunman's presence. At the same time she scoured the surrounding forest for a better place to hide. The evergreens that had seemed so dense earlier now appeared sparse and pathetically thin. *This is what it means to be the prey, to be hunted.* Her mind recoiled from the desolate, terrifying thought that threatened to paralyze her. So far she was unharmed. She could think at least as clearly as her opponent. As long as those two factors remained unchanged, she had a chance of escaping with her life.

The sound of icy snow crunching beneath heavy footsteps caused her to sink to her knees. Crouching as close to the evergreens as she could, Jordan watched a man moving stealthily among the trees. He was dressed in a hunter's green jacket and peaked Tyrolean cap, but it was the rifle he carried that caught her attention and held it with riveting force. She sucked in her breath when the man turned, and she recognized the bearded face of Count Boris Radetsky.

Radetsky frowned, his dark eyes narrowing against the white glare. From her meager hiding place, Jordan could tell that all his senses were on alert, attuned to the slightest motion or sound. *Please don't look this way. Please don't.* She repeated the irrational plea to herself, willing him not to turn yet another few inches.

Suddenly Radetsky's eyes widened, and he lifted his gun. Jordan could feel her heart hurling itself against her rib cage as she waited for him to turn toward her. Something in the distance had caught his attention, granting her a brief reprieve. Perhaps he hadn't seen her after all....

Another shot rang out, causing Jordan to flinch. She watched in horrified surprise as Radetsky dropped his weapon to press both hands against a red patch spreading across his right leg. Another shot, and he pitched forward into the snow.

A terror unlike any she had ever experienced seized Jordan, filled her veins with ice, turned her limbs to stone. There was another gunman. He had shot Radetsky. He had probably shot Gudrun. If she moved he would shoot her. If she stayed where she was he would find her—sooner or later.

Her only hope of evening the odds even slightly was to spot him first. If she could see him, at least she could anticipate his moves. Still not daring to move a muscle, Jordan looked in the direction Radetsky had glanced just before he had been hit.

The spreading branches of the tall evergreens provided a better cover than their slender trunks. Jordan had stared at the overlapping swaths of green needles for several seconds before she was able to pick out a small wooden platform constructed between the trees. It was a sportsman's roost, the kind favored by deer hunters. The darkly clad figure crouching near the edge of the platform was looking for other quarry, however. Jordan pressed her cold lips together as she recognized the hard, emotionless face from the photograph. Even more terrifying was the weapon he cradled against his hip, a high-powered rifle equipped with a scope.

He was scanning the landscape, his muscular body tensed for action. One false move from her and he would have her, easily, in his sights. The sound of something falling, a rock dislodging icy snow from branches, caused him to pivot and raise his gun. When a stone struck a tree in the opposite direction, he followed the sound with his gun. The gunman's body language revealed his heightened tension. Jordan could imagine his finger twitching on the trigger, eager to be done with business.

She gasped when she saw a man slipping between the trees to the gunman's rear. Nick! She recognized him just as he dropped out of sight behind a clump of brambles, only a few feet from the gunman's perch. What had prompted Nick to follow her to the estate? Had he heard the shots? He had surely thrown the stones that had distracted the gunman. Disordered thoughts raced wildly through Jordan's mind, but right now she didn't have the luxury to sort through them. Survival was the only thing demanding her attention.

No, Nick! Don't take the chance! Jordan watched, scarcely daring to breathe, as Nick crept from his hiding place and slipped beneath the hunter's platform. The gunman couldn't see him, Jordan knew—as long as Nick remained still. *Oh, my God! Be careful!* Jordan's eyes followed Nick's lean figure as he silently rose and then braced his shoulder against one leg of the hunter's platform. She mentally counted, uniting her strength with his across the distance. She could feel him poise himself, tense and then heave.

The flimsy structure's timbers creaked as it tipped to one side. With a splintering crash the platform broke in two, one side falling with the uprooted leg, the other dangling pathetically from the two legs that remained upright. The gunman fell on his back with a muffled thud. Before he could regain his senses or his gun, Nick leaped onto him. The two men rolled through the snow, locked in a fierce clench. Nick managed to throw a punch that connected solidly with his opponent's jaw, but the gunman recovered all too quickly. With a loud grunt he crashed his fist into Nick's temple and then shoved him backward against a stout pine. The impact of the blow had stunned Nick and he sank to his knees.

As the gunman grabbed his rifle, Jordan sprang to her feet. In horrific slow motion, she watched the long barrel rise, then level, saw it cut through the air, aim at Nick's head.

"No!" Raw fear tore the word from Jordan's chest.

The gunman swiveled. For an infinite second they stared at each other, eyes following the rifle barrel that connected them across the distance in a hideous rite. When the shot wailed through the air, Jordan closed her eyes, embracing the darkness. When she opened them again, she saw the gunman gape in uncomprehending amazement, stagger a few feet, and then fall backward.

Jordan turned to see Count Boris Radetsky slowly lower his gun.

Chapter Thirteen

Jordan pulled the bright woolen afghan close around her shoulders and huddled deeper into the corner of the sofa. Although Nick's apartment was comfortably warm, she had been unable to shake the chill that had clung to her bones since the horrifying incident at Radetsky's estate earlier that afternoon.

Nick leaned over the back of the sofa and gently lifted her hands, cupping them around a cup of hot spiced tea. He held her shoulders a moment, as if he needed to reassure himself that she was really there. When he slid onto the sofa beside her, she snuggled close to him, welcoming his embrace.

"Radetsky saved my life." Jordan repeated the sentence, still trying to get used to the startling turn of events.

"He saved mine, too," Nick reminded her. "To think that when I raced out to his estate I was convinced that he had hired Arvidsen to kill you!"

"We can discard that suspicion, once and for all. Poor man, the police said he would probably be in intensive care for some time. It seems the second bullet narrowly missed his heart. It's a miracle he was able to shoulder his gun and fire." Jordan took a careful sip of the scalding tea.

"I've never thought of Boris as a hero, but he certainly proved his mettle today," Nick conceded. "Lucky for both of us that he was out hunting when Arvidsen shot Gudrun. If he hadn't heard her scream—" He broke off, unwilling or unable to further explore the awful thought.

"To think that Gudrun learned about the appointment from Bertie Waxx!" Jordan shook her head, grappling with the bizarre twist of fate. "I would never have made that connection if the police hadn't found her calendar in her handbag, outlining the information Waxx had given her."

"I doubt if Bertie is going to be intercepting any more messages at your hotel. With the police on his back, we're probably rid of him for good." Nick's arm tightened around Jordan, pulling her closer to him. "I never wanted to see Gudrun come to this kind of fate, but I shudder to think what might have happened if Waxx hadn't given her the tip, and you had kept the bogus appointment."

Jordan frowned into the steam rising from the cup of tea. "It's clear Radetsky had nothing to do with the appointment. So who phoned Molly, posed as Radetsky and set things up to lure me out to the estate?"

"It could have been Arvidsen. Or whoever hired him." Nick thought for a moment. "The person had to have known about your previous efforts to contact Radetsky. He would have wanted to make it appear that Radetsky was the murderer, so he chose the estate as a meeting place. 'Why' is another question altogether."

"If only Arvidsen had lived to talk!" Jordan shook her head, arranging the afghan to cover her knees and Nick's.

"Maybe the police will be able to uncover something about Arvidsen's past that will link him with the person behind all this. Then again, I was so sure the Russian connection was what we had been looking for. All the pieces seemed to fit. Radetsky had learned you had some special information about the music box. He feared you either already possessed the music box or had a very good chance of finding it, so he began to worry about the implications of its recovery. Grandmama's right of inheritance could be substantiated, and he could lose a sizable portion of his fortune. Radetsky decided to stop you, at all costs. He would have learned about Arvidsen's capabilities from his fellow countryman in Paris. Many wealthy people have bodyguards, so he could have easily concealed his real intentions from everyone but Arvidsen, who had no scruples anyway. The scheme seemed so credible, and then, poof, my entire clever construction went up in a puff of gunsmoke, so to speak."

Jordan cradled the teacup in her chapped palms, not speaking for several minutes. "You know, Nick, I'm not so sure we should toss out your whole explanation. Boris is innocent, to be sure. But what if we were to keep the plan you just outlined and substitute someone else's name and motivation for his?"

Nick chuckled softly. "I'm all for considering things from every angle, but frankly I don't have any names or motives that spring to mind once we've eliminated Boris Radetsky. Do you?"

"I'm not sure." Jordan chose her words carefully. "The longer I think about all of this, the more I want to see a relationship between everything we've been investigating—the fate of the Radetsky music box, Kitty Ridgewood's heritage, the identity of your great-grandmother's betrayer."

"I agree. It does somehow seem logical that all those things are intrinsically connected. But what is the link?"

Jordan twisted on the sofa to face Nick. "I'm not sure yet, but I'd like a chance to talk with your grandmother."

"BUT YOU MUST HAVE SOME refreshments!" Nick's grandmother clasped both Jordan and Nick by the elbows as if to cut off their escape from her hospitality. "Sonja!" she called to the housekeeper as she led her two docile captives to the cozy fireside. "Please prepare coffee and some cakes for my guests." She seated them on the brocade settee, directing each into place as if they were children. Then she stepped back and beamed at them. "I am so happy that you have brightened my morning with a visit!" She gave Jordan an especially warm smile. "I have been telling Nick that I wanted to meet you, Miss MacKenzie. I am glad he has finally granted my wish."

Jordan glanced at Nick, who was tolerating the gentle gibe with good grace. "I'm very pleased to meet you, too," she said.

Privately, however, Jordan couldn't help but agree with his grandmother's reproving comment. If Nick had introduced them sooner, he would have saved her a lot of trouble, for she would have immediately recognized Natalie Gallinin as Kitty's relation.

As Nick's grandmother served coffee and chatted with her two guests, Jordan was struck by her close physical resemblance to Kitty. Perhaps when the two sisters were reunited, Kitty would acquire some of Natalie's gift for creating a pleasant, soothing atmosphere. At the very least, Kitty could find relief from her high-pressured life in her sister's gracious home. Jordan was enjoying the elderly woman's hospitality so much, she dreaded introducing a somber note to the gathering. As was appropriate, she waited for Nick to broach the subject of his grandmother's girlhood memories.

"Grandmama, I need to ask you some very important questions." He hesitated, then rose from the settee and seated himself on the hassock next to her chair. Nick took his grandmother's hands in his. "About the last days in Russia."

Natalie Gallinin said nothing, but Jordan noticed a faint throb beneath the fine skin of her temple.

Nick's voice dropped to a near whisper. "I know how painful these memories are for you, but it is very, very important."

His grandmother swallowed and then straightened her long, graceful ballerina's neck. "What do you wish to know, Nick?"

"What do you recall from the day you were to leave Kiev? I want to know as much as you can remember."

Natalie sighed, looking down at the two sets of hands clasped on her knee. "Mama woke us that morning and dressed us herself. The maid had long since disappeared, like so many of the other people and things from our earlier life. I remember what Mama was wearing, a lovely black silk dress with a high collar. She used to wear a gold lavaliere with that dress, but I suppose that by then she had already sold it with the rest of her jewelry. She said we were to begin a long journey that day, that we must be the brave girls that our papa would be proud of. She packed only a few of our belongings, for we could not carry much, and she needed to bring food along. There was so little to eat in those days." Natalie's voice caught, and she paused to compose herself.

"Mama gave us some bread for breakfast and then told me to look after Katya while she took care of some matters. She was gone an awfully long time, or so it seemed to me. Katya had become very fretful by the time she returned. Mama usually humored our moods, but not that day. She looked very worried, kept walking around the little room we all three shared. Finally, she knelt beside me and took me by the shoulders. Her face was so pale and serious, it frightened me. It was then she told me that we would be traveling without her. I started to cry, and I could see that Mama wanted to do the same. But she only held me for a bit. She promised that we would be safe and that we would all be together again very soon."

"Did you leave that day?" Nick asked gently.

His grandmother's silvery-white head nodded slowly. "Yes. Kuzov still had a sleigh, a wonder for the hard times, I assure you. Rachmanova came with the driver, and Mama and she began to pack our travel provisions into the sleigh. It was when they tried to tuck us in among the parcels of clothes and food that Katya started to wail. I have never heard a child cry in that way, before or since. She clung to Mama and would not let go. Finally, Mama relented and let Katya stay with her.

"I was so hurt and scared. I wanted to stay, too, but Mama gave Katya to Rachmanova for a moment and then took me aside. She told me she needed my help if everything was to go as planned. Now I realize she was only trying to soothe my feelings, distract me. I went with her back to the apartment and watched her dig beneath her cot. That is where she had hidden the music box. I held a blanket open and she wrapped the music box in it. I will never forget what she said. 'Natasha, your father's gift to me will buy our freedom, and that is the most precious gift of all.'"

A single tear trickled down Natalie's face, leaving a glistening path on the pale, dry skin. "Everything seemed to happen very quickly after that. I kissed Mama and Katya and then I was bundled into the sleigh. I have no idea how far we traveled. Children have no concept of distance as adults do. I do know it was very dark by the time we stopped. I was half-asleep—I had long since cried myself out—and I only vaguely remember a peasant woman carrying me into a place that smelled of dampness and animals. I must have spent the night in the barn, for when I awoke the next morning Rachmanova was there. I asked her about Mama and Katya, but she only said they would be coming later. But they never did."

Natalie began to cry softly, her slender shoulders shaking with each sob. "I never saw them again. Never."

Nick lifted his grandmother's hands and pressed them to his lips. When he spoke, his voice was choked with emotion. "Grandmama, you will soon see Katya."

Natalie blinked through her tears and then frowned at her grandson. "Katya? What can you possibly mean, Nicholas? Katya is dead!"

Nick shook his head, his mouth pulling shakily into a smile. "No, Grandmama, she isn't. By some great miracle she survived and now lives in California. She doesn't remember much from her childhood, but she hired Jordan to trace her family." When he glanced at Jordan, she noticed that his eyes were glistening. "Jordan found you, too."

Jordan wasn't sure Nick's grandmother had heard much of his explanation, for she could only stare in open-mouthed disbelief and repeat, "Katya is alive?"

Nick gave his grandmother a spontaneous hug. "Yes, she is, and she's going to be here within a few days."

Natalie was so delirious with joy she began to laugh and cry all at once. During the emotionally charged conversation between Nick and his grandmother, Jordan had tried to remain as inconspicuous as possible. She had felt slightly intrusive witnessing such a sensitive scene. At the same time, she had been deeply moved by Natalie's sad story and her ecstatic reaction to Nick's revelation about Kitty. Now Jordan could no longer restrain herself. Pushing up from the settee, she reached out to give the retired ballerina's hand a warm squeeze.

"I owe you so much, Miss MacKenzie. How can I ever thank you?" Natalie's hand trembled as it closed over Jordan's.

Jordan shook her head, not trusting her own voice to speak.

"Grandmama, there are still a few things that aren't clear in my mind about your journey from Russia." Nick sounded far less reluctant to discuss the subject now that the happy news about Katya had been revealed. "This coachman who drove you to the peasant's home, do you remember anything about him?"

Nick's grandmother thought for a few seconds. "Not much, really. He seemed like a very kind man. During the drive he sang to me in a language I didn't understand and that helped me stop crying. I don't think Maria Rachmanova thought much of him, however."

"Why do you say that?" Nick asked.

"I remember hearing a terrible argument between them after she arrived the next day. I didn't understand any of it, really, but I had never heard a servant defy a lady in that way. Rachmanova kept insisting that he take us somewhere, but he was determined to drive back to Kiev for some reason."

"To pick up your mother and Katya?" Jordan suggested.

"I don't know," Natalie replied. "Whatever the disagreement was about, the coachman got his way. He simply climbed into the sleigh and left. Rachmanova was furious, but she managed to pay one of the peasants to take us farther in his cart. The poor coachman, his defiance was to be his undoing."

"Why do you say that, Grandmama?"

Nick's grandmother shook her head sadly. "He was apparently overtaken by the same band of Bolshevik soldiers that captured Mama and Katya. We had been in Vienna for several months, living with Kuzov, when the news reached us. Until this day I thought they had all been killed.''

Jordan swallowed carefully before she posed her next question. "How did Kuzov react to the news?''

Natalie's brilliant blue eyes gazed into the fire. "He was heartbroken, I believe. Kuzov was a difficult man, but he treasured Mama. He had lost both a young friend and the dancer he had envisioned to carry on his work. But like me, he had someone to fall back on.''

Jordan's mouth went dry. "Who?''

Nick's grandmother looked up at her in surprise. "Why, Maria Rachmanova, of course.''

SEATED ON THE HEAVY velvet sofa with an antique porcelain cup balanced on her palm, Jordan felt as if she had stepped into a museum's vitrine. Even the smell pervading Maria Rachmanova's apartment seemed preserved from another era, a thick mélange of heavy fabric, incense and beeswax. The woman herself reminded Jordan of a costumed mannequin, with her floor-length tunic embroidered in the traditional Russian fashion and a turban crowning her white head.

"Isn't that incredibly marvelous news about Grandmama's sister?'' Daria commented, reaching to pass a crystal plate of sweets around the coffee table.

Rachmanova smiled slightly and nodded. "Yes, it is almost unbelievable. You are quite sure she is the lost sister?'' She fixed Jordan with an unflinching stare that demanded an answer.

"Absolutely,'' Jordan replied without hesitation.

"After all we've been through—and I include the awful shooting incident this week—it will be a real relief to have everything resolved,'' Nick remarked, picking a lump of sugar from the bowl with tiny silver tongs. "From what the police told me this morning, they plan to make an arrest very soon, perhaps before the week is out."

"They know who hired Arvidsen to try to kill me?" Jordan asked, carefully stirring the fragrant Russian tea.

Nick shrugged as he dropped the sugar lump into his tea. "You know how the police are. They won't give you any specifics. But they insisted that they had a conclusive lead. It seems they found some incriminating notes on Arvidsen, so in a way the dead do speak." He smiled at the little assembly, letting his eyes linger a bit longer on Rachmanova.

The aged ballerina's face remained impassive.

"I'm glad you don't have anything to be afraid of now," Daria said, reaching to give Jordan's arm a gentle pat.

"So am I," Jordan concurred heartily. "This is the first evening in a long time when I've felt safe going out after dark. Speaking of which, I fear we should be leaving if we want to catch that early show." She smiled at Nick.

Nick nodded agreement before finishing his tea. "I'm afraid Jordan is right, Maria Rachmanova. We do appreciate your having us for tea this afternoon. I've wanted her to meet you for so long. You've played such an important role in my family's history."

"It was my pleasure, Nicolai Rostovitch. Miss MacKenzie." Rachmanova's unblinking gaze shifted to Jordan for a moment. She moved to rise, but Daria quickly motioned her back into her seat.

"I'll show Nick and Jordan to the door for you, Maria Rachmanova," she offered.

After another round of thank-yous, Nick and Jordan followed Daria out of the sitting room to the foyer. They exchanged anxious looks as Daria opened the closet door and swept aside a cape and a Persian lamb coat. Without speaking, Nick and Jordan squeezed themselves into the closet. Daria gave them a thumbs-up before closing the door. From the dark cubicle, they heard her shut the front door soundly behind her. Several minutes later the door opened and closed once more.

Jordan took a slow, cautious breath, fighting back the claustrophobia creeping up on her. They had plenty of oxygen, she told herself, and who better to be cooped up with inside a closet than Nick. As if he had read her thoughts, Nick found her hand and gave it a firm squeeze.

After a brief period of time they heard Daria and Maria Rachmanova speaking Russian in the foyer, parting company for the evening. The door closed after Daria and then Rachmanova's almost inaudible steps disappeared into some other part of the apartment.

It could be a very long night, Jordan reflected. Their plan had hinged on the supposition that Rachmanova would act on Nick's casual account of the phony police story and the imminent arrest. There was a chance, of course, that she would do nothing. There was also the possibility that she wasn't the guilty party at all, in which case they would have to slip out of the apartment unnoticed before Rachmanova rose the next morning. In the meantime, Jordan tried to ignore her nervous legs and the irritating fact that she couldn't risk whispering to Nick.

She had let her mind drift to the still-thorny problem of finding Kitty Ridgewood and defusing her rage when Nick gave her sleeve a quick tug. Jordan was instantly alert to the sound of soft footsteps in the adjacent sitting room. Rachmanova was moving around at a surprisingly quick clip for one her age. Jordan could hear the drawers and cupboards being opened and closed in haste. When the steps retreated to another room in the apartment, Nick took her hand. With stealth worthy of a cat burglar, he silently eased open the closet door. After quickly checking the foyer, he led the way on tiptoe into the sitting room. Nick and Jordan crouched behind the camelback sofa where they could observe the foyer without being seen.

When Rachmanova emerged from the bedroom, she had changed into a charcoal gray suit tailored in the style of a half-century earlier. In one hand she carried an expensive leather handbag, in the other an alligator-skin valise. She moved anxiously, her schooled dancer's poise overridden by nerves. In the foyer she paused to pull the Persian lamb coat from the closet. She was struggling into the coat when Nick and Jordan appeared from behind the sofa.

"Going on a trip at this late hour, Maria Rachmanova?" Nick asked with studied casualness.

"What are you doing here? How dare you break into my apartment!" The former prima donna's eyes blazed with an anger that did not quite conceal their fear.

"Break in, did you say? Why don't you call the police, then?" Nick took a step toward Rachmanova, and she backed away from him.

"I will not have this in my own home!" Rachmanova sputtered.

"Answer my question, Maria Rachmanova. Why don't you call the police?" Nick repeated.

"You hired Arvidsen to kill me, didn't you?" Jordan put in, taking advantage of the woman's obvious confusion.

"I never told him to kill you or anyone," Rachmanova blurted out and then pressed her hand against her mouth. Her fearful eyes darted around the dimly lighted foyer. "I only wanted things to be as they always had. That is all."

"With Grandmama believing that you were her friend when you were really her mother's betrayer," Nick interjected bitterly.

"I never meant Olga any harm. Truly I did not. I only wanted her to stay behind in Russia." She sank to her knees, clutching the valise to her chest. "I did not want Olga to die. I did not," she insisted in a voice that had become a keening wail.

"But Olga did die. Only by the sheerest trick of fate did Katya survive. And Jordan would have been killed if Arvidsen's last plot had succeeded. All because of your damnable ambition," Nick reminded her without mercy.

Rachmanova sucked in her breath, struggling for her moorings. She seemed to be staring at some undefined spot in the distance. "Kuzov did not understand, he did not *see*. It was always Olga, Olga, *Olga*. He did not appreciate me, all I was willing to do for him. I would have given my life for him. He did not appreciate me." Her words dissolved into an incoherent gasping that eerily resembled laughter.

Stooping over Rachmanova, Nick took the valise from her grasp and clasped her arm. As he attempted to pull her to her feet, the valise fell open. Standing beside the broken figure of Maria Rachmanova, Nick and Jordan looked down into the valise at the Radetsky music box.

Chapter Fourteen

Jordan clamped one hand on Pedro's scruffy neck, holding him at bay while Nick climbed behind the wheel of the Porsche.

"Trust me. The trunk may be small, but nothing in your garment bag is going to be irreparably wrinkled," he assured her as he switched on the ignition.

"After the abuse my clothes have taken during the past couple of weeks, a few wrinkles will hardly be noticeable," Jordan remarked dryly. She glanced out the window. "I can hardly believe it's safe to go back to the hotel. On second thought, with Kitty there it may not be."

Nick chuckled, glancing away from the street for a split second to smile at Jordan. "Relax. The moment you tell her about finding Grandmama, those idiotic tabloid stories are suddenly going to seem very trivial."

"If I get a chance to tell her," Jordan put in.

If the phone conversation she had had with the Richtsberger Hof's concierge was any indication, Kitty Ridgewood had blown into town like a hurricane, her fury picking up steam as she homed in on Jordan. The poor man had sounded profoundly relieved when Jordan had phoned, as if his life had depended on her surfacing at that precise moment. Jordan could easily guess why after he had described how Miss Katharine Ridge had reserved a suite and then ordered him to find Jordan MacKenzie or else.

"It's funny how much alike siblings can be in some ways and how extraordinarily different in others," Jordan mused. "I was quite impressed with how little bitterness your grandmother harbors toward Rachmanova, considering the ills she brought upon your family."

"Seeing Katya again is all that Grandmama can think about right now. Then, too, Rachmanova is such a pathetic person. She was able to cause so much misery, and yet I do believe she honestly never meant to harm anyone. She let her obsession with Kuzov poison her judgment, drive her into a dream world of her own creation."

"I suspect the courts will take her delusional state of mind into consideration," Jordan commented.

"You know, I've always felt a little strange around her, as if I were talking with someone who never quite lived in the present. Now I realize what a sick woman she really is." When he braked for a red light, Nick took the chance to cast an admiring look at Jordan. "I always thought I was a pretty clever detective, at least where artworks are concerned, but I guess it takes someone who's accustomed to tracking down *people* to make the kind of connection you did with Rachmanova and Arvidsen."

Jordan shrugged modestly. "The profile Dad sent us said that Arvidsen worked for a Russian impresario in Paris, someone who not only shared Rachmanova's background but also her links with the theater and music. It seemed entirely plausible that she could have known the man and asked him to recommend a bodyguard. Because of her close association with Daria and your grandmother, Rachmanova had a convenient listening post. She always knew my travel plans and could direct Arvidsen. The clues that really cinched it for me, however, were all those nasty things Kuzov said about her in his journal. He considered her inferior to Olga and made no secret of it. And that gave Rachmanova a motive both to betray Olga and later to take measures to conceal her treachery forever."

"To think she had the music box all these years that Grandmama was struggling to prove her legitimacy!" Nick shook his head, frowning as he angled the car into the curb in front of the Richtsberger Hof.

"Once you've begun to live a lie, it's very difficult to face the truth," Jordan said philosophically. "Speaking of the moment of truth, wish me luck." She grimaced out the window at the hotel's staid facade.

Nick turned on his emergency lights and then jumped out of the car to fetch Jordan's luggage. "Bark if you see a policeman," he told Pedro as he followed Jordan into the hotel lobby.

The concierge's eyes widened in relief when he saw her. "Miss MacKenzie, how fortunate that you should arrive just now. Miss Ridge was asking about you only a few minutes ago." He hastened to retrieve Jordan's room key from its hook behind the desk. Then he hesitated, his eyes dilating yet another centimeter as he looked past Jordan to the elevator alcove.

Jordan turned to see Kitty Ridgewood striding across the lobby in her direction. What on earth did you say to someone who looked as if she were ready to strangle you with her bare hands? Somehow "Hi, Miss Ridgewood! How nice to see you!" didn't seem quite appropriate.

For better or for worse, Kitty relieved Jordan of her dilemma by speaking first. "So there you are!" she hissed through clenched teeth. "After flying all over Europe at my expense, cavorting with unsavory types, giving interviews to tabloid scum, you've finally come back to Vienna!"

"I can explain everything, Miss Ridgewood," Jordan began, but Kitty snapped her off.

"Yes, you will, Miss MacKenzie, to me and to my attorneys. I've been advised that I have grounds for a lawsuit, and believe me, I intend to exercise them. How could you drag my name into the papers—the *tabloids*—after I pleaded with you to keep my identity confidential?"

"That was an unfortunate accident. If you will just give me a chance to explain—"

"An accident?" Kitty sounded supremely offended. "And I suppose carrying on with this playboy was an accident, too?"

From the corner of her eye Jordan glanced at Nick, who had been watching the exchange from a safe distance. Before she could catch his reaction to the playboy moniker, however, Kitty launched a fresh assault. Jordan realized that if anyone was going to restore sanity, it would have to be her.

"I've never been so furious in my life—" Kitty began.

"Be quiet, Kitty!" Jordan ordered abruptly.

The bright blue eyes blinked in stunned surprise. "What did you say?"

"I said, be quiet. And if you don't do as I say I'm going to make a scene in this hotel lobby that will make those tabloid stories look like nothing in comparison."

"What do you mean—"

"I mean I'm going to announce your name so that people on the street can hear it, yell like a maniac, wave my arms, use profanity like *you've* never heard before, and generally attract as much attention as I can to *us*. Now do you understand?"

Kitty glared at Jordan, but for the first time she didn't try to say anything.

"That's more like it," Jordan told her. "Now you're going to come with me, and we're going to take a little ride in a taxi."

"You can't just order me—" Kitty started, lapsing back into her old habits.

Jordan lifted a cautionary finger. "Uh! Remember, yelling *and* loud profanity."

Mercifully, the threat was enough to persuade Kitty to follow Jordan out of the hotel to the taxi stand. After ushering her into the back of a Mercedes sedan, Jordan beckoned to Nick. He looked slightly intimidated as he joined her on the curb.

"Is your grandmother home now?" she asked him.

"She should be," Nick replied a little meekly.

"Good. We're going to deliver Katya to her. Please follow us. I may need your help," she added before ducking into the cab.

Jordan pretended not to notice Kitty, who was seething in the corner of the back seat, as she gave the cabbie directions. When she sat back against the seat, she regarded her unwilling traveling companion with a nod and a bemused smile. Amusement at her expense, however innocent, was not something Kitty accepted readily, and she prepared to retaliate.

"You know this is kidnapping, I suppose," she muttered, tight-lipped with rage.

Jordan nodded slightly toward the unwitting cab driver and then pressed her fingers to her lips. "Let's not embarrass this poor man, okay?"

The warning was enough to subdue Kitty into a sullen silence for the remainder of the drive. When they arrived at

Natalie Gallinin's elegant apartment building, Jordan reassured herself that she only need coerce her client a few steps farther and then the natural sequence of events would take over.

As soon as the cabbie braked, Kitty unlatched the door and climbed out. For an anxious moment Jordan feared that she might bolt, but curiosity seemed to have temporarily overridden her impulse to resist. She followed Jordan without protest into the building. Jordan caught her elbow gently, pulling her to a halt beside the elevator.

"Let's wait a minute for Nick," she suggested in a gentler tone than she had employed in the cab.

"Who on earth is Nick?" Kitty demanded, frowning at the handsome, dark-haired man pushing through the front door.

Jordan couldn't hold back any longer. As she guided Kitty into the elevator car, with Nick pulling the gate closed behind them, she smiled warmly at her. "Your greatnephew."

For several seconds Kitty's well-preserved face registered an astounding spectrum of human emotions. When she finally managed to recover her voice, she sounded shaken to her foundation. "He's . . . he's my family," she managed to get out, pointing awkwardly at Nick.

"Part of it," Jordan told her.

As the elevator shuddered to a stop, Nick and Jordan each took one of Kitty's arms and guided the dazed woman to Natalie Gallinin's apartment. Although Jordan had successfully constructed hundreds of family trees in her career, she had never experienced the peculiar twinge in her throat that she felt when she pressed the buzzer beside Natalie's door.

As the door opened, Nick and Jordan stepped back.

Nick's grandmother stood stock-still, as if she were afraid to move and break the precious dream surrounding her. "Katya?"

Kitty's lips silently formed the word, probing its flavor and the long-forgotten memories it awakened. For a long moment she could only stare at her sister, mesmerized by the flesh-and-blood image of herself she found standing before her. "You're...you're my sister?" Her normally commanding voice captured all the wonder of a child experiencing some marvelous aspect of the world for the first time.

"Your Natasha," Natalie supplied. She opened her arms, beckoning to her long-lost sister.

"Natasha," Kitty repeated. Then she fell into her sister's embrace, hugging her as if she could make up for those countless sad, lonely years they had been apart.

As the sisters walked arm in arm into the apartment, Nick and Jordan hung back at the door. The time was so intensely precious, belonging so exclusively to Natalie and Kitty, neither of them had any desire to intrude on it. From the foyer they watched Natalie take Kitty's hand as if she were still a very little sister and lead her to the polished mahogany sideboard. Smiling through her tears, Natalie rested one hand on the table, not far from the music box, just as she had for the camera long ago. Kitty brushed her wet cheek with her hand before she delicately touched the tiny horseman crowning the black Fabergé egg. Her lips trembled as she carefully twisted the silver figure. Joining hands across the table, the sisters smiled at each other as the sweet music transported them back to a time long, long ago.

"YOU'LL CALL ME AS SOON as you've checked into a hotel in Edinburgh. Promise?" Having lost track of her boss once, Molly Bledsoe was not taking any chances.

"I promise, Molly." Jordan cradled the receiver beneath her chin while her hands took a quick inventory of the credit cards, passport and plane tickets bulging from her daily planner.

"What time is your flight?" Molly persisted, determined to track Jordan's route as closely as possible.

"Six-something in the morning. I have a three-hour lay-over in London before connecting to Scotland."

"Grim," Molly sympathized. "All rightee, I'll put to-gether a copy of the Bellingrath file and express it to you as soon as I have an address. I must say, though, all of these cases seem pretty dull after the one you just completed."

They certainly do, Jordan reflected after she had bidden Molly goodbye and hung up the phone. Never had her in-vestigations yielded the spectacular results nor precipitated the dramatic changes as those Kitty Ridgewood's case had produced. Not only had her efforts reunited two sisters torn apart by a brutal revolution, she had helped recover a lost art treasure and established a woman's legitimacy. She had even uncovered evidence that might prove Nick Rostov to be the rightful heir to the Radetsky title.

Nick might be a count. Every time the thought surfaced in Jordan's mind, which was frequently enough these days, she had no idea what to do with it. Counts lived in palatial residences like Boris Radetsky. They attended glittering balls with their pedigreed friends, raced cars, got themselves photographed at glamorous places like Gstaad and Cannes. Nick was urbane enough to handle himself well in any sit-uation, but for some reason Jordan was having a difficult time picturing him in the aristocratic world she had con-jured.

It isn't Nick who doesn't fit. It's you. The thought stung her, intensified the strangely disjointed feeling that had shadowed her since the conclusion of Kitty Ridgewood's investigation. Such feelings were to be expected to some degree, she took pains to remind herself. After spending so much time working closely with Nick—living in his apartment for almost a week—she would naturally miss his company when circumstances drew them apart. Even in her weakest moment, she could not envy him the time he now spent with his family, the pleasure he derived from seeing his grandmother and her sister reunited after their long separation. And Nick had made an effort not to exclude her. He had even offered to drive her to the airport, an act of sheer gallantry considering the uncivilized departure time.

Still, as Jordan packed the few items remaining on the dresser, she felt an odd, gnawing longing. Something more than "it's been great" and "let's keep in touch" needed to be said, but Jordan was at a loss to pinpoint the exact words. If she had hoped to find them by the time Nick picked her up at four-thirty the following morning, she was sadly disappointed.

Perhaps it was only the early hour, but neither of them seemed able to find the easy plateau on which their conversations normally took place. At the airport they both invested a lot of attention in checking bags and negotiating metal detectors, far more than was needed to perform such routine functions. When her flight's boarding was announced over the loudspeaker, a mild panic seized Jordan. As they rushed to the gate, she struggled to organize her scrambled thoughts.

I care about you, Nick, and I'm going to miss you a lot. No, that wasn't what she really meant. *You're very special to me, so special I want us to stay in touch.* Stay in touch? That was the sort of thing you said to college roommates at graduation. *Let's not just say goodbye.* But rather? *I love you.* Something grabbed at Jordan's throat with such intensity she almost choked.

At the gate she turned to face him. Even in the ghastly air terminal light he looked smashingly handsome. His eyes were a bit weary from lack of sleep, but the characteristic spark of humor was still detectable. Here was her chance, her last chance, to tell him what she had been thinking.

"Well, I guess I'd better scoot before they give my seat to someone else." She shifted her briefcase to her other hand. "Let's definitely keep in touch."

"Definitely." Nick nodded in agreement. "Uh, say, if you have a little free time on your hands in Scotland, give me a call. Maybe I'll be able to get away for a day or so." He shoved his hands into his pockets. "I could catch up with you and we could, I don't know, go find the Loch Ness monster."

Jordan laughed, a little too loudly. "That sounds like fun." She glanced down the corridor leading onto the plane. "Okay, take care of yourself."

"You, too." Nick stooped to brush her lips with a light kiss. He waved as she trotted into the corridor.

Definitely keep in touch. She had really said that, hadn't she? Worse still, he had echoed her words. Jordan continued to ponder that last sobering realization as the aircraft carried her over the Alps and across the Channel. At least she hadn't made a complete fool of herself by declaring her love for someone who only wanted to keep in touch. Somehow that small consolation failed to banish the melancholy burdening her as she plodded through Gatwick Airport in search of a quiet spot to while away the next few hours.

Nick might be more realistic than she. He might be more willing to accept the differences between the worlds they each occupied, more ready to admit that a long-term relationship was simply not in the stars. She herself could acknowledge those truths on an intellectual level. That her mind could resign itself to reality, however, had no bearing at all on the inclination of her heart. She had fallen in love with Nick in a short time, but Jordan guessed it would take much longer to undo that sad condition.

Jordan was slumped in an uncomfortable plastic chair, trying to summon interest in the intricacies of the McDowell clan, when a shadow fell across her lap. Looking up, she blinked, at first not believing the tall, rangy apparition that had materialized before her eyes.

"Nick?"

He shook his head. "That's not your line, Jordan. You always say, 'What are you doing here?' "

Jordan began to smile. "Okay. What *are* you doing here?"

"What I always do. I followed you." Not breaking the gaze connecting them, Nick reached for her hands, pulling her to her feet.

The briefcase slid to the floor, scattering McDowellabilia across the carpet, but Jordan didn't even look at it. At that moment her eyes could focus only on the wonderful man smiling down at her.

"This is the last time I'm going to chase you down, Jordan MacKenzie," Nick warned her. "From now on, we've got to do better than this."

"Any suggestions how we go about that?" Jordan felt herself easing up onto her toes.

"I've given it some thought, and the best idea I've come up with is marriage. What about you?" His mouth hovered over hers, teasing her with its closeness.

"That's not only the most appropriate idea, it's also the most wonderful one I can think of." Jordan grazed Nick's lips with a short kiss. "So wonderful, in fact, that it's positively music to my ears."

Nick pulled Jordan even closer, and their embrace melted into a kiss that went unbroken even as a small child, led by her parents, brushed by holding a tiny music box playing the sweetest lullaby Jordan had ever heard.

COMING NEXT MONTH

#193 TRIAL BY FIRE by Rebecca York
43 Light Street
Though the Graveyard Murders happened in modern
Baltimore, they were linked to an old evil—black magic.
Herbalist Sabrina Barkley knew little about witchcraft, but
she and assistant D.A. Dan Cassidy feared their meeting in
the investigation was fated. The murders opened a door to
the past—a door they'd have to go through the fires of hell
to close. If they *ever* could...

#194 NOWHERE TO HIDE by Jasmine Cresswell
The only survivor of a fiery plane crash, Alyssa Humphrey
was lucky to be alive. But she'd lost her memory. The
Denver mansion no longer seemed like home; her fiancé
seemed a stranger. In a world where everything was
unfamiliar, financial advisor Adam Stryker was the only
man she could trust. Or was he?

#195 WHISTLEBLOWER by Tess Gerritsen
On a foggy highway, Cathy Weaver's headlights lit the
shadowy form of a man too late to avoid hitting him.
Victor Holland had the eyes of a hunted man—and a story
that sounded like the paranoid ravings of a madman. But
his kisses tasted of desperation and desire. Was he a man in
danger...or a dangerous man?

#196 CHILD'S PLAY by Bethany Campbell
Thornton Fuller was a young man with a child's mind who
knew a secret about death. When he told the children of
Rachel Dale and Jay Malone, Thornton knew he was in
trouble. Summer residents Rachel and Jay thought evil
couldn't touch idyllic Black Bear Lake. But they were
wrong. Even small towns had their demons....

HARLEQUIN®
AMERICAN ❖ ROMANCE®

MAKE YOUR GREAT ESCAPE...

Flee over icy passes to a remote mountain hideaway while Rafe pursues you.

Sail the high seas as a stowaway and get ready for an island tryst with a modern-day pirate.

Step from crashing waves into the arms of the right man... the Sand Man, and let him inspire your dreams.

Battle for control of a fancy ranch with a very determined and extremely sexy cowboy who entices you to fight dirty.

The American Romance you know has changed. Starting next month, step into the new world of American Romance—and test your mettle with our bold, brash, brave American men. They'll take you on rousing adventures that will make their dreams—and yours—come true.

See how we've changed. Join us next month for:

#453 **RAFE'S REVENGE** by Anne Stuart
#454 **ONCE UPON A TIME** by Rebecca Flanders
#455 **SAND MAN** by Tracy Hughes
#456 **THE COWBOY'S MISTRESS**
        by Cathy Gillen Thacker

The *new* American Romance—
Love has never been so exciting!

HANEW

OFFICIAL RULES • MILLION DOLLAR MATCH 3 SWEEPSTAKES
NO PURCHASE OR OBLIGATION NECESSARY TO ENTER

To enter, follow the directions published. If the "Match 3" Game Card is missing, hand print your name and address on a 3″×5″ card and mail to either: Harlequin "Match 3," 3010 Walden Ave., P.O. Box 1867, Buffalo, NY 14269-1867 or Harlequin "Match 3," P.O. Box 609, Fort Erie, Ontario L2A 5X3, and we will assign your Sweepstakes numbers. (Limit: one entry per envelope.) For eligibility, entries must be received no later than March 31, 1994 and be sent via first-class mail. No liability is assumed for printing errors, lost, late or misdirected entries.

Upon receipt of entry, Sweepstakes numbers will be assigned. To determine winners, Sweepstakes numbers will be compared against a list of randomly preselected prizewinning numbers. In the event all prizes are not claimed via the return of prizewinning numbers, random drawings will be held from among all other entries received to award unclaimed prizes.

Prizewinners will be determined no later than May 30, 1994. Selection of winning numbers and random drawings are under the supervision of D.L. Blair, Inc., an independent judging organization, whose decisions are final. One prize to a family or organization. No substitution will be made for any prize, except as offered. Taxes and duties on all prizes are the sole responsibility of winners. Winners will be notified by mail. Chances of winning are determined by the number of entries distributed and received.

Sweepstakes open to persons 18 years of age or older, except employees and immediate family members of Torstar Corporation, D.L. Blair, Inc., their affiliates, subsidiaries and all other agencies, entities and persons connected with the use, marketing or conduct of this Sweepstakes. All applicable laws and regulations apply. Sweepstakes offer void wherever prohibited by law. Any litigation within the province of Quebec respecting the conduct and awarding of a prize in this Sweepstakes must be submitted to the Régies des Loteries et Courses du Quebec. In order to win a prize, residents of Canada will be required to correctly answer a time-limited arithmetical skill-testing question. Values of all prizes are in U.S. currency.

Winners of major prizes will be obligated to sign and return an affidavit of eligibility and release of liability within 30 days of notification. In the event of non-compliance within this time period, prize may be awarded to an alternate winner. Any prize or prize notification returned as undeliverable will result in the awarding of that prize to an alternate winner. By acceptance of their prize, winners consent to use of their names, photographs or other likenesses for purposes of advertising, trade and promotion on behalf of Torstar Corporation without further compensation, unless prohibited by law.

This Sweepstakes is presented by Torstar Corporation, its subsidiaries and affiliates in conjunction with book, merchandise and/or product offerings. Prizes are as follows: Grand Prize—$1,000,000 (payable at $33,333.33 a year for 30 years). First through Sixth Prizes may be presented in different creative executions, each with the following appproximate values: First Prize—$35,000; Second Prize—$10,000; 2 Third Prizes—$5,000 each; 5 Fourth Prizes—$1,000 each; 10 Fifth Prizes—$250 each; 1,000 Sixth Prizes—$100 each. Prizewinners will have the opportunity of selecting any prize offered for that level. A travel-prize option, if offered and selected by winner, must be completed within 12 months of selection and is subject to hotel and flight accommodations availability. Torstar Corporation may present this Sweepstakes utilizing names other than Million Dollar Sweepstakes. For a current list of all prize options offered within prize levels and all names the Sweepstakes may utilize, send a self-addressed, stamped envelope (WA residents need not affix return postage) to: Million Dollar Sweepstakes Prize Options/Names, P.O. Box 4710, Blair, NE 68009.

For a list of prizewinners (available after July 31, 1994) send a separate, stamped, self-addressed envelope to: Million Dollar Sweepstakes Winners, P.O. Box 4728, Blair, NE 68009.   MSW7-92

HARLEQUIN SUPERROMANCE®

A PLACE IN HER HEART...

Somewhere deep in the heart of every grown woman is the little girl
she used to be....

In September, October and November 1992, the world of childhood
and the world of love collide in six very special romance titles. Follow
these six special heroines as they discover the sometimes heart-
wrenching, always heartwarming joy of being a Big Sister.

Written by six of your favorite Superromance authors, these
compelling and emotionally satisfying romantic stories will earn a
place in your heart!

SEPTEMBER 1992

#514   NOTHING BUT TROUBLE—Sandra James
#515   ONE TO ONE—Marisa Carroll

OCTOBER 1992

#518   OUT ON A LIMB—Sally Bradford
#519   STAR SONG—Sandra Canfield

NOVEMBER 1992

#522   JUST BETWEEN US—Debbi Bedford
#523   MAKE-BELIEVE—Emma Merritt

AVAILABLE WHEREVER
HARLEQUIN SUPERROMANCE
BOOKS ARE SOLD

BSIS92

HARLEQUIN®

I N T R I G U E ®

It looks like a charming old building near the Baltimore waterfront, but inside 43 Light Street lurks danger ... and romance.

Labeled a "true master of intrigue" by *Rave Reviews*, bestselling author Rebecca York continues her exciting series with #193 TRIAL BY FIRE, coming to you next month.

Sabrina Barkley, owner of an herbal shop at 43 Light Street, finds that the past has a bizarre way of affecting the present when she's called in by ADA Dan Cassidy to consult on a murder case—only to be herself accused of murder *and* witchcraft. Sabrina's only defense is four hundred years old and an ocean away. . . .

> "Rebecca York's 43 Light Street series just keeps getting better and better. (In TRIAL BY FIRE) the devilishly clever Ms. York brews up a mind-blowing concoction of black magic and timeless romance that will fire your imagination and sear your soul."
>
> —*Romantic Times*

Don't miss #193 TRIAL BY FIRE next month. And watch for all the upcoming 43 Light Street titles for the best in romantic suspense.   LS92-1R

JAYNE ANN KRENTZ

A two-part epic
tale from one of
today's most popular
romance novelists!

Dreams
Parts One & Two

The warrior died at her feet, his blood running out of the cave entrance and mingling with the waterfall. With his last breath he cursed the woman— told her that her spirit would remain chained in the cave forever until a child was created and born there....

So goes the ancient legend of the Chained Lady and the curse that bound her throughout the ages—until destiny brought Diana Prentice and Colby Savager together under the influence of forces beyond their understanding. Suddenly they were both haunted by dreams that linked past and present, while their waking hours were filled with danger. Only when Colby, Diana's modern-day warrior, learned to love, could those dark forces be vanquished. Only then could Diana set the Chained Lady free....

**Available in September
wherever Harlequin books are sold.**

JK92